A HANDFUL OF GOLD

Emmeline picked up the receiver, trembling as if it might give her a shock.

"Hullo?" she whispered.

And a voice – a faint, hoarse, distant voice – said,

"This is King Cunobel. I cannot speak for long. I am calling to warn you. There is danger on the way – great danger coming towards you and your friend. Take care! Watch well!"

Emmeline's lips parted. She could not speak.

"There is danger – danger!" the voice repeated. Then the line went silent.

Joan Aiken books in Red Fox

A HANDFUL OF
GOLD

Joan Aiken

With illustrations by
Quentin Blake

RED FOX

A Red Fox Book

Published by Random House Children's Books
20 Vauxhall Bridge Road, London SW1V 2SA

A division of Random House UK Ltd
London Melbourne Sydney Auckland
Johannesburg and agencies throughout the world

1 3 5 7 9 10 8 6 4 2

First published in Great Britain by
Jonathan Cape 1995

Red Fox edition 1997

Printed and bound in Great Britain by
Cox & Wyman Ltd, Reading, Berkshire

RANDOM HOUSE UK Limited Reg. No. 954009

Papers used by Random House UK Limited
are natural, recyclable products made from wood grown in
sustainable forests. The manufacturing processes conform to
the environmental regulations of the country of origin.

ISBN 0 09 9968361 X

'All You've Ever Wanted', 'The Rocking Donkey'
reprinted from *All You've Ever Wanted*, (1953); 'The People in the Castle',
'The Third Wish' from *More than You've Bargained For*, (1955); 'Miss Hooting's
Legacy', 'The Midnight Rose', 'The Cat Flap and the Apple Pie', from *Up the
Chimney Down*, (1984); 'A Harp of Fishbones, 'The Dark Streets of Kimball's Green',
'Mrs. Nutti's Fireplace' from *A Harp of Fishbones*, (1972); 'The Serial Garden',
'The Boy Who Read Aloud' from *A Small Pinch of Weather*, (1969);
'Moonshine in the Mustard Pot', 'The Man Who Pinched God's Letter',
'Crusader's Toby', from *The Faithless Lollybird*, (1977)

Contents

All You've Ever Wanted

MATILDA, YOU WILL AGREE, WAS A MOST unfortunate child. Not only had she three names each worse than the others – Matilda, Eliza and Agatha – but her father and mother died shortly after she was born, and she was brought up exclusively by her six aunts. These were all energetic women, and so on Monday Matilda was taught Algebra and Arithmetic by her Aunt Aggie, on Tuesday, Biology by her Aunt Beattie, on Wednesday Classics by her Aunt Cissie, on Thursday Dancing and Deportment by her Aunt Dorrie, on Friday Essentials by her Aunt Effie, and on Saturday French by her Aunt Florrie. Friday was the most alarming day, as Matilda never knew beforehand what Aunt Effie would decide on as the day's Essentials – sometimes it was cooking, or revolver practice, or washing, or boiler-making ("For you never know what a girl may need nowadays" as Aunt Effie rightly observed).

So that by Sunday, Matilda was often worn out, and thanked her stars that her seventh aunt, Gertie, had left

for foreign parts many years before, and never threatened
to come back and teach her Geology or Grammar on the
only day when she was able to do as she liked.

However, poor Matilda was not entirely free from her
Aunt Gertie, for on her seventh birthday, and each one
after it, she received a little poem wishing her well, written
on pink paper, decorated with silver flowers, and signed
'Gertrude Isabel Jones, to her niece, with much affection'.
And the terrible disadvantage of the poems, pretty though
they were, was that the wishes in them invariably came
true. For instance the one on her eighth birthday read:

> Now you are eight Matilda dear
> May shining gifts your place adorn
> And each day through the coming year
> Awake you with a rosy morn.

The shining gifts were all very well – they consisted of
a torch, a luminous watch, pins, needles, a steel soapbox
and a useful little silver brooch which said 'Matilda' in
case she ever forgot her name – but the rosy morns were
a great mistake. As you know, a red sky in the morning
is the shepherd's warning, and the fatal results of Aunt
Gertie's well-meaning verse was that it rained every day
for the entire year.

Another one read:

> Each morning make another friend
> Who'll be with you till light doth end,
> Cheery and frolicsome and gay,
> To pass the sunny hours away.

For the rest of her life Matilda was overwhelmed by the
number of friends she made in the course of that year –
three hundred and sixty-five of them. Every morning she
found another of them, anxious to cheer her and frolic

with her, and the aunts complained that her lessons were being constantly interrupted. The worst of it was that she did not really like all the friends – some of them were so *very* cheery and frolicsome, and insisted on pillow-fights when she had toothache, or sometimes twenty-one of them would get together and make her play hockey, which she hated. She was not even consoled by the fact that all her hours were sunny, because she was so busy in passing them away that she had no time to enjoy them.

> *Long miles and weary though you stray*
> *Your friends are never far away,*
> *And every day though you may roam,*
> *Yet night will find you back at home*

was another inconvenient wish. Matilda found herself forced to go for long, tiresome walks in all weathers, and it was no comfort to know that her friends were never far away, for although they often passed her on bicycles or in cars, they never gave her lifts.

However, as she grew older, the poems became less troublesome, and she began to enjoy bluebirds twittering in the garden, and endless vases of roses on her window-sill. Nobody knew where Aunt Gertie lived, and she never put in an address with her birthday greetings. It was there-fore impossible to write and thank her for her varied good wishes, or hint that they might have been more carefully worded. But Matilda looked forward to meeting her one day, and thought that she must be a most interest-ing person.

"You never knew what Gertrude would be up to next," said Aunt Cissie. "She was a thoughtless girl, and got into endless scrapes, but I will say for her, she was very good-hearted."

When Matilda was nineteen she took a job in the Minis-try of Alarm and Despondency, a very cheerful place where, instead of typewriter ribbon, they used red tape, and there was a large laundry basket near the main entrance labelled The Usual Channels where all the letters were put which people did not want to answer themselves. Once every three months the letters were re-sorted and dealt out afresh to different people.

Matilda got on very well here and was perfectly happy. She went to see her six aunts on Sundays, and had almost forgotten the seventh by the time that her twentieth birthday had arrived. Her aunt, however, had not forgotten.

On the morning of her birthday Matilda woke very late, and had to rush off to work cramming her letters unopened into her pocket, to be read later on in the morning. She had no time to read them until ten minutes to eleven, but that, she told herself, was as it should be, since, as she had been born at eleven in the morning, her birthday did not really begin till then.

Most of the letters were from her 365 friends, but the usual pink and silver envelope was there, and she opened it with the usual feeling of slight uncertainty.

> *May all your leisure hours be blest*
> *Your work prove full of interest,*
> *Your life hold many happy hours*
> *And all your way be strewn with flowers*

said the pink and silver slip in her fingers. 'From your affectionate Aunt Gertrude.'

Matilda was still pondering this when a gong sounded in the passage outside. This was the signal for everyone to leave their work and dash down the passage to a trolley which sold them buns and coffee. Matilda left her letters and dashed with the rest. Sipping her coffee and gossiping with her friends, she had forgotten the poem, when the voice of the Minister of Alarm and Despondency himself came down the corridor.

"What is all this? What does this mean?" he was saying.

The group round the trolley turned to see what he was talking about. And then Matilda flushed scarlet and spilt some of her coffee on the floor. For all along the respectable brown carpeting of the passage were growing flowers in the most riotous profusion – daisies, campanulas, crocuses, mimosa, foxgloves, tulips and lotuses. In some places the passage looked more like a jungle than anything else. Out of this jungle the little red-faced figure of the Minister fought its way.

"Who did it?" he said. But nobody answered.

Matilda went quietly away from the chattering group and pushed through the vegetation to her room, leaving a trail of buttercups and rhododendrons across the floor to her desk.

"I can't keep this quiet," she thought desperately. And she was quite right. Mr. Willoughby, who presided over the General Gloom Division, noticed almost immediately that when his secretary came in to his room, there was something unusual about her.

"Miss Jones," he said, "I don't like to be personal, but have you noticed that wherever you go, you leave a trail of mixed flowers?"

Poor Matilda burst into tears.

"I know, I don't know *what* I shall do about it," she sobbed.

Mr. Willoughby was not used to secretaries who burst into tears, let alone ones who left lobelias, primroses and the rarer forms of cactus behind them when they entered the room.

"It's very pretty," he said. "But not very practical. Already it's almost impossible to get along the passage, and I shudder to think what this room will be like when these have grown a bit higher. I really don't think you can go on with it, Miss Jones."

"You don't think I do it on purpose, do you?" said

11

Matilda sniffing into her handkerchief. "I can't stop it. They just keep on coming."

"In that case I am afraid," replied Mr. Willoughby, "that you will not be able to keep on coming. We really cannot have the Ministry overgrown in this way. I shall be very sorry to lose you, Miss Jones. You have been most efficient. What caused this unfortunate disability, may I ask?"

"It's a kind of spell," Matilda said, shaking the damp out of her handkerchief on to a fine polyanthus.

"But my dear girl," Mr. Willoughby exclaimed testily, "you have a National Magic Insurance card, haven't you? Good heavens – why don't you go to the Public Magician?"

"I never thought of that," she confessed. "I'll go at lunchtime."

Fortunately for Matilda the Public Magician's office lay just across the square from where she worked, so that she did not cause too much disturbance, though the Borough Council could never account for the rare and exotic flowers which suddenly sprang up in the middle of their dusty lawns.

The Public Magician received her briskly, examined her with an occultiscope, and asked her to state particulars of her trouble.

"It's a spell," said Matilda, looking down at a pink Christmas rose growing unseasonably beside her chair.

"In that case we can soon help you. Fill in that form, *if* you please." He pushed a printed slip at her across the table.

It said: 'To be filled in by persons suffering from spells, incantations, philtres, Evil Eye, etc.'

Matilda filled in name and address of patient, nature of spell, and date, but when she came to name and address of person by whom spell was cast, she paused.

"I don't know her address," she said.

"Then I'm afraid you'll have to find it. Can't do anything without an address," the Public Magician replied.

Matilda went out into the street very disheartened. The Public Magician could do nothing better than advise her to put an advertisement into *The Times* and the *International Sorcerers' Bulletin*, which she accordingly did:

AUNT GERTRUDE PLEASE COMMUNICATE MATILDA MUCH DISTRESSED BY LAST POEM

While she was in the Post Office sending off her advertisements (and causing a good deal of confusion by the number of forget-me-nots she left about), she wrote and posted her resignation to Mr. Willoughby, and then went sadly to the nearest Underground Station.

"Aintcher left something behind?" a man said to her at the top of the escalator. She looked back at the trail of daffodils across the station entrance and hurried anxiously down the stairs. As she ran round a corner at the bottom angry shouts told her that blooming lilies had interfered with the works and the escalator had stopped.

She tried to hide in the gloom at the far end of the platform, but a furious station official found her.

"Wotcher mean by it?" he said, shaking her elbow. "It'll take three days to put the station right, and look at my platform!"

The stone slabs were split and pushed aside by vast peonies, which kept growing, and threatened to block the line.

"It isn't my fault – really it isn't," poor Matilda stammered.

"The Company can sue you for this, you know," he began, when a train came in. Pushing past him, she squeezed into the nearest door.

She began to thank her stars for the escape, but it was too soon. A powerful and penetrating smell of onions

13

rose round her feet where the white flowers of wild garlic had sprung.

When Aunt Gertie finally read the advertisement in a ten-months' old copy of the *International Sorcerers' Bulletin*, she packed her luggage and took the next aeroplane back to England. For she was still just as Aunt Cissie had described her – thoughtless, but very good-hearted.

"Where is the poor child?" she asked Aunt Aggie.

"I should say she was poor," her sister replied tartly. "It's a pity you didn't come home before, instead of making her life a misery for twelve years. You'll find her out in the summerhouse."

Matilda had been living out there ever since she left the Ministry of Alarm and Despondency, because her aunts kindly but firmly, and quite reasonably, said that they could not have the house filled with vegetation.

She had an axe, with which she cut down the worst growths every evening, and for the rest of the time she kept as still as she could, and earned some money by doing odd jobs of typing and sewing.

"My poor dear child," Aunt Gertie said breathlessly, "I had no idea that my little verses would have this sort of effect. What ever shall we do?"

"Please do something," Matilda implored her, sniffing. This time it was not tears, but a cold she had caught from living in perpetual draughts.

"My dear, there isn't anything I can do. It's bound to last till the end of the year – that sort of spell is completely unalterable."

"Well, at least you can stop sending me the verses?" asked Matilda. "I don't want to sound ungrateful . . ."

"Even that I can't do," her aunt said gloomily. "It's a banker's order at the Magician's Bank. One a year from seven to twenty-one. Oh, dear, and I thought it would be such *fun* for you. At least you only have one more, though."

"Yes, but heaven knows what that'll be." Matilda sneezed despondently and put another sheet of paper into her typewriter. There seemed to be nothing to do but wait. However, they did decide that it might be a good thing to go and see the Public Magician on the morning of Matilda's twenty-first birthday.

Aunt Gertie paid the taxi-driver and tipped him heavily not to grumble about the mess of delphiniums sprouting out of the mat of his cab.

"Good heavens, if it isn't Gertrude Jones!" the Public Magician exclaimed. "Haven't seen you since we were at college together. How are you? Same old irresponsible Gertie? Remember that hospital you endowed with endless beds and the trouble it caused? And the row with the cigarette manufacturers over the extra million boxes of cigarettes for the soldiers?"

When the situation was explained to him he laughed heartily.

"Just like you, Gertie. Well-meaning isn't the word."

At eleven promptly, Matilda opened her pink envelope.

> *Matilda, now you're twenty-one,*
> *May you have every sort of fun;*
> *May you have all you've ever wanted,*
> *And every future wish be granted.*

"Every future wish be granted – then I wish Aunt Gertie would lose her power of wishing," cried Matilda; and immediately Aunt Gertie did.

But as Aunt Gertie with her usual thoughtlessness had said, 'May you have all you've *ever wanted*' Matilda had quite a lot of rather inconvenient things to dispose of, including a lion cub and a baby hippopotamus.

The Rocking Donkey

THERE WAS ONCE A LITTLE GIRL CALLED Esmeralda who lived with her wicked stepmother. Her father was dead. The stepmother, who was called Mrs. Mitching, was very rich, and lived in a large but hideous house in a suburb with a dusty, laurelly garden, an area, and a lot of ornamental iron fencing.

Mrs. Mitching was fond of opening things, and getting things up. The things she opened were mostly hospitals, or public libraries, or new by-passes, or civic centres, and the things she got up were sales of work, and bazaars, and flag days. She was in fact a public figure, and was very little at home. When she was, she spent her time receiving callers in her fringy, ornamented drawing-room.

"How is your little girl?" they would sometimes ask. "Is she still at home, or has she gone to boarding school?"

"Oh, she's at home," Mrs. Mitching would reply, "but she has her own play-room you know, so that we needn't

16

disturb one another. I don't believe in grown-ups bothering children all the time, do you?"

Mrs. Mitching could not afford school for Esmeralda, as she needed all her wealth for opening and getting up. She always took Esmeralda along to the openings, in a white muslin dress, painfully starched at the neck and wrists, because people liked to see a child on the platform. But for the rest of the time Esmeralda had to manage in her old brown dress, much too short now, and a torn pair of gym shoes. She had her meals in the kitchen, and they were horrible – bread and margarine, boiled fish and prunes.

But the most melancholy part of Esmeralda's life was that she had nothing to do. The play-room which Mrs. Mitching spoke of was a large dark basement room, shadowed by the laurels which overhung the area. There was nothing in it at all, not even a chair. No one ever came into it, and it would have been thick with dust had not Esmeralda, who was a tidy creature, once a week borrowed a broom from the housemaid's cupboard and swept it. She had no toys. Once, Mr. Snye, the man who came to cut the laurels, had given her a length of garden twine, and she used this as a skipping rope, to keep herself warm. She became a very good skipper, and could polka, double-through, swing the rope, and other fancy variations, while if she felt inclined to do plain skipping she could go on almost all day without a fault.

There were no books to read in the house, and she was not encouraged to go into Mrs. Mitching's rooms or outside, because of her shabby clothes, though she sometimes took a stroll at dusk.

One day Mrs. Mitching was to open a jumble sale. She was being driven to it by the Mayor in his Rolls Royce, so she told Hooper, the housemaid, to bring Esmeralda by bus, dressed in her white muslin, and meet her at the Hall. Then she went off to keep an appointment.

17

"Drat," said Hooper. "Now what am I to do? Your muslin's still at the laundry from last week."

"I'll have to go as I am," said Esmeralda, who quite liked openings. At least they made a change from wandering about in the basement.

"I don't know what Madam'll say," said Hooper doubtfully, "but I should catch it if I didn't take you, sure enough." So they went as they were, Esmeralda in her old brown dress and shoes.

When Mrs. Mitching saw them she gave a cry of dismay. "I can't let you be seen like that! You must go home at once," and she hurriedly left them, before anyone should connect her with the shabby child.

Hooper had set her heart on a violet satin pincushion she noticed on one of the stalls, so she pushed Esmeralda into a corner, and said, "You wait there, I shan't be a moment. It won't matter, no one will know who you are."

Esmeralda stood looking quietly about her. An elderly gentleman, Lord Mauling, making his way to the platform, noticed what seemed to him a forlorn-looking little creature, and stopping by her he took a coin from his pocket and said: "Here, my dear. Buy yourself a pretty toy."

Esmeralda gave him a startled look as he went on his way, and then stared at the coin she held in her hand. It was a shilling. She had never had any money before and was quite puzzled to know what she should buy with it. Almost without realizing what she was doing she began to wander along the stalls, looking at the different things offered for sale. There were books, clothes, bottles of scent, flowers – all the things she saw seemed beautiful, but she could not imagine buying any of them. Then she came to the toy counter. Toys! She had never had one. The only time she ever touched a toy was sometimes when Mrs. Mitching opened a children's ward at a hospital, and she would present a ceremonial teddy-bear to a little patient. She gazed at dolls, puzzles, engines, without notic-

18

her house for the wives of chimney sweeps, and it occurred to her that the basement play-room would be just the right size for the purpose. She went along to inspect it, and found Esmeralda having her weekly clean-out with brush and dustpan.

"That's right, that's right," she said absently, glancing about. "But what is this? A rocking horse?" Esmeralda stood mute.

"Do you not think you are a little old for such toys? Yes, yes, I think it had better be given away to some poor child. It is the duty of children who live in rich houses, such as you, Esmeralda, to give away your old toys to the little slum children who have nothing. It can be taken away when the van for the Bombed Families calls here tomorrow morning. But you must certainly clean it up a little first. You should be quite ashamed to pass on such a shabby old toy without doing your best to improve its appearance. After all, you know, it may gladden some poor little life in Stepney or Bethnal Green. So give it a good scrub this evening. Now what was I doing? Ah yes, seventeen feet by sixteen, ten tables – let me see—"

Esmeralda passed the rest of the day in a sort of numbness. After tea she took some sugar-soap and a scrubbing brush from the housemaid's cupboard and started to scrub Prince.

"Well," she thought, "perhaps I didn't *deserve* to be so happy. I never thought of scrubbing him. Perhaps some-one else will take better care of him. But oh, what shall I do, what shall I do?"

She scrubbed and scrubbed, and as the shabby grey peeled away, a silvery gleam began to show along Prince's back and sides, and his mane and tail shone like floss. By the time she had finished it was quite dark, and a long ray of moonlight, striking across the floor, caught his head and for a moment dazzled her eyes.

For the last time she went up, fetched her blankets,

and settled herself beside him. Just before she fell asleep it seemed to her that his nose came down and lightly touched her wet cheek.

Next day Esmeralda hid herself. She did not want to see Prince taken away. Mrs. Mitching superintended his removal.

"Good gracious," she said, when she saw him shining in the sun. "That is far too valuable to be taken to Stepney. I shall give it to the museum." So the Bombed Families van dropped Prince off at the museum before going on to Stepney.

All day Esmeralda avoided the basement play-room. She felt that she could not bear to look at the empty patch in the middle of the floor.

In the evening Hooper felt sorry for her, she seemed so restless and moping, and took her out for a stroll. They went to the museum, where Hooper liked to look at the models of fashions through the ages. While she was studying crinolines and bustles Esmeralda wandered off, and soon, round a corner she came on Prince, railed off from the public with a red cord, and a notice beside him which read: "Donated by the Hon. Mrs. Mitching, November 19—."

Esmeralda stretched out her hand, but she could not quite touch him over the cord.

"Now, Miss," said an attendant. "No touching the exhibits, please." So she looked and looked at him until Hooper said it was time to go home.

Every day after that she went to the museum and looked at Prince, and Hooper said to Cook, "That child doesn't look well." Mrs. Mitching was away from home a good deal, organizing the grand opening of a new welfare centre and clinic, so she did not notice Esmeralda's paleness, or her constant visits to the museum.

One night something woke Esmeralda. It was a long finger of moonlight which lay lightly across her closed lids. She got up quietly and put on her old brown dress and thin shoes. It was easy to steal out of that large house without anyone hearing, and once outside she slipped along the empty streets like a shadow. When she reached the museum she went at once, as if someone had called her, to a little door at one side. Someone had left it unlocked, and she opened it softly and went into the thick dark.

The museum was a familiar place by now, and she went confidently forward along a passage, and presently came out into the main hall. It did not take her long to find Prince, for there he was, shining like silver in the moonlight. She walked forward, stepped over the rope, and put her hand on his neck.

"Esmeralda," he said. His voice was like a faint, silvery wind.

"You never spoke to me before."

"How could I? I was choked with grey paint."

"Oh," she cried, "I'm so terribly lonely without you. What shall I do?"

"You never rode on me," he said.

"I didn't like to. You were so old and tired, it would have seemed like taking a liberty."

"Ride on me now."

Timidly she put her foot into the stirrup and swung herself on to his back.

"Settle yourself in the saddle and hold tight. Are you all right?"

"Yes," she said.

Like a feather in the wind they went rocking up the ray of moonlight and passed through the high window as if it had been mist. Neither of them was ever seen again.

The People in the Castle

THE CASTLE STOOD ON A STEEP HILL ABOVE the town. Round the bottom of the hill ran the outer castle wall with a massive gateway, and inside this gate was the doctor's house. People could only approach the castle by going in through his surgery door, out through his garden door, and up a hundred steps; but nobody bothered to do this, because the castle was supposed to be haunted, and in any case who wants to go and see an empty old place falling into ruins? Let the doctor prowl round it himself if he wanted to.

The doctor was thought to be rather odd by the townspeople. He was very young to be so well established, he was always at work writing something, and he was often quite rude to his patients if they took too long about describing their symptoms, and would abruptly tell them to get on and not beat about the bush.

He had arranged his surgery hour in a very businesslike way. The patients sat in rows in the large waiting-room amusing themselves with the illustrated papers or with the view of the castle, which filled up the whole of one window in a quite oppressive manner. Each patient picked up a little numbered card from a box as he arrived and then waited until the doctor rang the bell and flashed his number on the indicator. Then the patient hurried to the surgery, breathlessly recited his symptoms before the doctor grew impatient, received his medicine, dropped his card into another little box, paid for his treatment (or not, after the National Health Service arrived), and hurried out by another door which led straight back to the main castle gateway.

By this means the incoming and outgoing patients were not allowed to become entangled in halls and passageways creating confusion and holding up proceedings. The doctor was not very fond of people, and the sooner he could clear them all out of his house and get back to his writing, the better he was pleased.

One evening there were fewer patients than usual. It was late in October. The wind had been blowing in from the sea all day, but it dropped before sunset, and what leaves remained on the trees were hanging motionless in the clear dusk.

"Is there anyone after you?" the doctor asked old Mrs. Daggs, as he gave her some sardine ointment.

"Just one young lady, a stranger I reckon. Never seen her in the town."

"All right – good night," said the doctor quickly, and opened the door for the old woman, at the same time pressing the buzzer for the next number. Then he thought of a phrase for the paper he was writing on speech impediments and twiddled round in his revolving chair to put it down in the notebook on his desk. He was automatically listening for the sound of the waiting-room door, but as he heard nothing he impatiently pressed the buzzer again, and turning round shouted:

"Come along there."

Then he stopped short, for his last patient had already arrived and was sitting in the upright chair with her hands composedly folded in her lap.

"Oh – sorry," he said. "You must have come in very quietly. I didn't know you were in here."

She inclined her head a little, as if acknowledging his apology. She was very white-faced, with the palest gold hair he had ever seen, hanging in a mass to her shoulders. Even in that dusky room it seemed to shine. Her dress was white, and over it she wore a grey plaid-like cloak, flung round her and fastening on her shoulder.

"What's your trouble?" asked the doctor, reaching for his prescription block.

She was silent.

"Come along for goodness' sake – speak up," he said testily. "We haven't got all night." Then he saw, with surprise and some embarrassment, that she was holding out a slate to him. On it was written:

"I am dumb."

He gazed at her, momentarily as speechless as she, and she gently took the slate back again and wrote on it:

"Please cure me."

It seemed impolite to answer her in speech, almost like taking an unfair advantage. He felt inclined to write his message on the slate too, but he cleared his throat and said:

"I don't know if I can cure you, but come over to the light and I'll examine you." He switched on a cluster of bright lights by his desk, and she obediently opened her mouth and stood trustfully while he peered and probed with his instruments.

He gave an exclamation of astonishment, for at the back of her mouth he could see something white sticking up. He cautiously pulled it further forward with his forceps and discovered that it was the end of a long piece of cotton wool. He pulled again, and about a foot of it came out of her mouth, but that seemed to be nowhere near the end. He glanced at the girl in astonishment, but as she appeared quite calm he went on pulling, and the stuff kept reeling out of her throat until there was a tangle of it all over the floor.

At last the end came out.

"Can you speak now?" he asked, rather anxiously.

She seemed to be clearing her throat, and presently said with some difficulty:

"A little. My throat is sore."

"Here's something to suck. I'll give you a prescription for that condition – it's a result of pulling out the wool, I'm afraid. This will soon put it right. Get it made up as soon as you can."

He scribbled on a form and handed it to her. She looked at it in a puzzled manner.

"I do not understand."

"It's a prescription," he said impatiently.

"What is that?"

"Good heavens – where *do* you come from?"

She turned and pointed through the window to the castle, outlined on its hill, against the green sky.

"From *there?* Who are you?"

"My name is Helen," she said, still speaking in the same husky, hesitant manner. "My father is King up there on the hill." For the first time the doctor noticed that round her pale, shining hair she wore a circlet of gold, hardly brighter than the hair beneath. She was then a princess?

"I had a curse laid on me at birth – I expect you know the sort of thing?" He nodded.

"A good fairy who was there said that I would be cured of my dumbness on my eighteenth birthday by a human doctor."

"Is it your birthday today?"

"Yes. Of course we all knew about you, so I thought I

27

would come to you first." She coughed, and he jumped up and gave her a drink of a soothing syrup, which she took gratefully.

"Don't try to talk too much at first. There's plenty of time. Most people talk too much anyway. I'll have the prescription made up" – "and bring it round," he was going to say, but hesitated. Could one go and call at the castle with a bottle of medicine as if it was Mrs. Daggs?

"Will you bring it?" she said, solving his problem. "My father will be glad to see you."

"Of course. I'll bring it tomorrow evening."

Again she gravely inclined her head, and turning, was gone, though whether by the door or window he could not be sure.

He crossed to the window and stood for some time staring up at the black bulk of the castle on the thorn-covered hill, before returning to his desk and the unfinished sentence. He left the curtains open.

Next morning, if it had not been for the prescription lying on his desk, he would have thought that the incident had been a dream. Even as he took the slip along to Boots to have the medicine made up he wondered if the white-coated woman there would suddenly tell him that he was mad.

That evening dusk was falling as the last of his surgery patients departed. He went down and locked the large gates and then, with a beating heart, started the long climb up the steps to the castle. It was lighter up on the side of the knoll. The thorns and brambles grew so high that he could see nothing but the narrow stairway in front of him. When he reached the top he looked down and saw his own house below, and the town with its crooked roofs running to the foot of the hill, and the river wriggling away to the sea. Then he turned and walked under the arch into the great hall of the castle.

The first thing he noticed was the scent of lime. There

was a big lime tree which, in the daytime, grew in the middle of the grass carpeting the great hall. He could not see the tree, but why was a lime tree blossoming in October?

It was dark inside, and he stood hesitating, afraid to step forward into the gloom, when he felt a hand slipped into his. It was a thin hand, very cool; it gave him a gentle tug and he moved forward, straining his eyes to try and make out who was leading him. Then, as if the pattern in a kaleidoscope had cleared, his eyes flickered and he began to see.

There were lights grouped round the walls in pale clusters, and below them, down the length of the hall, sat a large and shadowy assembly; he could see the glint of light here and there on armour, or on a gold buckle or the jewel in a head-dress as somebody moved.

At the top of the hall, on a dais, sat a royal figure, cloaked and stately, but the shadows lay so thick in between that he could see no more. But his guide plucked him forward; he now saw that it was Helen, in her white dress with a gold belt and bracelets. She smiled at him gravely and indicated that he was to go up and salute the King.

With some vague recollection of taking his degree he made his way up to the dais and bowed.

"I have brought the Princess's linctus, Sire," he said, stammering a little.

"We are pleased to receive you and to welcome you to our court. Henceforth come and go freely in this castle whenever you wish."

The doctor reflected that he always *had* come and gone very freely in the castle; however, it hardly seemed the same place tonight, for the drifting smoke from the candles made the hall look far larger.

He lifted up his eyes and took a good look at the King,

who had a long white beard and a pair of piercing eyes. Helen had seated herself on a stool at his feet.

"I see you are a seeker after knowledge," said the King suddenly. "You will find a rich treasure-house to explore here – only beware that your knowledge does not bring you grief."

The doctor jumped slightly. He had indeed been thinking that the King looked like some Eastern sage and might have information which the doctor could use in his study on occult medicine.

"I suppose all doctors are seekers after knowledge," he said cautiously, and handed Helen her bottle of medicine. "Take a teaspoonful after meals – or – or three times a day." He was not sure if the people in the castle had meals in the ordinary way, though some kind of feast seemed to be in progress at the moment.

From that time on the doctor often made his way up to the castle after evening had fallen, and sat talking to the King, or to some of the wise and reverend knights who formed his court, or to Helen. During the daytime the castle brooded, solitary and crumbling as always, save for some occasional archaeologist taking pictures for a learned monthly.

On Christmas Eve the doctor climbed up with a box of throat tablets for Helen, who still had to be careful of her voice, and a jar of ointment for the King who had unfortunately developed chilblains as a result of sitting in the chill and draughty hall.

"You really should get him away from here, though I'd miss him," he told Helen. "I don't know how old he is—"

"A thousand— " she interjected.

"—Oh," he said, momentarily taken aback. "Well in any case it really is too damp and cold for him here. And you should take care of your throat too; it's important not to strain it these first months. This castle really is no place for either of you."

She obediently flung a fold of her grey cloak round her neck.

"But we are going away tomorrow," she said. "Didn't you know? From Christmas to Midsummer Day my father holds his court at Avignon."

The doctor felt as if the ground had been cut from under his feet.

"You're going away? You mean you'll none of you be here?"

"No," she answered, looking at him gravely.

"Helen! Marry me and stay with me here. My house is very warm – I'll take care of you, I swear it—." He caught hold of her thin, cold hand.

"Of course I'll marry you," she said at once. "You earned the right to my hand and heart when you cured me – didn't you know that either?"

She led him to her father and he formally asked for her hand in marriage.

"She's yours," said the King. "I can't prevent it, though I don't say I approve of these mixed marriages. But mind you cherish her – the first unkind word, and she'll vanish like a puff of smoke. That's one thing we *don't* have to put up with from mortal man."

As soon as Helen married the doctor and settled in his house she became a changed creature. The people in the town were surprised and charmed to find what a cheerful, pretty wife their hermit-like doctor had found himself. She left off her magic robes and put on check aprons; she learned to cook and flitted around dusting and tidying; moreover as her newly won voice gathered strength she chattered like a bird and hummed the whole day long over her work.

She abolished the buzzer in the surgery because she said it frightened people. She used to look through the door herself and say:

"The doctor will see you now, Mrs. Jones, and will you

try not to keep him waiting please – though I know it's hard for you with your leg. Is it any better, do you think? And how's your husband's chest?'

"She's like a ray of sunshine, bless her," people said.

The doctor was not sure about all this. What he had chiefly loved in her was the sense of magic and mystery; she had been so silent and moved with such stately grace. Still, it was very pleasant to have this happy creature in his house attending to his comfort – only she did talk so. In the daytime it was not so bad, but in the evenings when he wanted to get on with his writing it *was* trying.

By and by he suggested that she might like to go to the cinema, and took her to a Disney. She was enchanted, and after that he was ensured peace and quiet on at least two evenings a week, for she was quite happy to go off by herself and leave him, only begging him not to work too hard.

One night he had nearly finished the chapter on Magic and its Relation to Homeopathic Medicine, and was wishing that he could go up and discuss it with the King. He heard her come in and go to the kitchen to heat the soup for their late supper.

Soon she appeared with a tray.

"It was a Western," she said, her eyes sparkling. "The hero comes riding into this little town, you see, and he pretends he's a horse-dealer but really he's the D.A. in disguise. So he finds that the rustling is being run by the saloon keeper—"

"Oh, for goodness' sake, *must* you talk all the time," snapped the doctor. Then he stopped short and looked at her aghast.

A dreadful change had come over her. The gay print apron and hair ribbon dropped off her and instead he saw her clad in her white and grey robes and wreathed about with all her magic. Even as she held out her hands to him despairingly she seemed to be drawn away and vanished through the thick curtains.

"Helen!" he cried. There was no answer. He flung open the door and ran frantically up the steps to the castle. It was vacant and dark. The grass in the great hall was stiff with frost and the night sky showed pale above him in the roofless tower.

"Helen, Helen," he called, until the empty walls re-echoed, but no one replied. He made his way slowly down the steps again and back to his warm study where the steam was still rising from the two bowls of soup.

From that day the townspeople noticed a change in their doctor. He had been hermit-like before; now he was morose. He kept the castle gates locked except for the surgery hour and disconnected his telephone. No longer was there a pretty wife to tell them that the doctor would see them now; instead they were confronted by a closed door with a little grille, through which they were expected to recite their symptoms. When they had done so, they were told to go round by an outside path to another door, and by the time they reached it they found the necessary pill or powder and written instructions lying outside on the step. So clever was the doctor that even with this unsatisfactory system he still cured all his patients, and indeed it seemed as if he could tell more about a sick person through a closed door than other doctors could face to face; so that although people thought his treatment strange, they went on coming to him.

There were many queer tales about him, and everyone agreed that night after night he was heard wandering in the ruined castle calling "Helen! Helen!" but that no one ever answered him.

Twenty years went by. The doctor became famous for his books, which had earned him honorary degrees in all the universities of the world. But he steadfastly refused to leave his house, and spoke to no one, communicating with the tradespeople by means of notes.

One day as he sat writing he heard a knock on the outer gate, and something prompted him to go down and open it. Outside stood a curious looking little woman in black academic robes and hood, who nodded to him.

"I am Dr. Margaret Spruchsprecher, Rector of the University of Freiherrburg," she said, walking composedly up the path before him and in at his front door. "I have come to give you the degree of Master of Philosophy at our University, as you would not come to us or answer our letters."

He bowed awkwardly and took the illuminated parchment she offered him.

"Would you like a cup of coffee?" he said, finding his voice with difficulty. "I am most honoured that you should come all this way to call on me."

"Perhaps now that I have come so far I can help you," she said. "You are seeking something, are you not? Something besides knowledge? Something that you think is in the castle, up there on the hill?"

He nodded, without removing his gaze from her. The keen, piercing look in her old eyes reminded him vividly of the King.

"Well! Supposing that all this time, what you seek is not *inside*, but has gone *outside*; supposing that you have been sitting at the mouth of an empty mouse-hole; what then?" There was something brisk, but not unkindly in her laugh as she turned and made off down the path again, clutching the voluminous black robes round herself as the wind blew them about. The gate slammed behind her.

"Wait—" the doctor called and ran after her, but it was too late. She was lost in the crowded High Street.

He went out into the town and wandered distractedly about the streets staring into face after face, in search of he hardly knew what.

"Why, it's the doctor, isn't it," a woman said. "My Teddy's been a different boy since that medicine you gave him, Doctor."

Someone else came up and told him how thankful they were for his advice on boils.

"My husband's never forgotten how you cured his ear-ache when he thought he'd have to throw himself out of the window, the pain was so bad."

"I've always wanted to thank you, Doctor, for what you did when I was so ill with the jaundice—"

"You saved my Jennifer that time when she swallowed the poison—"

The doctor felt quite ashamed and bewildered at the chorus of thanks and greetings which seemed to rise on every side. He finally dived into a large doorway which seemed to beckon him, and sank relieved into a dark and sound-proof interior – the cinema.

For a long time he took no notice of the film which was in progress on the screen, but when he finally looked up his attention was attracted by the sight of galloping horses; it was a Western. All of a sudden the memory of Helen came so suddenly and bitterly into his mind that he nearly cried aloud.

"Excuse me, sir, that's the one and nine's you're sitting in. You should be in the two and three's."

He had no recollection of having bought any ticket, but obediently rose and followed his guide with her darting torch. His eyes were full of tears and he stumbled; she waited until he had caught her up and then gave him a hand.

It was a thin hand, very cool; it gave him a gentle tug. He stood still, put his other hand over it and muttered:

"Helen."

"Hush, you'll disturb people."

"Is it you?"

"Yes. Come up to the back and we can talk."

The cinema was pitch dark and full of people. As he followed her up to the rampart at the back he could feel them all about him.

"Have you been here all these years?"

"All these years?" she whispered, mocking him. "It was only yesterday."

"But I'm an old man, Helen. What are you? I can't see you. Your hands feel as young as ever."

"Don't worry," she said soothingly. "We must wait till this film ends – this is the last reel – and then we'll go up to the castle. My father will be glad to see you again. He likes your books very much."

He was too ashamed to ask her to come back to him, but she went on:

"And you had better come up and live with us in the castle now."

A feeling of inexpressible happiness came over him as he stood patiently watching the galloping horses and feeling her small, cool hand in his.

Next day the castle gates were found standing ajar, and the wind blew through the open doors and windows of the doctor's house. He was never seen again.

Miss Hooting's Legacy

For weeks before cousin elspeth's visit, mrs. Armitage was, as her son Mark put it, 'flapping about like a wet sheet in a bramble bush'.

"What shall we do about the unicorn? Cousin Elspeth doesn't approve of keeping pets."

"But she can't disapprove of him. He's got an angelic nature – haven't you, Candleberry?"

Harriet patted the unicorn and gave him a lump of sugar. It was a hot day in early October and the family were having tea in the garden.

"He'll have to board out for a month or two at Coldharbour Farm." Mrs. Armitage made a note on her list. "And you," she said to her husband, "must lay in at least five cases of Glensporran. Cousin Elspeth will only drink iced tea with whisky in it."

"Merciful powers! What this visit is going to cost us! How long is the woman going to stay?"

"Why does she have to come?" growled Mark, who had

been told to dismantle his home-made nuclear turbine, which was just outside the guest-room window.

"Because she's a poor old thing and her sister's just died, and she's lonely. Also, she's very rich, and if she felt like it, she could easily pay for you and Harriet to go to college, or art school, or something of that sort."

"But that's *years* ahead!"

"*Someone* has to think ahead in this family," said Mrs. Armitage, writing down *Earl Grey tea, new face-towels* on her list. "And, Harriet, you are not to encourage the cat to come upstairs and sleep on your bed. It would be awful if he got into Cousin Elspeth's room and disturbed her. She writes that she is a very light sleeper—"

"Oh, poor Walrus. Where *can* he sleep, then?"

"In his basket, in the kitchen. And, Mark, will you ask Mr. Peake to stay out of the guest bathroom for a few months? He's very obliging, but it always takes a long time to get an idea into his head."

"Well, he *is* three hundred years old, after all," said Harriet. "You can't expect a ghost to respond quite as quickly as ordinary people."

"Darling," said Mrs. Armitage to her husband, "some time this week, could you find a few minutes to hang up the big mirror that I bought at Dowbridges' sale? It's been down in the cellar for the last two months—"

"Hang it, where?" said Mr. Armitage, reluctantly coming out of his evening paper.

"In the guest-room, of course! To replace the one that Mark broke when his turbine exploded—"

"I'll do it, if you like," said Mark, who loved banging in nails. "After all, it was my fault the other one got broken."

"And I'll help," said Harriet, who wanted another look at the new mirror.

She had accompanied her mother to the furniture sale, a couple of months ago, when three linen tablecloths, one wall mirror, ten flowerpots, and a rusty pressure cooker had been knocked down to Mrs. Armitage for £12 in the teeth of spirited and urgent bidding from old Miss Hooting, who lived at the other end of the village. For some reason the old lady seemed particularly keen to acquire this lot, though there were several other mirrors in the sale. At £11.99, however, she ceased to wave her umbrella, and limped out of the sale hall, scowling, muttering, and casting angry glances at Mrs. Armitage. Since then she had twice dropped notes, in black spidery handwriting, through the Armitage letterbox offering to buy the mirror, first for £12.50, then for £13, but Mrs. Armitage, who did not much like Miss Hooting, politely declined to sell.

"I wonder *why* the old girl was so keen to get hold of the glass?" remarked Harriet, holding the jam-jar full of nails while Mark tapped exploringly on the wall, hunting for reliable spots. The mirror was quite a big heavy one, about two metres long by one metre wide, and required careful positioning.

"It seems ordinary enough." Mark glanced at it casually. The glass, plainly quite old, had a faint silvery sheen; the frame, wooden and very worn, was carved with vine leaves and little grinning creatures.

"It doesn't give a very good reflection." Harriet peered in. "Makes me look frightful."

"Oh I dunno; about the same as usual, I'd say," remarked her brother. He selected his spot, pressed a nail into the plaster, and gave it one or two quick bangs. "There. Now another here. Now pass us the glass."

They heard the doorbell ring as Mark hung up the mirror, and a few minutes later, when they came clattering downstairs with the hammer and nails and the stepladder, they saw their mother on the doorstep, engrossed in a long, earnest conversation with old Mrs. Lomax, Miss Hooting's neighbour. Mrs. Lomax was not a close friend of the Armitage family, but she had once obligingly restored the Armitage parents to their proper shape when Miss Hooting, in a fit of temper, had changed them into ladybirds.

Odd things frequently happened to the Armitages.

"What did Mrs. Lomax want, Ma?" Harriet asked her mother at supper.

Mrs. Armitage frowned, looking half worried, half annoyed.

"It's still this business about the mirror," she said. "Old Miss Hooting had really set her heart on it, for some reason. Why didn't she just *tell* me so? Now she has got pneumonia, she's quite ill, Mrs. Lomax says, and she keeps tossing and turning, and saying she has to have the glass, and if not, she'll put a curse on us by dropping a bent pin down our well. Perhaps, after all, I had better let the poor thing have the glass."

"Why? You bought it," said Harriet. "She could have gone on bidding."

"Perhaps £11.99 was all she had."

"There were other glasses that went for less."

Mr. Armitage was inclined to make light of the matter. "I don't see what dropping a bent pin into the well could do. I expect she's delirious. Wait till she's better; then you'll find the whole thing has died down, very likely."

Next day, however, the Armitages learned that old Miss Hooting had died in the night.

"And not before it was time," said Mr. Armitage. "She must have been getting on for a hundred. Anyway, that solves your problem about the mirror."

"I hope so," said the wife.

"Now all we have to worry about is Cousin Elspeth. Did you say she takes cubes of frozen tea in her whisky, or frozen whisky in her tea?"

"Either way will do, so long as the tea is Earl Grey..."

Cousin Elspeth's arrival coincided with old Miss Hooting's funeral.

The funeral of a witch (or 'old fairy lady' as they were always politely referred to in the Armitages' village, where a great many of them resided) is always a solemn affair, and Miss Hooting, because of her great age and explosive temper, had generally been regarded as the chairwitch of the village community. So the hearse, drawn by four black griffins and carrying a glass coffin with Miss Hooting in it, looking very severe in her black robes and hat, was followed by a long straggling procession of other old ladies, riding in vehicles of all kinds, from rickety perch phaetons with half the springs gone, to moth-eaten flying carpets and down-at-the-wheel chariots.

Mark and Harriet would very much have liked to attend the ceremony, but were told firmly that, since the family had not been on very good terms with Miss Hooting, they were to stay at home and not intrude. They heard later from their friend Rosie Perrow that there had been a considerable fuss at the graveside, because Miss Hooting had left instructions that her coffin was not to be covered over until November 1st, and the vicar had very strong objections to this.

"Specially as the coffin was made of glass," Rosie reported.

"I suppose he thought kids might come and smash it," said Mark.

"So they might. Miss Hooting wasn't at all popular."

Cousin Elspeth, when she arrived, was in a state of high indignation.

"Rickety, ramshackle equipages all along the village street, holding up the traffic! My taxi took twenty-eight minutes to get here, and cost me £9.83! Furthermore, I am accustomed to take my tea at four-thirty precisely, and it is now twelve meenutes past five!"

Cousin Elspeth was a tall, rangy lady, with teeth that

41

Mr. Armitage said reminded him of the cliffs of Dover, a voice like a chain-saw, cold, granite-coloured eyes that missed nothing, hair like the English Channel on a grey choppy day, and an Aberdeen accent as frigid as chopped ice.

In a way, Mark thought, it was a shame that she had just missed Miss Hooting; the two of them might have hit it off.

Tea, with three kinds of scones, two kinds of shortbread, and cubes of frozen Glensporran in her Earl Grey, was just beginning to soothe Cousin Elspeth's ruffled feelings when there came a peal at the front doorbell.

"Inconseederate!" Cousin Elspeth sniffed again.

The caller proved to be Mr. Glibchick, the senior partner in the legal firm of Wright, Wright, Wright, Wright, and Wrong, who had their offices on the village green. All the Wrights and the Wrongs had long since passed away, and Mr. Glibchick ran the firm with the help of his junior partner, Mr. Wrangle.

"What was it, dear?" inquired Mrs. Armitage, when her husband returned, looking rather astonished, from his conversation with the lawyer.

"Just imagine – Miss Hooting has left us something in her Will!"

Cousin Elspeth was all ears at once. Making and remaking her own Will had been her favourite hobby for years past; and since arriving at the Armitage house she had already mentally subtracted £400 and a writing-desk from Mark's legacy, because he had neglected to pass her the jam, and was deliberating at present about whether to bequeath a favourite brown mohair stole to Harriet, who had politely inquired after her lumbago.

"Left us a legacy? What – in the name of goodness?" exclaimed Mrs. Armitage. "I thought the poor old thing hadn't two pennies to rub together."

"Not money. Two mechanical helots, was what Mr. Glib-chick said."

"Helots? What are they?"

"Helots were a kind of slave."

"Fancy Miss Hooting keeping slaves!" Harriet looked horrified. "I bet she beat them with her umbrella and made them live on burnt toast-crusts."

"Little gels should be seen and not hairrd," remarked Cousin Elspeth, giving Harriet a disapproving glance, and changing her mind about the brown mohair stole.

Next day the mechanical slaves were delivered by Ernie Perrow in his tractor-trailer.

They proved to be two figures, approximately human in shape, one rather larger than life-size, one rather smaller, constructed out of thin metal piping, with plastic boxes for their chests containing a lot of electronic gadgetry. Their feet were large, round, and heavy, and they had long, multi-hinged arms ending in prehensile hands with hooks on the fingers. They had eyes made of electric light-bulbs and rather vacant expressions. Their names were stencilled on their feet: *Tinthea* and *Nickelas*.

"What gruesome objects!" exclaimed Mrs. Armitage. "For mercy's sake, let's give them to the next jumble-sale; the very sight of them is enough to give me one of my migraines!"

Cousin Elspeth entirely agreed. "Whit seengularly ree-pulsive airrticles!"

But Mark and his father, seeing eye to eye for once, were most anxious to get the mechanical slaves into working order, if possible.

"Besides, it would be very tactless to give them to a sale. Miss Hooting's friends would be sure to get to know."

"The things are in a horrible condition," pronounced Mark, after some study of the helots. "All damp and dirty and rusty; the old girl must have kept them in some dismal outhouse and never oiled them."

"What makes them go?" inquired Harriet, peering at a damp, tattered little booklet, entitled *Component Identification*, which hung on a chain round Tinthea's neck.

"It seems to be lunar energy," said her father. "Which is pretty dicey, if you ask me. I never heard of anything running on lunar energy before. But that seems to be the purpose of those glass plates on the tops of their heads."

"More to 'em than meets the eye," agreed Mark, wagging his own head.

As it happened, the month of October was very fine. Hot, sunny days were succeeded by blazing moonlit nights. Tinthea and Nickelas were put out in the greenhouse to warm up and dry off. Meanwhile Mark and his father, each guided by a booklet, spent devoted hours cleaning, drying, oiling and de-rusting the family's new possessions.

" 'Clean glazed areas with water and ammonia solution', it says."

" 'Brush cassette placement with household detergent.' "

"Which is the cassette placement?"

"I think it must be that drawer affair in the chest."

"Chest of drawers," giggled Harriet.

Tinthea, on whom Mark was working, let out something that sounded like a snort.

" 'Keep latched prehensile work/monitor selector function aligners well lubricated with sunflower or cottonseed oil.' Which do you think those are?"

"Its hands?" suggested Harriet.

Mr. Armitage, doing his best to clean the feet of Nickelas, which were in a shocking state, matted with dirt and old, encrusted furniture polish, accidentally touched a concealed lever in the heel, and Nickelas began to hop about, in a slow, ungainly, but frantic way, like a toad in a bed of thistles. The helot's hand, convulsively opening and shutting, grasped the handle of Mr. Armitage's metal tool-box, picked up the box, and swung it at its owner's head. Mr. Armitage just managed to save himself from a cracked skull by falling over sideways into a tray of flowerpots. Nickelas then clumsily but effectively smashed eight greenhouse panes with the end of the tool-box, using it like a sledge-hammer, before Mark, ducking low, managed to grab the helot's leg and flick down the switch.

"Oh, I see, *that*'s how they work!" Harriet pressed Tinthea's switch.

"Don't, idiot!" shouted Mark, but it was too late. Tinthea picked up a bucket of dirty, soapy water and dashed it into Harriet's face just before Mr. Armitage, with great presence of mind, hooked the helot's feet from under her with the end of a rake. Tinthea fell flat on the ground, and Mark was able to switch her off.

"We have got to learn to programme them properly before we switch them on. They seem to have charged up quite a lot of lunar energy," said Mr. Armitage, trying to prize Nickelas's steel fingers loose from the handle of the tool-chest.

He read aloud: " 'To programme the helots: turn the percept/accept/monitor/selector to zero. If the helot is in multiple cycle, depress the Clear key. The memory will then return to State o ½. Bring the memory factor into play by raising shutter of display window, simultaneously depressing locking lever, opening upper assembly carriage masker, sliding drum axle out of tab rack, shifting wheel track chain into B position, and moving preset button to ←> signal.' Is that clear?" said Mr. Armitage, after a little thought.

"No," said Mark. "Do these things have memories then?"

"I think so. I'm not quite sure about that Stage o ½. Maybe they still have some instructions programmed into them by old Miss Hooting. I don't quite see how to get rid of those. Here, it says, 'The helot will remember the previous day's instructions and repeat for an indefinite number of operations unless the memory factor is cancelled by opening 'R' slot and simultaneously depressing all function keys.' I must say," said Mr. Armitage, suddenly becoming enthusiastic, "if we could get Nickelas, for instance, to take over all the digging and lawn mowing, and carry the garbage bin to the street, I should be quite grateful to old Miss Hooting for her legacy, and I'm sorry I ever called her a trouble-making old so-and-so."

"And maybe we can programme Tinthea to wash dishes and make beds?" Harriet suggested hopefully.

But there was a long way to go before the helots could be set to perform any useful task with the slightest certainty that it would be carried out properly.

Tinthea, programmed to make the beds, showered sunflower oil liberally all over the blankets, and then tore up the sheets into shreds; she finished by scooping handfuls of foam rubber out of the mattresses, and unstringing all the bed-springs. The only bed spared was that of Cousin Elspeth, who always kept her bedroom door locked. Tinthea was unable to get into her room, though she returned to rattle vainly at the door handle all day long.

Nickelas, meanwhile, ran amok with the motor mower, trundling it back and forth across the garden, laying flat all Mrs. Armitage's begonias and dahlias in fifteen minutes; Mark was able to lasso him and switch him off just before he began on the sweet peas.

"We'd better get rid of them before they murder us all in our beds," said Mrs. Armitage.

"It seems a shame not to get *some* use out of them," said Harriet. "Don't you think we could teach Tinthea to do the cooking?"

But Tinthea's notion of cooking was to pile every article from the refrigerator into the oven, including ice-cubes and Mr. Armitage's special film for his Japanese camera. And then Harriet found her supplying buckets of strong

Earl Grey tea to Nickelas, who was pouring them over Mr. Armitage's cherished asparagus bed.

Instructed to pick blackberries for jam, Nickelas came back with a basket containing enough Deadly Nightshade berries to poison the entire village. Tinthea, set to polish the stairs, covered them with salad oil; Harriet was just in time to catch Cousin Elspeth as she slid down the last six steps. The results of this were quite advantageous, for Harriet was, on the spot, reappointed to the brown mohair stole in Cousin Elspeth's Will (though not informed of the fact) and Cousin Elspeth's lumbago, as it proved subsequently, was cured for ever by the shock of the fall; still, the Armitage household began to feel that the helots were more of a liability than an asset.

But how to dispose of them?

"If I were ye, I'd smesh 'em with a hetchit," snapped Cousin Elspeth.

"I don't think *that* would be advisable. A witch's legacy, you know, should be treated with caution."

"A witch! Hech!"

Mr. Armitage telephoned the local museum to ask if they would accept the helots; but Mr. Muskin, the curator, was away for a month in Tasmania, collecting ethnological curiosities. The nearest National Trust mansion had to refer the possibility of being given two lunar-powered helots to its Acquisitions Board; and the librarian at the village library was quite certain she didn't want them; nor did the Primary School.

For the time, Tinthea and Nickelas were locked in the cellar. "They won't pick up much lunar power there," said Mr. Armitage. They could be heard gloomily thumping about from time to time.

"I think they must have learned how to switch each other on," said Mark.

"It's a bit spooky having them down there," shivered

Harriet. "I wish Mr. Muskin would come back from Tasmania and decide to have them."

Meanwhile, to everybody's amazement, a most remarkable change was taking place in Cousin Elspeth. This was so noticeable, and so wholly unexpected, that it even distracted the family's attention from the uncertainty of having two somewhat unbiddable helots in the cellar.

In fact, as Mr. Armitage said to his wife, it was almost impossible to believe the evidence of one's own eyes.

In the course of three weeks Cousin Elspeth's looks and her temper improved daily and visibly. Her cheeks grew pink, her eyes blue, and her face no longer looked like a craggy mountain landscape, but became simply handsome and distinguished. She was heard to laugh, several times, and told Mrs. Armitage that it didn't matter if the tea wasn't always Earl Grey; she remembered a limerick she had heard in her youth about the Old Man of Hoy, restored the writing-desk to Mark in her Will, and began to leave her bedroom door unlocked.

Curiously enough, after a week or two, it was Mrs. Armitage who began to think rather wistfully of the wasted helot manpower lying idle down there in the cellar. She told Mark to fetch Tinthea to help with the job of washing blankets, which Cousin Elspeth pointed out should be done before the winter.

"After all, as we've got the creatures we might as well make *some* use of them. Just carrying blankets to and fro, Tinthea can't get up to much mischief. But don't bring Nickelas, I can't stand his big staring eyes."

So Mark, assisted by Harriet, fetched the smaller helot from the cellar. They were careful not to switch her on until she was in the utility room, and the cellar door locked again on the inert Nickelas.

But Harriet did afterwards recall that Tinthea's bulbous, sightless eyes seemed to watch the process of locking and unlocking very attentively.

For once, however, the smaller helot appeared to be in a co-operative mood, and she hoisted wet blankets out of the washing machine and trundled off with them into the garden, where she hung them on the line without doing anything un-programmed or uncalled-for, returning three or four times for a new load. It was bright, blowy autumn weather, the leaves were whirling off the trees, and the blankets dried so quickly that they were ready to put back on the beds after a couple of hours.

"Ech! Bless my soul!" sighed Cousin Elspeth at tea, which was, again, taken in the garden as the weather was so fine. "This veesit has passed so quickly, it's harrd to realise that it will be November on Thurrsday. I must be thinking of reeturrning to my ain wee naist."

"Oh, but you mustn't think of leaving before our Hallowe'en party," said Mrs. Armitage quickly. "We have *so* much enjoyed having you, Cousin Elspeth, you must make this visit an annual event. It has been a real pleasure."

"Indeed it has! I've taken a grand fancy to your young folk." Cousin Elspeth beamed benevolently at Mark and Harriet, who were lying on their stomachs on the grass, doing homework between bites of bread and damson jam.

"Where's Tinthea?" Harriet suddenly said to Mark. "Did you put her away?"

"No I didn't. Did you?"

Harriet shook her head.

Quietly she and Mark rose, left the group round the garden table, and went indoors.

"I can hear something upstairs," said Mark.

A thumping could be heard from the direction of Cousin Elspeth's room.

Harriet armed herself with a broom, Mark picked a walking-stick from the front-door stand, and they hurried up the stairs.

As they entered Cousin Elspeth's room, Tinthea could be seen apparently admiring herself in the large looking-glass. Then, advancing to it with outstretched monitor selection function aligners, she was plainly about to remove it from the wall when Mark, stepping forward, tapped down her main switch with the ferrule of the walking-stick. Tinthea let out what sounded like a cry of rage and spun half round before she lost her power and became inert, with dangling mandibles and vacant receiving panel; but even so it seemed to Harriet that there was a very malevolent expression in her sixty-watt eyes.

"What was *really* queer, though," Harriet said to her brother, "was that just before you hooked down her switch I caught sight of her reflection in the glass, and she looked – well, not like a helot, more like a person. There *is* something peculiar about that mirror."

She studied herself in the glass.

"The first time I saw myself in it I thought I looked horrible. But now I look better—"

Mark eyed his reflection and said, "Perhaps that's what's been happening to Cousin Elspeth; seeing herself in the glass day after day . . ."

"Of *course!* Aren't you clever! So that's why old Miss Hooting wanted it! But what shall we do about Tinthea?"

"Put her back in the cellar. You take her legs. Don't touch the switch." Tinthea sagged heavily between them as they carried her back to the cellar. And when she was set down next to Nickelas, it seemed to Harriet that a wordless message flashed between the two bulbous pairs of sightless eyes.

The Armitages' Hallowe'en party was always a great success.

This year Mrs. Armitage, with Cousin Elspeth and Harriet helping, produced a magnificent feast, including several Scottish delicacies such as haggis and Aberdeen Bun; Mark and Harriet organised apple-bobbing, table-turning, and fortune-telling with tea-leaves (large Earl

Grey ones), flour, lighted candles, and soot. The guests came dressed as trolls, kelpies, banshees, werewolves, or boggarts, and the sensation of the evening was the pair of helots, Tinthea and Nickelas, who, carefully and lengthily programmed during days of hard work by Mr. Armitage, passed round trays of cheese tarts, chestnut crunch fancies, and tiny curried sausages.

"But they're not real, are they?" cried Mrs. Pontwell, the vicar's wife. "I mean – they are Mark and Harriet, cleverly dressed up, aren't they, really?"

When she discovered that the helots were *not* Mark and Harriet she gave a slight scream and kept well out of their way for the rest of the evening.

Many of the guests remained, playing charades, until nearly midnight, but Cousin Elspeth, who intended to leave the following morning, retired to bed at half past ten.

"Och! I've just had a grand time," she said. "I never thocht I'd enjoy a party so well. But old bones, ye ken, need plainty of rest; I'll e'en take maself off to ma wee bed, for I must be up bricht and airrly the morn."

Her absence did not diminish the gaiety of the party, and Mrs. Armitage was serving cups of hot chocolate with rum in it while everybody sang "Widecombe Fair", when piercing shrieks were heard from upstairs. Simultaneously all the lights went out.

"Och, maircy! Mairder! Mairder! Mairder!"

"Sounds as if someone's strangling Cousin Elspeth," said Mark, starting for the stairs.

"Where did you put the matches?" said Harriet.

There were plenty of candles and matches lying around, but in the confusion, with guests and members of the family bumping about in the dark, it was some time before a rescue party, consisting of Mark, Mr. Armitage, and Mr. Shepherd from next door, was able to mount the stairs with candles and make their way to Cousin Elspeth's room.

They found that lady sitting up in bed in shawl and nightcap, almost paralytic with indignation.

"A deedy lot you are, upon my worrd! I could have been torrn leemb fra leemb before ye lifted a feenger!"

"But what happened?" said Mr. Armitage, looking round in perplexity.

"The mirror's gone!" said Mark.

"Whit happened? Whit *happened*? Yon unco' misshapen stravaiging shilpit monsters of yours cam' glomping intil ma room – bauld as brass! – removed the meerror fra the wall, and glomped off oot again, as calm as Plato! Wheer they have taken it, I dinna speer – nor do I care – but thankful I am this is the last nicht in life I'll pass under *this* roof, and I'll ne'er come back afore death bears me awa', and it's only a wonder I didna die on the spot wi' petrification!" And Cousin Elspeth succumbed to a fit of violent hysterics, needing to be ministered to with burnt feathers, sal volatile, brandy, snuff, hotwater bottles and antiphlogistine poultices.

While this was happening, Mark said to Harriet,

"Where do you suppose the helots have taken the mirror?"

"Back to the cellar? How did they get out?"

By this time most of the guests had gone. The blown fuse had been mended and the lights restored. Mark and Harriet went down, a little cautiously, to inspect the cellar, but found it empty; the lock had been neatly picked from inside.

As they returned to the hall the telephone rang. Mark picked up the receiver and heard the vicar's voice.

"Mark, is that you, my boy? I'm afraid those two mechanical monsters of yours are up to something very fishy in the churchyard. I can see them from my study window in the moonlight. Will you ask your father to come along, and tell him I've phoned P.C. Loiter."

"Oh, *now* what?" groaned Mr. Armitage on hearing this news, but he accompanied his children to the churchyard, which was only a five-minute run along the village street, leaving Mrs. Armitage in charge of the stricken Cousin Elspeth.

A large bright hunter's moon was sailing overhead, and by its light it was easy to see Nickelas and Tinthea hoisting up Miss Hooting's glass coffin. They had excavated the grave with amazing speed, and now carefully placed the coffin on the grass to one side of it. Then they laid the mirror, reflecting surface down, on top of the coffin.

As the Armitages arrived at one gate, the vicar and P.C. Loiter came from the vicarage garden.

"Here! What's going on!" shouted P.C. Loiter, outraged. "Just you stop that – whatever you're doing! – If you ask me," he added in an undertone to Mr. Pontwell, "that's what comes of burying these here wit – these old fairy ladies in churchyards along with decent folk."

"Oh dear me," said the vicar, "but we must be broadminded, you know, and Miss Hooting had been such a long-established member of our community—"

At this moment Nickelas and Tinthea, taking no notice of P.C. Loiter's shouts, raised the mirror high above the coffin, holding it like a canopy.

"What's the idea, d'you suppose?" Mark muttered to Harriet.

"So as to get the reflection of Miss Hooting inside the coffin—"

"Ugh!"

The coffin suddenly exploded with the kind of noise that a gas oven makes when somebody has been too slow in lighting the match. The helots fell backwards, letting go of the mirror, which fell and smashed.

A large owl was seen to fly away from where the coffin had been.

P.C. Loiter, very reluctantly, but encouraged by the presence of Mr. Pontwell and Mr. Armitage on either side, went forward and inspected the coffin. But there was nothing in it, except a great deal of broken glass. Nor was the body of Miss Hooting ever seen again.

"*I* think it was a plan that went wrong," said Harriet to Mark. "*I* think she hoped, if she had the mirror, it would make her young and handsome and stop her from dying."

"So she sent the helots to get it? Maybe," said Mark.

"What a shame the mirror got smashed. Because, look at Cousin Elspeth!"

Cousin Elspeth, overnight, had gone back to exactly what she had been at the beginning of the visit – sour, dour, hard-featured, and extremely bad-tempered.

"Ye might have provided a drap of Earl Grey for my last breakfast!" she snapped. "And, as for that disgreeceful occurrence last nicht – aweel, the less said the better!" After which she went on to say a great deal more about it, and, as she left, announced that Mark would certainly not get the writing-desk nor Harriet the mohair stole, since they were undoubtedly responsible for the goings-on in the night.

"Somehow I don't see Cousin Elspeth putting us through art school," mused Harriet, as the taxi rolled away with their cousin along the village street.

"That's a long way off," said Mark peacefully.

Mr. Armitage was on the telephone to Dowbridges, the auctioneers.

"I want you to come and fetch two robots and enter them in your Friday sale. Please send a truck at once; I'd like them out of the house by noon. Yes, *robots*; two lunar-powered robots, in full working order, complete with instruction booklets. Handy for workshop, kitchen, or garden; a really useful pair; you can price the large one at £90 and the small at £50."

On Friday Mrs. Armitage and Harriet attended the sale, and returned to report with high satisfaction that both helots had been sold to old Admiral Lycanthrop.

"*He*'ll give them what-for, I bet," said Mark. "*He* won't stand any nonsense from them."

But, alas, it turned out that the admiral, who was rather hard of hearing, thought he was bidding for two row-boats, and when he discovered that his purchase consisted instead of two lunar-powered mechanical slaves with awkward dispositions, he returned them, demanding his money back.

The Armitages came down to breakfast on Saturday to find Nickelas and Tinthea standing mute, dogged, and expectant, outside the back door . . .

The Third Wish

ONCE THERE WAS A MAN WHO WAS DRIVING
in his car at dusk on a spring evening through part
of the forest of Savernake. His name was Mr. Peters. The
primroses were just beginning but the trees were still bare,
and it was cold; the birds had stopped singing an hour
ago.

As Mr. Peters entered a straight, empty stretch of road
he seemed to hear a faint crying, and a struggling and
thrashing, as if somebody was in trouble far away in the
trees. He left his car and climbed the mossy bank beside
the road. Beyond the bank was an open slope of beech
trees leading down to thorn bushes through which he saw
the gleam of water. He stood a moment waiting to try
and discover where the noise was coming from, and presently heard a rustling and some strange cries in a voice
which was almost human – and yet there was something
too hoarse about it at one time and too clear and sweet
at another. Mr. Peters ran down the hill and as he neared

the bushes he saw something white among them which was trying to extricate itself; coming closer he found that it was a swan that had become entangled in the thorns growing on the bank of the canal.

The bird struggled all the more frantically as he approached, looking at him with hate in its yellow eyes, and when he took hold of it to free it, hissed at him, pecked him, and thrashed dangerously with its wings which were powerful enough to break his arm. Nevertheless he managed to release it from the thorns, and carrying it tightly with one arm, holding the snaky head well away with the other hand (for he did not wish his eyes pecked out), he took it to the verge of the canal and dropped it in.

The swan instantly assumed great dignity and sailed out to the middle of the water, where it put itself to rights with much dabbling and preening, smoothing its feathers with little showers of drops. Mr. Peters waited, to make sure that it was all right and had suffered no damage in its struggles. Presently the swan, when it was satisfied with its appearance, floated in to the bank once more, and in a moment, instead of the great white bird, there was a little man all in green with a golden crown and long beard, standing by the water. He had fierce glittering eyes and looked by no means friendly.

"Well, Sir," he said threateningly, "I see you are presumptuous enough to know some of the laws of magic. You think that because you have rescued – by pure good fortune – the King of the Forest from a difficulty, you should have some fabulous reward."

"I expect three wishes, no more and no less," answered Mr. Peters, looking at him steadily and with composure.

"Three wishes, he wants, the clever man! Well, I have yet to hear of the human being who made any good use of his three wishes – they mostly end up worse off than they started. Take your three wishes then—" he flung three dead leaves in the air "—don't blame me if you spend the last wish in undoing the work of the other two."

Mr. Peters caught the leaves and put two of them carefully in his notecase. When he looked up the swan was sailing about in the middle of the water again, flicking the drops angrily down its long neck.

Mr. Peters stood for some minutes reflecting on how he should use his reward. He knew very well that the gift of three magic wishes was one which brought trouble more often than not, and he had no intention of being like the forester who first wished by mistake for a sausage, and then in a rage wished it on the end of his wife's nose, and then had to use his last wish in getting it off again. Mr. Peters had most of the things which he wanted and was very content with his life. The only thing that troubled him was that he was a little lonely, and had no companion for his old age. He decided to use his first wish and to keep the other two in case of an emergency. Taking a thorn he pricked his tongue with it, to remind himself not to utter rash wishes aloud. Then holding the third leaf and gazing round him at the dusky undergrowth, the primroses, great beeches and the blue-green water of the canal, he said:

"I wish I had a wife as beautiful as the forest."

A tremendous quacking and splashing broke out on the surface of the water. He thought that it was the swan laughing at him. Taking no notice he made his way through the darkening woods to his car, wrapped himself up in the rug and went to sleep.

When he awoke it was morning and the birds were beginning to call. Coming along the track towards him was the most beautiful creature he had ever seen, with eyes as blue-green as the canal, hair as dusky as the bushes, and skin as white as the feathers of swans.

"Are you the wife that I wished for?" asked Mr. Peters.

"Yes I am," she replied. "My name is Leita."

She stepped into the car beside him and they drove off to the church on the outskirts of the forest, where they were married. Then he took her to his house in a remote and lovely valley and showed her all his treasures – the bees in their white hives, the Jersey cows, the hyacinths, the silver candlesticks, the blue cups and the lustre bowl for putting primroses in. She admired everything, but what pleased her most was the river which ran by the foot of his garden.

"Do swans come up here?" she asked.

"Yes, I have often seen swans there on the river," he told her, and she smiled.

Leita made him a good wife. She was gentle and friendly, busied herself about the house and garden, polished the bowls, milked the cows and mended his socks. But as time went by Mr. Peters began to feel that she was not happy. She seemed restless, wandered much in the garden, and sometimes when he came back from the fields he would find the house empty and she would only return after half an hour or so with no explanation of where she had been. On these occasions she was especially tender and would put out his slippers to warm and cook his favourite dish – Welsh rarebit with wild strawberries – for supper.

One evening he was returning home along the river path when he saw Leita in front of him, down by the water. A swan had sailed up to the verge and she had her arms round its neck and the swan's head rested against her cheek. She was weeping, and as he came nearer he saw that tears were rolling, too, from the swan's eyes.

"Leita, what is it?" he asked, very troubled.

"This is my sister," she answered. "I can't bear being separated from her."

Now he understood that Leita was really a swan from

the forest, and this made him very sad because when a human being marries a bird it always leads to sorrow.

"I could use my second wish to give your sister human shape, so that she could be a companion to you," he suggested.

"No, no," she cried. "I couldn't ask that of her."

"Is it so very hard to be a human being?" asked Mr. Peters sadly.

"Very, very hard," she answered.

"Don't you love me at all, Leita?"

"Yes, I do, I do love you," she said, and there were tears in her eyes again. "But I miss the old life in the forest, the cool grass and the mist rising off the river at sunrise and the feel of the water sliding over my feathers as my sister and I drifted along the stream."

"Then shall I use my second wish to turn you back into a swan again?" he asked, and his tongue pricked to remind him of the old King's words, and his heart swelled with grief inside him.

"Who would darn your socks and cook your meals and see to the hens?"

"I'd do it myself as I did before I married you," he said, trying to sound cheerful.

She shook her head. "No, I could not be as unkind to you as that. I am partly a swan, but I am also partly a human being now. I will stay with you."

Poor Mr. Peters was very distressed on his wife's account and did his best to make her life happier, taking her for drives in the car, finding beautiful music for her to listen to on the radio, buying clothes for her and even suggesting a trip round the world. But she said no to that; she would prefer to stay in their own house near the river.

He noticed that she spent more and more time baking wonderful cakes – jam puffs, petits fours, éclairs and meringues. One day he saw her take a basketful down to the river and he guessed that she was giving them to her sister.

He built a seat for her by the river, and the two sisters spent hours together there, communicating in some wordless manner. For a time he thought that all would be well, but then he saw how thin and pale she was growing.

One night when he had been late doing the accounts he came up to bed and found her weeping in her sleep and calling:

"Rhea! Rhea! I can't understand what you say! Oh, wait for me, take me with you!"

Then he knew that it was hopeless and she would never be happy as a human. He stooped down and kissed her goodbye, then took another leaf from his notecase, blew it out of the window, and used up his second wish.

Next moment instead of Leita there was a sleeping swan lying across the bed with its head under its wing. He carried it out of the house and down to the brink of the river, and then he said "Leita! Leita!" to waken her, and gently put her into the water. She gazed round her in astonishment for a moment and then came up to him and rested her head lightly against his hand; next instant she was flying away over the trees towards the heart of the forest.

He heard a harsh laugh behind him, and turning round saw the old King looking at him with a malicious expression.

"Well, my friend! You don't seem to have managed so wonderfully with your first two wishes, do you? What will you do with the last? Turn yourself into a swan? Or turn Leita back into a girl?"

"I shall do neither," said Mr. Peters calmly. "Human beings and swans are better in their own shapes."

But for all that he looked sadly over towards the forest where Leita had flown, and walked slowly back to his empty house.

Next day he saw two swans swimming at the bottom of the garden, and one of them wore the gold chain he had given Leita after their marriage; she came up and rubbed her head against his hand.

Mr. Peters and his two swans came to be well known in that part of the country; people used to say that he talked to the swans and they understood him as well as his neighbours. Many people were a little frightened of him. There was a story that once when thieves tried to break into his house they were set upon by two huge white birds which carried them off bodily and dropped them in the river.

As Mr. Peters grew old everyone wondered at his contentment. Even when he was bent with rheumatism he would not think of moving to a drier spot, but went slowly about his work, milking the cows and collecting the honey and eggs, with the two swans always somewhere close at hand.

Sometimes people who knew his story would say to him: "Mr. Peters, why don't you wish for another wife?"

"Not likely," he would answer serenely. "Two wishes were enough for me, I reckon. I've learned that even if your wishes are granted they don't always better you. I'll stay faithful to Leita."

One autumn night, passers-by along the road heard the mournful sound of two swans singing. All night the song went on, sweet and harsh, sharp and clear. In the morning Mr. Peters was found peacefully dead in his bed with a smile of great happiness on his face. In between his hands, which lay clasped on his breast, were a withered leaf and a white feather.

A Harp of Fishbones

LITTLE NERRYN LIVED IN THE HALF-RUINED mill at the upper end of the village, where the stream ran out of the forest. The old miller's name was Timorash, but she called him uncle. Her own father and mother were dead, long before she could remember. Timorash was no real kin, nor was he particularly kind to her; he was a lazy old man. He never troubled to grow corn as the other people in the village did, little patches in the clearing below the village before the forest began again. When people brought him corn to grind he took one-fifth of it as his fee and this, with wild plums which Nerryn gathered and dried, and carp from the deep millpool, kept him and the child fed through the short bright summers and the long silent winters.

Nerryn learned to do the cooking when she was seven or eight; she toasted fish on sticks over the fire and baked cakes of bread on a flat stone; Timorash beat her if the food was burnt, but it mostly was, just the same, because

63

so often half her mind would be elsewhere, listening to the bell-like call of a bird or pondering about what made the difference between the stream's voice in winter and in summer. When she was a little older Timorash taught her how to work the mill, opening the sluice-gate so that the green, clear mountain water could hurl down against the great wooden paddle-wheel. Nerryn liked this much better, since she already spent hours watching the stream endlessly pouring and plaiting down its narrow passage. Old Timorash had hoped that now he would be able to give up work altogether and lie in the sun all day, or crouch by the fire, slowly adding one stick after another and dreaming about barley wine. But Nerryn forgot to take flour in payment from the villagers, who were in no hurry to remind her, so the old man angrily decided that this plan would not answer, and sent her out to work.

First she worked for one household, then for another. The people of the village had come from the plains; they were surly, big-boned, and lank, with tow-coloured hair and pale eyes; even the children seldom spoke. Little Nerryn sometimes wondered, looking at her reflection in the millpool, how it was that she should be so different from them, small and brown-skinned, with dark hair like a bird's feathers and hazelnut eyes. But it was no use asking questions of old Timorash, who never answered except by grunting or throwing a clod of earth at her. Another difference was that she loved to chatter, and this was perhaps the main reason why the people she worked for soon sent her packing.

There were other reasons too, for, though Nerryn was willing enough to work, things often distracted her.

"She let the bread burn while she ran outside to listen to a curlew," said one.

"When she was helping me cut the hay she asked so many questions that my ears have ached for three days," complained another.

"Instead of scaring off the birds from my corn-patch she sat with her chin on her fists, watching them gobble down half a winter's supply and whistling to them!" grumbled a third.

Nobody would keep her more than a few days, and she had plenty of beatings, especially from Timorash, who had hoped that her earnings would pay for a keg of barley wine. Once in his life he had had a whole keg, and he still felt angry when he remembered that it was finished.

At last Nerryn went to work for an old woman who lived in a tumbledown hut at the bottom of the street. Her name was Saroon and she was by far the oldest in the village, so withered and wrinkled that most people thought she was a witch; besides, she knew when it was going to rain and was the only person in the place who did not fear to venture a little way into the forest. But she was growing weak now, and stiff, and wanted somebody to help dig her corn-patch and cut wood. Nevertheless she hardly seemed to welcome help when it came. As Nerryn moved about at the tasks she was set, the old woman's little red-rimmed eyes followed her suspiciously; she hobbled round the hut watching through cracks, grumbling and chuntering to herself, never losing sight of the girl for a moment, like some cross-grained old animal that sees a stranger near its burrow.

On the fourth day she said,

"You're singing girl,"

"I – I'm sorry," Nerryn stammered. "I didn't mean to – I wasn't thinking. Don't beat me, please."

"Humph," said the old woman, but she did not beat Nerryn that time. And next day, watching through the window-hole while Nerryn chopped wood, she said,

"You're not singing."

Nerryn jumped. She had not known the old woman was so near.

"I thought you didn't like me to," she faltered.

"I didn't say so, did I?"

Muttering, the old woman stumped off to the back of the hut and began to sort through a box of mildewy nuts. "As if I should care," Nerryn heard her grumble, "whether the girl sings or not!" But next day she put her head out of the door, while Nerryn hoed the corn-patch, and said,

"Sing, child!"

Nerryn looked at her, doubtful and timid, to see if she really meant it, but she nodded her head energetically, till the tangled grey locks bounced on her shoulders, and repeated,

"Sing!"

So presently the clear, tiny thread of Nerryn's song began again as she sliced off the weeds; and old Saroon came out and sat on an upturned log beside the door, pounding roots for soup and mumbling to herself in time to the sound. And at the end of the week she did not dismiss the girl, as everyone else had done, though what she paid was so little that Timorash grumbled every time Nerryn brought it home. At this rate twenty years would go by before he had saved enough for a keg of barley wine.

One day Saroon said,

"Your father used to sing."

This was the first time anyone had spoken of him.

"Oh," Nerryn cried, forgetting her fear of the old woman. "Tell me about him."

"Why should I?" old Saroon said sourly. "He never did anything for *me*." And she hobbled off to fetch a pot of water. But later she relented and said,

"His hair was the colour of ash buds, like yours. And he carried a harp."

"A harp, what is a harp?"

"Oh, don't pester, child. I'm busy."

But another day she said, "A harp is a thing to make music. His was a gold one, but it was broken."

"Gold, what is gold?"

"This," said the old woman, and she pulled out a small, thin disc which she wore on a cord of plaited grass round her neck.

"Why!" Nerryn exclaimed. "Everybody in the village has one of those except Timorash and me. I've often asked what they were but no one would answer."

"They are gold. When your father went off and left you and the harp with Timorash, the old man ground up the harp between the millstones. And he melted down the gold powder and made it into these little circles and sold them to everybody in the village, and bought a keg of barley wine. He told us they would bring good luck. But I have never had any good luck and that was a long time ago. And Timorash has long since drunk all his barley wine."

"Where did my father go?" asked Nerryn.

"Into the forest," the old woman snapped. "I could have told him he was in for trouble. I could have warned him. But he never asked *my* advice."

She sniffed, and set a pot of herbs boiling on the fire. And Nerryn could get no more out of her that day.

But little by little, as time passed, more came out.

"Your father came from over the mountains. High up yonder, he said, there was a great city, with houses and palaces and temples, and as many rich people as there are fish in the millpool. Best of all, there was always music playing in the streets and houses and in the temples. But then the goddess of the mountain became angry, and fire burst out of a crack in the hillside. And then a great cold came, so that people froze where they stood. Your father said he only just managed to escape with you by running very fast. Your mother had died in the fire."

"Where was he going?"

"The king of the city had ordered him to go for help."

"What sort of help?"

67

"Don't ask *me*," the old woman grumbled. "You'd think he'd have settled down here like a person of sense, and mended his harp. But no, on he must go, leaving you behind so that he could travel faster. He said he'd fetch you again on his way back. But of course he never did come back – one day I found his bones in the forest. The birds must have killed him."

"How do you *know* they were my father's bones?"

"Because of the tablet he carried. See, here it is, with his name on it, Heramon the harper."

"Tell me more about the harp!"

"It was shaped like this," the old woman said. They were washing clothes by the stream, and she drew with her finger in the mud. "Like this, and it had golden strings across, so. All but one of the strings had melted in the fire from the mountain. Even on just one string he could make very beautiful music, that would force you to stop whatever you were doing and listen. It is a pity he had to leave the harp behind. Timorash wanted it as payment for looking after you. If your father had taken the harp with him, perhaps he would have been able to reach the other side of the forest."

Nerryn thought about this story a great deal. For the next few weeks she did even less work than usual and was mostly to be found squatting with her chin on her fists by the side of the stream. Saroon beat her, but not very hard. Then one day Nerryn said,

"I shall make a harp."

"Hah!" sniffed the old woman. "You! What do you know of such things?"

After a few minutes she asked,

"What will you make it from?"

Nerryn said, "I shall make it of fishbones. Some of the biggest carp in the millpool have bones as thick as my wrist, and they are very strong."

"Timorash will never allow it."

"I shall wait till he is asleep, then."

So Nerryn waited till night, and then she took a chunk of rotten wood, which glows in the dark, and dived into the deep millpool, swimming down and down to the depths where the biggest carp lurk, among the mud and weeds and old sunken logs.

When they saw the glimmer of the wood through the water, all the fish came nosing and nibbling and swimming round Nerryn, curious to find if this thing which shone so strangely was good to eat. She waited as long as she could bear it, holding her breath, till a great barrel-shaped monster slid nudging right up against her; then, quick as a flash, she wrapped her arms round his slippery sides and fled up with a bursting heart to the surface.

Much to her surprise, old Saroon was there, waiting in the dark on the bank. But the old woman only said,

"You had better bring the carp to my hut. After all, you want no more than the bones, and it would be a pity to waste all that good meat. I can live on it for a week." So she cut the meat off the bones, which were coal-black but had a sheen on them like mother-of-pearl. Nerryn dried them by the fire, and then she joined together the three biggest, notching them to fit, and cementing them with a glue she made by boiling some of the smaller bones together. She used long, thin, strong bones for strings, joining them to the frame in the same manner.

All the time old Saroon watched closely. Sometimes she would say,

"That was not the way of it. Heramon's harp was wider," or "You are putting the strings too far apart. There should be more of them, and they should be tighter."

When at last it was done, she said,

"Now you must hang it in the sun to dry."

So for three days the harp hung drying in the sun and wind. At night Saroon took it into her hut and covered it with a cloth. On the fourth day she said,

"Now, play!"

Nerryn rubbed her finger across the strings, and they gave out a liquid murmur, like that of a stream running over pebbles, under a bridge. She plucked a string, and the noise was like that a drop of water makes, falling in a hollow place.

"That will be music," old Saroon said, nodding her head, satisfied. "It is not quite the same as the sound from your father's harp, but it is music. Now you shall play me tunes every day, and I shall sit in the sun and listen."

"No," said Nerryn, "for if Timorash hears me playing he will take the harp away and break it or sell it. I shall go to my father's city and see if I can find any of his kin there."

At this old Saroon was very angry. "Here have I taken all these pains to help you, and what reward do I get from it? How much pleasure do you think I have, living among dolts in this dismal place? I was not born here, any more than you were. You could at least play to me at night, when Timorash is asleep."

"Well, I will play to you for seven nights," Nerryn said.

Each night old Saroon tried to persuade her not to go, and she tried harder as Nerryn became more skilful in playing, and drew from the fishbone harp a curious watery music, like the songs that birds sing when it is raining. But Nerryn would not be persuaded to stay, and when she saw this, on the seventh night, Saroon said,

"I suppose I shall have to tell you how to go through the forest. Otherwise you will certainly die, as your father did. When you go among the trees you will find that the grass underfoot is thick and strong and hairy, and the farther you go, the higher it grows, as high as your waist. And it is sticky and clings to you, so that you can only go forward slowly, one step at a time. Then, in the middle of the forest, perched in the branches, are vultures who

70

will drop on you and peck you to death if you stand still for more than a minute."

"How do you know all this?" Nerryn said.

"I have tried many times to go through the forest, but it is too far for me; I grow tired and have to turn back. The vultures take no notice of me, I am too old and withered, but a tender young piece like you would be just what they fancy."

"Then what must I do?" Nerryn asked.

"You must play music on your harp till they fall asleep; then, while they sleep, cut the grass with your knife and go forward as fast as you can."

Nerryn said, "If I cut you enough fuel for a month, and catch you another carp, and gather you a bushel of nuts, will you give me your little gold circle, or my father's tablet?"

But this Saroon would not do. She did, though, break off the corner of the tablet which had Heramon the harper's name on it, and give that to Nerryn.

"But don't blame me," she said sourly, "if you find the city all burnt and frozen, with not a living soul to walk its streets."

"Oh, it will all have been rebuilt by this time," Nerryn said. "I shall find my father's people, or my mother's, and I shall come back for you, riding a white mule and leading another."

"Fairy tales!" old Saroon said angrily. "Be off with you, then. If you don't wish to stay I'm sure *I* don't want you idling about the place. All the work you've done this last week I could have done better myself in half an hour. Drat the woodsmoke! It gets in a body's eyes till they can't see a thing." And she hobbled into the hut, working her mouth sourly and rubbing her eyes with the back of her hand.

Nerryn ran into the forest, going cornerways up the

mountain, so as not to pass too close to the mill where old Timorash lay sleeping in the sun.

Soon she had to slow down because the way was so steep. And the grass grew thicker and thicker, hairy, sticky, all twined and matted together, as high as her waist. Presently, as she hacked and cut at it with her bone knife, she heard a harsh croaking and flapping above her. She looked up, and saw two grey vultures perched on a branch, leaning forward to peer down at her. Their wings were twice the length of a man's arm and they had long, wrinkled, black, leathery necks and little fierce yellow eyes. As she stood, two more, then five, ten, twenty others came rousting through the branches, and all perched round about, craning their long black necks, swaying back and forth, keeping balanced by the way they opened and shut their wings.

Nerryn felt very much afraid of them, but she unslung the harp from her back and began to play a soft, trickling tune, like rain falling on a deep pool. Very soon the vultures sank their necks down between their shoulders and closed their eyes. They sat perfectly still.

When she was certain they were asleep, Nerryn made haste to cut and slash at the grass. She was several hundred yards on her way before the vultures woke and came cawing and jostling through the branches to cluster again just overhead. Quickly she pulled the harp round and strummed on its fishbone strings until once again, lulled by the music, the vultures sank their heads between their grey wings and slept. Then she went back to cutting the grass, as fast as she could.

It was a long, tiring way. Soon she grew so weary that she could hardly push one foot ahead of the other, and it was hard to keep awake; once she only just roused in time when a vulture, swooping down, missed her with his beak and instead struck the harp on her back with a loud strange twang that set echoes scampering through the trees.

At last the forest began to thin and dwindle; here the tree-trunks and branches were all draped about with grey-green moss, like long dangling hanks of sheepswool. Moss grew on the rocky ground, too, in a thick carpet. When she reached this part, Nerryn could go on safely; the vultures rose in an angry flock and flew back with harsh croaks of disappointment, for they feared the trailing moss would wind round their wings and trap them.

As soon as she reached the edge of the trees Nerryn lay down in a deep tussock of moss and fell fast asleep.

She was so tired that she slept almost till nightfall, but then the cold woke her. It was bitter on the bare mountainside; the ground was all crisp with white frost, and when Nerryn started walking uphill she crunched through it, leaving deep black footprints. Unless she kept moving she knew that she would probably die of cold, so she climbed on, higher and higher; the stars came out, showing more frost-covered slopes ahead and all around, while the forest far below curled round the flank of the mountain like black fur.

Through the night she went on climbing and by sunrise she had reached the foot of a steep slope of ice-covered boulders. When she tried to climb over these she only slipped back again.

What shall I do now? Nerryn wondered. She stood blowing on her frozen fingers and thought, "I must go on or I shall die here of cold. I will play a tune on the harp to warm my fingers and my wits."

She unslung the harp. It was hard to play, for her fingers were almost numb and at first refused to obey but, while she had climbed the hill, a very sweet, lively tune had come into her head, and she struggled and struggled until her stubborn fingers found the right notes to play it. Once she played the tune – twice – and the stones on

73

the slope above began to roll and shift. She played a third time and, with a thunderous roar, the whole pile broke loose and went sliding down the mountain-side. Nerryn was only just able to dart aside out of the way before the frozen mass careered past, sending up a smoking dust of ice.

Trembling a little she went on up the hill, and now she came to a gate in a great wall, set about with towers. The gate stood open, and so she walked through.

"Surely this must be my father's city," she thought.

But when she stood inside the gate, her heart sank, and she remembered old Saroon's words. For the city that must once have been bright with gold and coloured stone and gay with music was all silent; not a soul walked the streets and the houses, under their thick covering of frost, were burnt and blackened by fire.

And, what was still more frightening, when Nerryn looked through the doorways into the houses, she could see people standing or sitting or lying, frozen still like statues, as the cold had caught them while they worked, or slept, or sat at dinner.

"Where shall I go now?" she thought. "It would have been better to stay with Saroon in the forest. When night comes I shall only freeze to death in this place."

But still she went on, almost tiptoeing in the frosty silence of the city, looking into doorways and through gates, until she came to a building that was larger than any other, built with a high roof and many pillars of white marble. The fire had not touched it.

"This must be the temple," she thought, remembering the tale Saroon had told, and she walked between the pillars, which glittered like white candles in the light from the rising sun. Inside there was a vast hall, and many people standing frozen, just as they had been when they came to pray for deliverance from their trouble. They had offerings with them, honey and cakes and white doves and lambs and precious ointment. At the back of the hall the people wore rough clothes of homespun cloth, but farther forward Nerryn saw wonderful robes, embroidered with gold and copper thread, made of rich materials, trimmed with fur and sparkling stones. And up in the very front, kneeling on the steps of the altar, was a man who was finer than all the rest and Nerryn thought he must have been the king himself. His hair and long beard were white, his cloak was purple, and on his head were three crowns, one gold, one copper, and one of ivory. Nerryn stole up to him and touched the fingers that held a gold staff, but they were ice-cold and still as marble, like all the rest.

A sadness came over her as she looked at the people and she thought, "What use to them are their fine robes now? Why did the goddess punish them? What did they do wrong?"

But there was no answer to her question.

"I had better leave this place before I am frozen as well," she thought. "The goddess may be angry with me too, for coming here. But first I will play for her on my harp, as I have not brought any offering."

So she took her harp and began to play. She played all the tunes she could remember, and last of all she played the one that had come into her head as she climbed the mountain.

At the noise of her playing, frost began to fall in white showers from the roof of the temple, and from the rafters and pillars and the clothes of the motionless people. Then the king sneezed. Then there was a stirring noise, like the sound of a winter stream when the ice begins to melt. Then someone laughed – a loud, clear laugh. And, just as, outside the town, the pile of frozen rocks had started to move and topple when Nerryn played, so now the whole gathering of people began to stretch themselves, and turn round, and look at one another, and smile. And as she went on playing they began to dance.

The dancing spread, out of the temple and down the streets. People in the houses stood up and danced. Still dancing, they fetched brooms and swept away the heaps of frost that kept falling from the rooftops with the sound of the music. They fetched old wooden pipes and tabors out of cellars that had escaped the fire, so that when Nerryn stopped playing at last, quite tired out, the music still went on. All day and all night, for thirty days, the music lasted, until the houses were rebuilt, the streets clean, and not a speck of frost remained in the city.

But the king beckoned Nerryn aside when she stopped playing and they sat down on the steps of the temple.

"My child," he said, "where did you get that harp?"

"Sir, I made it out of fishbones after a picture of my father's harp that an old woman made for me."

"And what was your father's name, child, and where is he now?"

"Sir, he is dead in the forest, but here is a piece of a tablet with his name on it."

And Nerryn held out the little fragment with Heramon the harper's name written. When he saw it, great tears formed in the king's eyes and began to roll down his cheeks.

"Sir," Nerryn said, "what is the matter? Why do you weep?"

"I weep for my son Heramon, who is lost, and I weep for joy because my grandchild has returned to me."

Then the king embraced Nerryn and took her to his palace and had robes of fur and velvet put on her, and there was great happiness and much feasting. And the king told Nerryn how, many years ago, the goddess was angered because the people had grown so greedy for gold from her mountain that they spent their lives in digging and mining, day and night, and forgot to honour her

76

with music, in her temple and in the streets, as they had been used to do. They made tools of gold, and plates and dishes and musical instruments; everything that could be was made of gold. So at last the goddess appeared among them, terrible with rage, and put a curse on them, of burning and freezing.

"Since you prefer gold, got by burrowing in the earth, to the music that should honour me," she said, "you may keep your golden toys and little good may they do you! Let your golden harps and trumpets be silent, your flutes and pipes be dumb! I shall not come among you again until I am summoned by notes from a harp that is not made of gold, nor of silver, nor any precious metal, a harp that has never touched the earth but came from deep water, a harp that no man has ever played."

Then fire burst out of the mountain, destroying houses and killing many people. The king ordered his son Heramon, who was the bravest man in the city, to cross the dangerous forest and seek far and wide until he should find the harp of which the goddess spoke. Before Heramon could depart a great cold had struck, freezing people where they stood; only just in time he caught up his little daughter from her cradle and carried her away with him.

"But now you are come back," the old king said, "you shall be queen after me, and we shall take care that the goddess is honoured with music every day, in the temple and in the streets. And we will order everything that is made of gold to be thrown into the mountain torrent, so that nobody ever again shall be tempted to worship gold before the goddess."

So this was done, the king himself being the first to throw away his golden crown and staff. The river carried all the golden things down through the forest until they came to rest in Timorash's millpool, and one day, when he was fishing for carp, he pulled out the crown. Overjoyed, he ground it to powder and sold it to his neighbours for barley wine. Then he returned to the pool, hoping for more gold, but by now he was so drunk that he fell in and drowned among a clutter of golden spades and trumpets and goblets and pickaxes.

But long before this Nerryn with her harp on her back and astride a white mule with knives bound to its hoofs, had ridden down the mountain to fetch Saroon as she had promised. She passed the forest safely, playing music for the vultures while the mule cut its way through the long grass. Nobody in the village recognized her, so splendidly was she dressed in fur and scarlet.

But when she came to where Saroon's hut had stood, the ground was bare, nor was there any trace that a dwelling had ever been there. And when she asked for Saroon, nobody knew the name, and the whole village declared that such a person had never lived there.

Amazed and sorrowful, Nerryn returned to her grandfather. But one day, not long after, when she was alone, praying in the temple of the goddess, she heard a voice that said,

"Sing, child!"

And Nerryn was greatly astonished, for she felt she had heard the voice before, though she could not think where.

While she looked about her, wondering, the voice said again,

"Sing!"

And then Nerryn understood, and she laughed, and, taking her harp, sang a song about chopping wood, and about digging, and fishing, and the birds of the forest, and how the stream's voice changes in summer and in winter. For now she knew who had helped her to make her harp of fishbones.

The Serial Garden

"COLD RICE PUDDING FOR BREAKFAST?" SAID Mark, looking at it with disfavour.

"Don't be fussy," said his mother. "You're the only one who's complaining." This was unfair, for she and Mark were the only members of the family at table, Harriet having developed measles while staying with a school friend, while Mr. Armitage had somehow managed to lock himself in the larder. Mrs. Armitage never had anything but toast and marmalade for breakfast anyway.

Mark went on scowling at the chilly-looking pudding. It had come straight out of the fridge, which was not in the larder.

"If you don't like it," said Mrs. Armitage, "unless you want Daddy to pass you cornflakes through the larder ventilator, flake by flake, you'd better run down to Miss Pride and get a small packet of cereal. She opens at eight; Hickmans don't open till nine. It's no use waiting till the

79

blacksmith comes to let your father out; I'm sure he won't be here for hours yet."

There came a gloomy banging from the direction of the larder, just to remind them that Mr. Armitage was alive and suffering in there.

"*You're* all right," shouted Mark heartlessly as he passed the larder door, "there's nothing to stop you having cornflakes. Oh I forgot, the milk's in the fridge. Well, have cheese and pickles then. Or treacle tart."

Even through the zinc grating on the door he could hear his father shudder at the thought of treacle tart and pickles for breakfast. Mr. Armitage's imprisonment was his own fault, though; he had sworn that he was going to find out where the mouse got into the larder if it took him all night, watching and waiting. He had shut himself in, so that no member of the family should come bursting in and disturb his vigil. The larder door had a spring catch, which sometimes jammed; it was bad luck that this turned out to be one of the times.

Mark ran across the field to Miss Pride's shop at Sticks Corner and asked if she had any cornflakes.

"Oh, I don't think I have any left, dear," Miss Pride said woefully. "I'll have a look ... I think I sold the last packet a week ago Tuesday."

"What about the one in the window?"

"That's a dummy, dear."

Miss Pride's shop-window was full of nasty old cardboard cartons with nothing inside them, and several empty display stands which had fallen down and never been propped up again. Inside the shop were a few small tired-looking tins and jars, which had a worn and scratched appearance as if mice had tried them and given up. Miss Pride herself was small and wan, with yellowish grey hair; she rooted rather hopelessly in a pile of empty boxes. Mark's mother never bought any groceries from Miss Pride if she could help it, since the day when she had found a label inside the foil wrapping of a cream cheese saying 'This cheese should be eaten before May 11th, 1899'.

"No cornflakes, I'm afraid, dear."

"Any Wheat Crispies? Puffed Corn? Rice Nuts?"

"No, dear. Nothing left, only Brekkfast Brikks."

"Never heard of *them*," said Mark doubtfully.

"Or I've a jar of Ovo here. You spread it on bread. That's nice for breakfast," said Miss Pride with a sudden burst of salesmanship. Mark thought the Ovo looked beastly, like yellow paint, so he took the packet of Brekkfast Brikks. At least it wasn't very big ... On the front of the box was a picture of a fat, repulsive, fair-haired boy, rather like the chubby Augustus, banging on his plate with his spoon.

"They look like tiny doormats," said Mrs. Armitage, as Mark shovelled some Brikks into his bowl.

"They taste like them too. Gosh," said Mark, "I must hurry or I'll be late for school. There's rather a nice little cut-out garden on the back of the packet, though; don't throw it away when it's empty. Goodbye, Daddy," he shouted through the larder door. "Hope Mr. Ellis comes soon to let you out." And he dashed off to catch the school bus.

At breakfast next morning Mark had a huge helping of Brekkfast Brikks and persuaded his father to try them.

"They taste just like esparto grass," said Mr. Armitage fretfully.

"Yes I know, but do take some more, Daddy. I want to cut out the model garden, it's so lovely."

"Rather pleasant, I must say. It looks like an eighteenth-century German engraving," his father agreed. "It certainly was a stroke of genius putting it on the packet. No one would ever buy these things to eat for pleasure. Pass me the sugar, please. And the cream. And the strawberries."

It was half-term, so after breakfast Mark was able to take the empty packet away to the playroom and get on with the job of cutting out the stone walls, the row of little trees, the fountain, the yew-arch, the two green lawns, and the tiny clumps of brilliant flowers. He knew better than to 'stick tabs in slots and secure with paste' as the directions suggested; he had made models off packets before and knew they always fell to pieces unless they were firmly bound together with transparent sticky tape.

It was a long, fiddling, pleasurable job.

Nobody interrupted him. Mrs. Armitage only cleared the playroom once every six months or so, when she made a ferocious descent on it and tidied up the tape-recorders, roller-skates, meteorological sets, and dismantled railway-engines, and threw away countless old magazines, stringless tennis rackets, abandoned paintings, and unsuccessful models. There were always bitter complaints from Mark and Harriet; then they forgot and things piled up again till next time.

As Mark worked his eye was caught by a verse on the side of the packet:

> *Brekkfast Brikks to start the day*
> *Make you fit in every way.*
> *Children bang their plates with glee*
> *At Brekkfast Brikks for lunch and tea!*
> *Brekkfast Brikks for supper too*
> *Give peaceful sleep the whole night through.*

"Blimey," thought Mark, sticking a cedar tree into the middle of the lawn and then bending a stone wall round at dotted lines A, B, C and D. "I wouldn't want anything for breakfast, lunch, tea and supper, not even Christmas pudding. Certainly not Brekkfast Brikks."

He propped a clump of gaudy scarlet flowers against the wall and stuck them in place.

The words of the rhyme kept coming into his head as he worked and presently he found that they went rather well to a tune that was running through his mind, and he began to hum, and then to sing; Mark often did this when he was alone and busy.

"Brekkfast Brikks to sta-art the day,
Ma-ake you fi-it in every way—

Blow, where did I put that little bit of sticky tape? Oh, there it is.

Children bang their pla-ates with glee
At Brekkfast Brikks for lunch and tea.

Slit gate with razor-blade, it says, but it'll have to be a penknife.

Brekkfast Brikks for supper toohoo
Give peaceful sleep the whole night throughoo . . .

Hullo. That's funny," said Mark.

It was funny. The openwork iron gate he had just stuck in position now suddenly towered above him. On either side, to right and left ran the high stone wall, stretching away into the foggy distance. Over the top of the wall he could see tall trees, yews and cypresses and others he didn't know.

"Well, that's the neatest trick I ever saw," said Mark. "I wonder if the gate will open?"

He chuckled as he tried it, thinking of the larder door. The gate did open, and he went through into the garden.

One of the things that had already struck him as he cut them out was that the flowers were not at all in the right proportions. But they were all the nicer for that. There were huge velvety violets and pansies the size of saucers; the hollyhocks were as big as dinner-plates and the turf was sprinkled with enormous daisies. The roses, on the other hand, were miniature, no bigger than cuff-buttons. There were real fish in the fountain, bright pink.

"*I* made all this," thought Mark, strolling along the mossy path to the yew-arch. "Won't Harriet be surprised when she sees it. I wish she could see it now. I wonder what made it come alive like that?"

He passed through the yew-arch as he said this and discovered that on the other side there was nothing but grey, foggy blankness. This, of course, was where his cardboard garden ended. He turned back through the archway and gazed with pride at a border of huge scarlet tropical flowers which were perhaps supposed to be geraniums but certainly hadn't turned out that way. "I know! Of course it was the rhyme, the rhyme on the packet."

He recited it. Nothing happened. "Perhaps you have to sing it," he thought and (feeling a little foolish) he sang it through to the tune that fitted so well. At once, faster than blowing out a match, the garden drew itself together and shrank into its cardboard again, leaving Mark outside.

"What a marvellous hiding-place it'll make when I don't want people to come bothering," he thought. He sang the spell once more, just to make sure that it worked, and there was the high mossy wall, the stately iron gate, and the tree-tops. He stepped in and looked back. No playroom to be seen, only grey blankness.

At that moment he was startled by a tremendous clanging, the sort of sound the Trump of Doom would make if it were a dinner-bell. "Blow," he thought, "I suppose that's lunch." He sang the spell for the fourth time; immediately he was in the playroom, and the garden was on the table, and Agnes was still ringing the dinner-bell outside the door.

"All right, I heard," he shouted. "Just coming."

He glanced hurriedly over the remains of the packet

to see if it bore any mention of the fact that the cut-out garden had magic properties. It did not. He did, however, learn that this was Section Three of the Beautiful Brekkfast Brikks Garden Series, and that Sections One, Two, Four, Five and Six would be found on other packets. In case of difficulty in obtaining supplies, please write to Frühstücksgeschirrziegelsteinindustrie (Great Britain), Lily Road, Shepherd's Bush.

"Elevenpence a packet," Mark murmured to himself, going to lunch with unwashed hands. "Five elevens are thirty-five. Thirty-five pennies are – no, that's wrong. Five elevens are fifty-five. Father, if I mow the lawn and carry coal every day for a month, can I have fifty-five pence?"

"You don't want to buy another space-gun, do you?" said Mr. Armitage looking at him suspiciously. "Because one is quite enough in this family."

"No, it's not a space-gun, I swear."

"Oh, very well."

"And can I have fifty-five pence now?"

Mr. Armitage gave it reluctantly. "But that lawn has to be like velvet, mind," he said. "And if there's any falling-off in the coal supply I shall demand my money back."

"No, no, there won't be," Mark promised earnestly. As soon as lunch was over he dashed down to Miss Pride's. Was there a chance that she would have Sections One, Two, Four, Five and Six? He felt certain that no other shop had even heard of Brekkfast Brikks, so she was his only hope, apart from the address in Shepherd's Bush.

"Oh, I don't know, I'm sure," Miss Pride said, sounding very doubtful – and more than a little surprised. "There might just be a couple on the bottom shelf – yes, here we are."

They were Sections Four and Five, bent and dusty, but intact, Mark saw with relief. "Don't you suppose you have any more anywhere?" he pleaded.

"I'll look in the cellar but I can't promise. I haven't

85

had deliveries of any of these for a long time. Made by some foreign firm they were; people didn't seem very keen on them," Miss Pride said aggrievedly. She opened the door revealing a flight of damp stone stairs. Mark followed her down them like a bloodhound on the trail.

The cellar was a fearful confusion of mildewed, tattered and toppling cartons, some full, some empty. Mark was nearly knocked cold by a shower of pilchards in tins which he dislodged on to himself from the top of a heap of boxes. At last Miss Pride with a cry of triumph unearthed a little cache of Brekkfast Brikks, three packets, which turned out to be the remaining Sections, Six, One and Two.

"There, isn't that a piece of luck now!" she said, looking quite faint with all the excitement. It was indeed rare for Miss Pride to sell as many as five packets of the same thing at one time.

Mark galloped home with his booty and met his father in the porch. Mr. Armitage let out a groan of dismay.

"I'd almost rather you'd bought a space-gun," he said.

> *"Brekkfast Brikks for supper too*
> *Give peaceful sleep the whole night through."*

"I don't want peaceful sleep," Mr. Armitage said. "I intend to spend tonight mouse-watching again. I'm tired of finding footprints in the Stilton."

During the next few days Mark's parents watched anxiously to see, as Mr. Armitage said, whether Mark would start to sprout esparto grass instead of hair. For he doggedly ate Brekkfast Brikks for lunch, with soup, or sprinkled over his pudding, for tea, with jam, and for supper lightly fried in dripping, not to mention, of course, the immense helping he had for breakfast with sugar and milk. Mr. Armitage for his part soon gave up; he said he wouldn't taste another Brekkfast Brikk even if it were wrapped in an inch-thick layer of *pâté-de-foie*. Mark regretted Harriet, who was a handy and uncritical eater, but she was still away convalescing from her measles with an aunt.

In two days the second packet was finished (sundial, paved garden, and espaliers). Mark cut it out, fastened it together, and joined it on to Section Three with trembling hands. Would the spell work for this section too? He sang the rhyme in rather a quavering voice, but luckily the playroom door was shut and there was no one to hear him. Yes! The gate grew again above him, and when he opened it and ran across the lawn through the yew-arch he found himself in a flagged garden full of flowers like huge blue cabbages.

Mark stood hugging himself with satisfaction, and then began to wander about smelling the flowers, which had a spicy perfume most unlike any flower he could think of. Suddenly he pricked up his ears. Had he caught a sound? There! It was like somebody crying, and seemed to come from the other side of the hedge. He ran to the next opening and looked through. Nothing: only grey mist and emptiness. But, unless he had imagined it, just before he got there he thought his eye had caught the flash of white-and-gold draperies swirling past the gateway.

"Do you think Mark's all right?" Mrs. Armitage said to her husband next day. "He seems to be in such a dream all the time."

"Boy's gone clean off his rocker if you ask me," grumbled Mr. Armitage. "It's all these doormats he's eating. Can't be good to stuff your insides with mouldy jute. Still I'm bound to say he's cut the lawn very decently and seems to be remembering the coal. I'd better take a day off from the office and drive you over to the shore for a picnic; sea air will do him good."

Mrs. Armitage suggested to Mark that he should slack off on the Brekkfast Brikks, but he was so horrified that she had to abandon the idea. But, she said, he was to run four times round the garden every morning before breakfast. Mark almost said "Which garden?" and stopped just in time. He had cut out and completed another large lawn, with a lake and weeping willows, and on the far side of the lake had a tantalizing glimpse of a figure dressed in white and gold who moved away and was lost before he could get there.

After munching his way through the fourth packet he was able to add on a broad grass walk bordered by curiously clipped trees. At the end of the walk he could see the white-and-gold person, but when he ran to the spot no one was there – the walk ended in the usual grey mist.

When he had finished and cut out the fifth packet (an orchard) a terrible thing happened to him. For two days he could not remember the tune that worked the spell. He tried other tunes, but they were no use. He sat in the playroom singing till he was hoarse, or silent with despair. Suppose he never remembered it again?

His mother shook her head at him that evening and said he looked as if he needed a dose. "It's lucky we're going to Shinglemud Bay for the day tomorrow," she said. "That ought to do you good."

"Oh, *blow.* I'd forgotten about that," Mark said. "Need I go?"

His mother stared at him in utter astonishment.

But in the middle of the night he remembered the right tune, leapt out of bed in a tremendous hurry, and ran down to the playroom without even waiting to put on his dressing-gown and slippers.

The orchard was most wonderful, for instead of mere apples its trees bore oranges, lemons, limes, and all sorts of tropical fruits whose names he did not know, and there were melons and pineapples growing, and plantains and avocados. Better still, he saw the lady in her white and gold waiting at the end of an alley and was able to draw near enough to speak.

"Who are you?" she asked. She seemed very astonished at the sight of him.

"My name is Mark Armitage," he said politely. "Is this your garden?"

Close to, he saw that she was really very grand indeed. Her dress was white satin embroidered with pearls, and swept the ground; she had a gold scarf and her hair, dressed high and powdered, was confined in a small gold-and-pearl tiara. Her face was rather plain, pink with a long nose, but she had a kind expression and beautiful grey eyes.

"Indeed it is," she announced with hauteur. "I am Princess Sophia Maria Louisa of Saxe-Hoffenpoffen-und-Hamster. What are you doing here, pray?"

"Well," Mark explained cautiously, "it seemed to come about through singing a tune."

"Indeed? That is most interesting. Did the tune, perhaps, go like this?" The princess hummed a few bars.

"That's it! How did you know?"

"Why, you foolish boy, it was I who put the spell on the garden, to make it come alive when the tune is played or sung."

"I say!" Mark was full of admiration. "Can you do magic as well as being a princess?"

She drew herself up. "Naturally! At the court of Saxe-Hoffenpoffen where I was educated all princesses were taught a little magic – not much as to be vulgar, just enough to get out of social difficulties."

"Jolly useful," Mark said. "How did you work the spell for the garden, then?"

"Why, you see," (the princess was obviously delighted to have somebody to talk to; she sat on a stone seat and patted it, inviting Mark to do likewise) "I had the misfortune to fall in love with Herr Rudolf, the Court Kapellmeister, who taught me music. Oh, he was so kind and handsome! And he was most talented, but my father, of course, would not hear of my marrying him because he was only a common person."

"So what did you do?"

"I arranged to vanish, of course. Rudi had given me a beautiful book with many pictures of gardens. My father kept strict watch to see I did not run away, so I slipped between the pages of the book, having first asked my maid to take it to Rudi that evening. And I posted him a note telling him to play the tune when he received the book. But I believe that spiteful Gertrud must have played me false and never taken the book, for more than fifty years have now passed and I have been here all alone, waiting in the garden, and Rudi has never come. Oh, Rudi, Rudi," she exclaimed, wringing her hands and crying a little, "where can you be? It is so long – so long!"

"Fifty years," Mark said kindly, reckoning that must make her nearly seventy. "I must say you don't look it."

"Of course I do not, dumbhead. For me, I make it that time does not touch me. But tell me, how did you know the tune that works the spell? It was taught me by my dear Rudi."

"I'm not sure where I picked it up," Mark confessed. "For all I know it may be one of the Top Ten. I'll ask my music teacher, he's sure to know. Perhaps he'll have heard of your Rudolf too."

Privately Mark feared that Rudolf might very well have died by now, but he did not like to depress Princess Sophia Maria by such a suggestion, so he bade her a polite good night, promising to come back as soon as he could with another section of garden and any news he could pick up.

He planned to go and see Mr. Johansen, his music teacher, next morning, but he had forgotten the family trip to the beach. There was just time to scribble a hasty postcard to the British office of Frühstücksgerschirrziegel-steinindustrie, asking them if they could inform him from what source they had obtained the pictures used on the packets of Brekkfast Brikks. Then Mr. Armitage drove his wife and son to Shinglemud Bay, gloomily prophesying wet weather.

In fact the weather turned out fine, and Mark found it quite restful to swim and play beach cricket and eat ham sandwiches and lie in the sun. For he had been struck by a horrid thought: suppose he should forget the tune again when he was inside the garden – would he be stuck there, like Father in the larder? It was a lovely place to go and wander at will, but somehow he didn't fancy spending the next fifty years there with Princess Sophia Maria. Would she oblige him by singing the spell if he forgot it, or would she be too keen on company to let him go? He was not inclined to take any chances.

It was late when they arrived home, too late, Mark thought, to disturb Mr. Johansen, who was elderly and kept early hours. Mark ate a huge helping of sardines-on-Brekkfast Brikks for supper – he was dying to finish Section Six – but did not visit the garden that night.

Next morning's breakfast (Brikks with hot milk for a change) finished the last packet – and just as well, for the larder mouse, which Mr. Armitage still had not caught, was discovered to have nibbled the bottom left-hand corner of the packet, slightly damaging an ornamental grotto in a grove of lime-trees. Rather worried about this, Mark decided to make up the last section straight away, in case the magic had been affected. By now he was becoming very skilful at the tiny fiddling task of cutting out the little tabs and slipping them into the little slots; the job did not take long to finish. Mark attached Section Six to Section Five and then, drawing a deep breath, sang the incantation once more. With immense relief he watched the mossy wall and rusty gate grow out of the playroom floor; all was well.

He raced across the lawn, round the lake, along the avenue, through the orchard, and into the lime-grove. The scent of the lime-flowers was sweeter than a cake baking.

Princess Sophia Maria came towards him from the grotto, looking slightly put out.

"Good morning!" she greeted Mark. "Do you bring me any news?"

"I haven't been to see my music teacher yet," Mark confessed. "I was a bit anxious because there was a hole—"

"Ach, yes, a hole in the grotto! I have just been looking. Some wild beast must have made its way in, and I am afraid it may come again. See, it has made tracks like those of a big bear." She showed him some enormous footprints in the soft sand of the grotto floor. Mark stopped up the hole with prickly branches and promised to bring a dog when he next came, though he felt fairly sure the mouse would not return.

"I can borrow a dog from my teacher – he has plenty. I'll be back in an hour or so – see you then," he said.

"*Auf Wiedersehen*, my dear young friend."

Mark ran along the village street to Mr. Johansen's house, Houndshaven Cottage. He knew better than to knock at the door because Mr. Johansen would be either practising his violin or out in the barn at the back, and in any case the sound of barking was generally loud enough to drown any noise short of gun-fire.

Besides giving music lessons at Mark's school, Mr. Johansen kept a guest-house for dogs whose owners were abroad or on holiday. He was extremely kind to the guests and did his best to make them feel at home in every way, finding out from their owners what were their favourite foods, and letting them sleep on his own bed, turn about.

92

He spent all his spare time with them, talking to them and playing either his violin or LP records of domestic sounds likely to appeal to the canine fancy – such as knives being sharpened, cars starting up, and children playing ball-games.

Mark could hear Mr. Johansen playing Brahms' Lullaby in the barn, so he went out there; the music was making some of the more susceptible inmates feel homesick: howls, sympathetic moans, and long shuddering sighs came from the numerous comfortably carpeted cubicles all the way down the barn.

Mr. Johansen reached the end of the piece as Mark entered. He put down his fiddle and smiled welcomingly.

"Ach, how *gut*! It is the young Mark."

"Hullo, sir."

"You know," confided Mr. Johansen, "I play to many audiences in my life all over the world, but never anywhere do I get such a response as from zese dear doggies – it is really remarkable. But come in, come in to ze house and have some coffee-cake."

Mr. Johansen was a gentle, white-haired elderly man; he walked slowly with a slight stoop and had a kindly sad face with large dark eyes; he looked rather like some sort of dog himself, Mark always thought, perhaps a collie or a long-haired dachshund.

"Sir," Mark said, "if I whistle a tune to you, can you write it down for me?"

"Why yes, I shall be most happy," Mr. Johansen said, pouring coffee for both of them.

So Mark whistled his tune once more; as he came to the end he was surprised to see the music master's eyes fill with tears, which slowly began to trickle down his thin cheeks.

"It recalls my youth, zat piece," he explained, wiping them away and rapidly scribbling crochets and minims on a piece of music paper. "Many times I am whistling it myself – it is wissout doubt from me you learn it – but always it is reminding me of how happy I was long ago when I wrote it."

"You *wrote* that tune?" Mark said, much excited.

"Why yes. What is so strange in zat? Many, many tunes haf I written."

"Well—" Mark said, "I won't tell you just yet in case I'm mistaken – I'll have to see somebody else first. Do you mind if I dash off right away? Oh, and might I borrow a dog – preferably a good ratter?"

"In zat case, better have my dear Lotta – alzough she is so old she is ze best of zem all," Mr. Johansen said proudly. Lotta was his own dog, an enormous shaggy lumbering animal with a tail like a palm-tree and feet the size of electric polishers; she was reputed to be of incalcuable age; Mr. Johansen called her his strudel-hound. She knew Mark well and came along with him quite biddably, though it was rather like leading a mammoth.

Luckily his mother, refreshed by her day at the sea, was heavily engaged with Agnes the maid in spring-cleaning. Furniture was being shoved about and everyone was too busy to notice Mark and Lotta slip into the playroom.

A letter addressed to Mark lay among the clutter on the table; he opened and read it while Lotta foraged happily among the piles of magazines and tennis nets and cricket bats and rusting electronic equipment, managing to upset several things and increase the state of hugger-mugger in the room.

The letter was from Messrs Digit, Digit & Rule, a firm of chartered accountants, and said:

Dear Sir,
    We are in receipt of your inquiry as to the source of pictures on packets of Brekkfast Brikks. We are pleased to inform you that these were reproduced from the illustrations of a little-known eighteenth-

century German work, Steinbergen's *Gartenbuch*. Unfortunately the only known remaining copy of this book was burnt in the disastrous fire which destroyed the factory and premises of Messrs Frühstücks-geschirrziegelsteinindustrie two months ago. The firm has now gone into liquidation and we are winding up their effects.

Yours faithfully,
P. J. ZERO, Gen. Sec.

"Steinbergen's *Gartenbuch*," Mark thought. "That must have been the book that Princess Sophia used for the spell – probably the same copy. Oh well, since it's burnt, it's lucky the pictures were reproduced on the Brekkfast Brikk packs. Come on, Lotta, let's go and find a nice princess then. Good girl! Rats! Chase 'em!"

He sang the spell and Lotta, all enthusiasm, followed him into the garden.

They did not have to go far before they saw the princess – she was sitting sunning herself on the rim of the fountain. But what happened then was unexpected. Lotta let out the most extraordinary cry – whine, bark and howl all in one – and hurled herself towards the princess like a rocket.

"Hey! Look out! Lotta! *Heel!*" Mark shouted in alarm. But Lotta, with her great paws on the princess's shoulders, had about a yard of salmon-pink tongue out, and was washing her face all over with frantic affection.

The princess was just as excited. "Lotta! Lotta! She knows me, it's dear Lotta, it must be! Where did you get her?" she cried to Mark, hugging the enormous dog whose tail was going round faster than a turbo-prop.

"Why, she belongs to my music master, Mr. Johansen, and it's he who made up the tune," Mark said.

The princess turned quite white, and had to sit down on the fountain's rim again.

"*Johansen?* Rudolf Johansen? My Rudi! At last! After all these years! Oh, run, run, and fetch him immediately, please! Immediately!"

Mark hesitated a moment.

"Please make haste!" she besought him. "Why do you wait?"

"It's only – well, you won't be surprised if he's quite *old*, will you? Remember he hasn't been in a garden keeping young like you."

"All that will change," the princess said confidently. "He has only to eat the fruit of the garden. Why, look at Lotta – when she was a puppy, for a joke I gave her a fig from this tree, and you can see she is a puppy still, though she must be older than any other dog in the world! Oh, please hurry to bring Rudi here."

"Why don't you come with me to his house?"

"That would not be correct etiquette," she said with dignity. "After all, I *am* royal."

"Okay," said Mark. "I'll fetch him. Hope he doesn't think I'm crackers."

"Give him this." The princess took off a locket on a gold chain. It had a miniature of a romantically handsome young man with dark curling hair. "My Rudi," she explained fondly. Mark could just trace a faint resemblance to Mr. Johansen.

He took the locket and hurried away. At the gate something made him look back: the princess and Lotta were sitting at the edge of the fountain, side by side. The princess had an arm round Lotta's neck; with the other hand she waved to him, just a little.

"Hurry!" she called again.

Mark made his way out of the house, through the spring-cleaning chaos, and flew down the village to Houndshaven Cottage. Mr. Johansen was in the house this time, boiling up a noisome mass of meat and bones for the dogs' dinner. Mark said nothing at all, just handed him the locket. He took one look at it and staggered, putting his hand to his heart; anxiously, Mark led him to a chair.

"Are you all right, sir?"

"Yes, yes! It was only ze shock. Where did you get ziss, my boy?"

So Mark told him.

Surprisingly, Mr. Johansen did not find anything odd about the story; he nodded his head several times as Mark related the various points.

"Yes, yes, her letter, I have it still—" he pulled out a worn little scrap of paper – "but ze *Gartenbuch* it reached me never. Zat wicked Gertrud must haf sold it to some bookseller who sold it to Frühstücksgeschirrziegelstein-industrie. And so she had been waiting all ziss time! My poor little Sophie!"

"Are you strong enough to come to her now?" Mark asked.

"*Natürlich!* But first we must give ze dogs zeir dinner; zey must not go hungry."

So they fed the dogs, which was a long job, as there were at least sixty, and each had a different diet, including some very odd preferences like Swiss Roll spread with Marmite, and yeast pills wrapped in slices of caramel. Privately, Mark thought the dogs were a bit spoilt, but Mr. Johansen was very careful to see that each visitor had just what it fancied.

"After all, zey are not mine! Must I not take good care of zem?"

At least two hours had gone by before the last willow-pattern plate was licked clean and they were free to go. Mark made rings round Mr. Johansen all the way up the village; the music master limped quietly along, smiling a little; from time to time he said, "Gently, my friend. We do not run a race. Remember I am an old man."

This was just what Mark did remember. He longed to see Mr. Johansen young and happy once more.

The chaos in the Armitage house had changed its location: the front hall was now clean, tidy and damp; the rumpus of vacuuming had shifted to the playroom. With a black hollow of apprehension in his middle, Mark ran through the open door, and stopped, aghast. All the toys, tools, weapons, boxes, magazines and bits of machinery had been rammed into the cupboards; the table where his garden had been laid out was bare. Mrs. Armitage was in there taking down the curtains.

"*Mother!* Where's my Brekkfast Brikks garden?"

"Oh, darling, you didn't want it, did you? It was all dusty, I thought you'd finished with it. I'm afraid I've burnt it in the furnace. Really you *must* try not to let this room get into such a clutter, it's perfectly disgraceful. — Why, hullo, Mr. Johansen," she added in embarrassment, "I didn't see you, I'm afraid you've called at the worst possible moment. But I'm sure you'll understand how it is at spring-cleaning time."

She rolled up her bundle of curtains, glancing worriedly at Mr. Johansen; he looked rather odd, she thought. But he gave her his tired, gentle smile, and said,

"Why, yes, Mrs. Armitage, I understand, I understand very well. Come, Mark. We have no business here, you can see."

Speechlessly, Mark followed him. What was there to say?

"Never mind," Mrs. Armitage called after Mark. "The Rice Nuts packets has a helicopter on it."

Every week in *The Times* newspaper you will see this advertisement:

"BREKKFAST BRIKKS PACKETS. £100 offered for any in good condition, whether empty or full."

So if you have any, you know where to send them.

The Dark Streets of Kimball's Green

"Em! you, em! where has that dratted child got to? Em! Wait till I lay hold of you, I won't half tan you!"

Mrs. Bella Vaughan looked furiously up and down the short street. She was a stocky woman, with short, thick, straight grey hair, parted on one side and clamped back by a grip; a cigarette always dangled from one corner of her mouth and, as soon as it dwindled down, another grew there. "Em! Where have you got to?" she yelled again.

"Here I am, Mrs. Vaughan!" Emmeline dashed anxiously round the corner.

"Took long enough about it! The Welfare Lady's here, wants to know how you're getting on. Here, let's tidy you up."

Mrs. Vaughan pulled a comb and handkerchief out of her tight-stretched apron pocket, dragged the comb sharply through Emmeline's hair, damped the hankerchief with spit and scrubbed it over Emmeline's flinching face.

"Hullo, Emmeline. Been out playing?" said the Welfare Lady, indoors. "That's right. Fresh air's the best thing for them, isn't it, Mrs. Vaughan?"

"She's always out," grunted Mrs. Vaughan. "Morning, noon and night. I don't hold with kids frowsting about indoors. Not much traffic round here."

'Well, Emmeline, how are you getting on? Settling down with Mrs. Vaughan, quite happy, are you?"

Emmeline looked at her feet and muttered something. She was thin and small for her age, dark-haired and pale-cheeked.

"She's a mopey kid," Mrs. Vaughan pronounced. "Always want to be reading, if I didn't tell her to run out of doors."

"Fond of reading, are you?" the Welfare Lady said kindly. "And what do you read, then?"

"Books," muttered Emmeline. The Welfare Lady's glance strayed to the huge, untidy pile of magazines on the telly.

"Kid'll read anything she could lay hands on, if I let her," Mrs. Vaughan said. "I don't though. What good does reading do you? None that I know of."

"Well, I'm glad you're getting on all right, Emmeline. Be a good girl and do what Mrs. Vaughan tells you. And I'll see you next month again." She got into her tiny car and drove off to the next of her endless list of calls.

"Right," said Mrs. Vaughan. "I'm off too, down to the town hall to play bingo. So you hop it, and mind you're here on the doorstep at eleven sharp or I'll skin you."

Emmeline murmured something.

"Stay indoors? Not on your nelly! And have them saying, if the house burnt down, that I oughtn't to have left you on your own?"

"It's so cold out." A chilly September wind scuffled the

bits of paper in the street. Emmeline shivered in her thin coat.

"Well, run about then, and keep warm! Fresh air's good for you, like that interfering old busybody said. Anyway she's come and gone for the month, that's something. Go on, hop it now."

So Emmeline hopped it.

Kimball's Green where Mrs. Vaughan had her home, was a curious, desolate little corner of London. It lay round the top of a hill, which was crowned with a crumbling, blackened church, St Chad's. The four or five streets of tiny, aged houses were also crumbling and blackened, all due for demolition and most of them empty. The houses were so old that they seemed shrunk and wrinkled, like old apples or old faces, and they were immeasurably, unbelievably dirty, with the dirt of hundreds of years. Around the little hill was a flat, desolate tract of land, Wansea Marshes, which nobody had even tried to use until the nineteenth century; then it became covered with railway goods yards and brick-works and gas-works and an electric power station, all of which belched their black smoke over the little island of Kimball's Green on the hilltop.

You could hardly think anybody would *choose* to live in such a cut-off part, but Mrs. Vaughan had been born in Sylvan Street, near the top of the hill, and she declared she wasn't going to shift until they came after her with a bulldozer. She took in foster children when they grew too old for the Wansea Orphanage, and, though it wasn't a very healthy neighbourhood, what with the smoke and the damp from the marshes, there were so many orphans, and so few homes for them to go to, that Emmeline was the latest of a large number who had stayed with Mrs. Vaughan. But there were very few other children in the district now; very few inhabitants at all, except old and queer ones who camped secretly in the condemned houses. Most people found it too far to go to the shops: an eight-penny bus-ride, all the way past the goods yards and the gas-works, to Wansea High Street.

So far as anyone knew, Emmeline belonged in the neighbourhood; she had been found on the step of St Chad's one windy March night; but in spite of this, or because of it, she was rather frightened by the nest of little dark empty streets. She was frightened by many things, among which were Mrs. Vaughan and her son Colin. And she particularly hated the nights, five out of seven, when Mrs. Vaughan went off to play bingo, leaving Emmeline outside in the street. Indeed, if it hadn't been for two friends, Emmeline really didn't know how she could have borne those evenings.

As Mrs. Vaughan's clumping steps died away down the hill, one of the friends appeared: his thin form twined out from between some old black railings and he rubbed encouragingly against Emmeline's ankles, sticking up his tail in welcome.

"Oh, Scrawny! there you are," she said with relief. "Here, I've saved you a piece of cheese-rind from tea."

Old Scrawny was a tattered, battered tabby, with ragged whiskers, crumpled ears, and much fur missing from his tail; he had no owner and lived on what he could find; he ate the cheese-rind with a lot of loud, vulgar, guzzling noise, and hardly washed at all afterwards; but Emmeline loved him dearly, and he loved her back. Every night she left her window open and old Scrawny climbed in, by various gutters, drain-pipes, and the wash-house roof. Mrs. Vaughan wouldn't have allowed such a thing for a minute if she had known, but Emmeline always took care that old Scrawny had left long before she was called in the morning.

When the rind was finished Scrawny jumped into Emmeline's arms and she tucked her hands for warmth under his scanty fur; they went up to the end of the street by the church, where there was a telephone booth. Like the houses around it was old and dirty, and it had been out of order for so many years that now nobody even bothered to thump its box for coins. The only person who used it was Emmeline, and she used it almost every night, unless gangs were roaming the streets and throwing stones, in which case she hid behind a dustbin or under a flight of area steps. But when the gangs had gone elsewhere the call-box made a very convenient shelter; best of all, it was even light enough to read there, because although the bulb in the call-box had been broken long ago, a street lamp shone right overhead.

"No book tonight, Scrawny, unless Mr. Yakkymo comes and brings me another," said Emmeline, "so what shall we do? Shall we phone somebody, or shall I tell you a story?"

Scrawny purred, dangling round her neck like a striped scarf.

"We'll ring somebody up, shall we? All right."

She let the heavy door close behind her. Inside it was not exactly warm, but at least they were out of the wind. Scrawny climbed from Emmeline's shoulder into the compartment where the telephone books would have been if somebody hadn't made off with them; Emmeline picked up the broken receiver and dialled.

"Hullo, can I speak to King Cunobel? Hullo, King Cunobel, I am calling to warn you. A great army is approaching your fort – the Tribe of the Children of Darkness. Under their wicked queen Belavaun they are coming to attack your stronghold with spears and chariots. You must tell your men to be extra brave; each man must arm himself with his bow and a sheaf of arrows, two spears and a sword. Each man must have his faithful wolfhound by his side." She stroked old Scrawny, who seemed to be listening intently. "Your men are far outnumbered by the Children of Dark, King Cunobel, so you must tell your

Chief Druid to prepare a magic drink, made from vetch and mallow and succory, to give them courage. The leaves must be steeped in mead and left to gather dew for two nights, until you have enough to wet each man's tongue. Then they will be brave enough to beat off the Children of Dark and save your camp."

She listened for a moment or two with her ear pressed against the silent receiver, and then said to old Scrawny,

"King Cunobel wants to know what will happen if the Children of Dark get to the fort before the magic drink is prepared?"

"Morow," said Scrawny. He jumped down from the bookshelf and settled himself on Emmeline's feet, where there was more room to stretch out.

"My faithful wolfhound says you must order your men to make high barricades of brambles and thorns," Emmeline told King Cunobel. "Build them in three rings round the encampment, and place one-third of your men inside each ring. King Cunobel and the Druids will be in the middle ring. Each party must fight to the death in order to delay the Children of Dark until the magic drink is ready. Do you understand? Then good-bye and good luck."

She listened again.

"He wants to know who *I* am," she told Scrawny, and she said into the telephone, "I am a friend, the Lady Emmeline, advised by her faithful enchanted wolfhound Catuscraun. I wish you well."

Then she rang off and said to Scrawny, "Do you think I had better call the Chief Druid and tell him to hurry up with that magic drink?"

Old Scrawny shut his eyes.

"No," she agreed, "you're right, it would only distract him. I know, I'll ring up the wicked Queen of Dark."

She dialled again and said:

"Hullo, is that the wicked Queen Belavaun? This is your

greatest enemy, ringing up to tell you that you will never, never capture the stronghold of King Cunobel. Not if you besiege it for three thousand years! King Cunobel has a strong magic that will defeat you. All your tribes, the Trinovans and the Votadins and the Damnons and the Bingonii will be eaten by wolves and wild boars. Not a man will remain! And you will lose all your wealth and power and your purple robes and fur cloaks, you will have nothing left but a miserable old mud cabin outside King Cunobel's stronghold, and every day his men will look over the walls and laugh at you. Goodbye, and bad luck to you forever!"

She rang off and said to Scrawny: "That frightened her."

Scrawny was nine-tenths asleep, but at this moment footsteps coming along the street made him open his eyes warily. Emmeline was alert, too. The call-box made a good look-out point, but it would be a dangerous place in which to be trapped.

"It's all right," she said to Scrawny, then. "It's only Mr. Yakkymo."

She opened the door and they went to meet their other friend.

Mr. Yakkymo (he spelt his name Iachimo, but Yakkymo was the way it sounded) came limping slightly up the street until he reached them; then he rubbed the head of old Scrawny (who stuck his tail up) and handed Emmeline a book. It was old and small, with a mottled binding and gilt-edged leaves; it was called *The Ancient History of Kimball's Green and Wansea Marshes*, and it came from Wansea Borough Library.

Emmeline's eyes opened wide with delight. She began reading the book at once, skipping from page to page.

"Why, this tells all about King Cunobel! It's even better than the one you brought about ancient London. Have you read this, Mr. Yakkymo?"

He nodded, smiling. He was a thin, bent old man with rather long white hair; as well as the book he carried a leather case, which contained a flute, and when he was not speaking he would often open this case and run his fingers absently up and down the instrument.

"I thought you would find it of interest," he said. "It's a pity Mrs. Vaughan won't let you go to the public library yourself."

"She says reading only puts useless stuck-up notions in people's heads," Emmeline said dreamily, her eyes darting up and down the pages of the book. "Listen! It tells what King Cunobel wore – a short kilt with a gold belt. His chest was painted blue with woad, and he had a gold collar round his neck and a white cloak with gold embroidery. He carried a shield of beaten brass and a short sword. On his head he wore a fillet of gold, and on his arm gold armlets. His house was built of mud and stone, with a thatched roof; the walls were hung with skins and the floor strewn with rushes."

They had turned and were walking slowly along the street; old Scrawny, after the manner of cats, sometimes loitered behind investigating doorsteps and dark crannies, sometimes darted ahead and then waited for them to come up with him.

"Do you think any of King Cunobel's descendants still live here?" Emmeline said.

"It is just possible."

"Tell me some more about what it was like here then."

"All the marshes – the part where the brick-works and the goods yards are now – would have been covered by forest and threaded by slow-flowing streams."

"Threaded by slow-flowing streams," Emmeline murmured to herself.

"All this part would be Cunobel's village. Little mud huts, each with a door and a chimney hole, thatched with reeds."

Emmeline looked at the pavements and rows of houses, trying to imagine them away, trying to imagine forest trees and little thatched huts.

"There would be a stockade of logs and thorns all round. A bigger hall for the king, and one for the Druids near the sacred grove."

"Where was that?"

"Up at the top of hill, probably. With a specially sacred oak in the middle. There is an oak tree, still, in St Chad's churchyard; maybe it's sprung from an acorn of the Druid's oak."

"Maybe it's the same one? Oaks live a long time, don't they?"

"Hark!" he said checking. "What's that?"

The three of them were by the churchyard wall; they kept still and listened. Next moment they all acted independently, with the speed of long practice: Mr. Iachimo, murmuring, "Good night, my child," slipped away round a corner; Emmeline wrapped her precious book in a polythene bag and poked it into a hole in the wall behind a loose stone; then she and old Scrawny raced downhill, back to Mrs. Vaughan's house. She crouched panting on the doorstep, old Scrawny leapt up on to a shed roof and out of reach, just as a group of half a dozen people came swaggering and singing along the street.

"What was that?" one of them called.

"A cat."

"Let's go after it!"

"No good. It's gone."

When they got to Mrs. Vaughan's their chief left the others and came over to Emmeline.

"It's you, is it, Misery?" he said. "Where's Ma?"

"Out at bingo."

"She would be. I wanted to get a bit of the old girl's pension off her before she spent it all."

He gave Emmeline's hair a yank and flipped her nose,

hard and painfully, with his thumbnail. She looked at him in stony silence, biting her lip.

"Who's *she*, Col?" a new gang-member asked. "Shall we chivvy her?"

"She's one of my Ma's orphanage brats – just a little drip. Ma won't let me tease her, so long as she's indoors, or on the step. But watch it, you, if we catch you in the street." Colin flipped Emmeline's nose again and they drifted off, kicking at anything that lay on the pavement.

At half-past eleven Mrs. Vaughan came home from her bingo and let in the shivering Emmeline, who went silently up to her bed in the attic. At eleven thirty-five old Scrawny jumped with equal silence on to her stomach, and the two friends curled round each other for warmth.

Colin was not at breakfast next morning. Often he spent nights on end away from home; his mother never bothered to ask where.

Emmeline had to run errands and do housework in the morning but in the afternoon Mrs. Vaughan, who wanted a nap, told her to clear off and not show her face a minute before six. That gave her five whole hours for reading; she dragged on her old coat and flew up to the churchyard.

The door in the high black wall was always kept locked, but somebody had once left a lot of rusty old metal pipes stacked in an angle of the wall; Emmeline, who weighed very little more than old Scrawny, clambered carefully up them, and so over.

Inside, the churchyard was completely overgrown. Blackthorn, plane and sycamore trees were entangled with great clumps of bramble. Groves of mares'-tails, chin-high to Emmeline, covered every foot of the ground. It made a perfect place to come and hide by day, but was too dark at night and too full of pitfalls; pillars and stone slabs leaned every which way, hidden in the vegetation.

Emmeline flung herself down on the flat tomb of Admiral Sir Horace Tullesley Campbell and read her book; for three hours she never moved; then she closed it with a sigh, so as to leave some for the evening in case Mrs. Vaughan went out.

A woodpecker burst yammering from the tallest tree as Emmeline shut the book. Could that be the Druid's oak, she wondered, and started to push her way through to it. Brambles scratched her face and tore her clothes; Mrs. Vaughan would punish her but that couldn't be helped. And at last she was there. The tree stood in a little clear space of bare leaf-mould. It was an oak, a big one, with a gnarled, massive trunk and roots like knuckles thrusting out of the ground. This made an even better secret place for reading than the Admiral's tomb, and Emmeline wished once again that it wasn't too dark to read in the churchyard at night.

St Chad's big clock said a quarter to six, so she left *The Ancient History of Kimball's Green* in its plastic bag hidden in a hollow of the tree and went draggingly home; then realized, too late, that her book would be exceedingly hard to find once dark had fallen.

Mrs. Vaughan, who had not yet spent all her week's money, went out to bingo again that evening, so Emmeline returned to the telephone box and rang up King Cunobel.

"Is that the King? I have to tell you that your enemies are five miles nearer. Queen Belavaun is driving a chariot with scythes on its wheels, and her wicked son Coluon leads a band of savage followers; he carries a sling and a gold-handled javelin and is more cruel than any of the band. Has the Chief Druid prepared the magic drink yet?"

She listened and old Scrawny, who as usual was sitting at her feet, said "Prtnrow?"

"The Chief Druid says they have made the drink,

Scrawny, and put it in a flagon of beaten bronze, which has been set beneath the sacred oak until it is needed. Meanwhile the warriors are feasting on wheat-cakes, boars' flesh and mead."

Next she rang up Queen Belavaun and hissed, "Oh wicked queen, your enemies are massing against you! You think that you will triumph, but you are wrong! Your son will be taken prisoner, and you will be turned out of your kingdom; you will be forced to take refuge with the Iceni or the Brigantes."

It was still only half-past nine, and Mr. Iachimo probably would not come this evening, for two nights out of three he went to play his flute outside a theatre in the West End of London.

"Long ago I was a famous player and people came from all over Europe to hear me," he had told Emmeline sadly, one wet evening when they were sheltering together in the church porch.

"What happened? Why aren't you famous now?"

"I took to drink," he said mournfully. "Drink gives you hiccups. You can't play the flute with hiccups."

"You don't seem to have hiccups now."

"Now I can't afford to drink any longer."

"So you can play the flute again," Emmeline said triumphantly.

"True," he agreed; he pulled out his instrument and blew a sudden dazzling shower of notes into the rainy dark. "But now it is too late. Nobody listens; nobody remembers the name of Iachimo. And I have grown too old and tired to make them remember."

"Poor Mr. Yakkymo," Emmeline thought, recalling this conversation. "*He* could do with a drop of King Cunobel's magic drink; then he'd be able to make people listen to him."

She craned out of the telephone box to look at St Chad's clock: quarter to ten. The streets were quiet tonight; Colin's gang had got money from somewhere and were down at the Wansea Palais.

"I'm going to get my book," Emmeline suddenly decided. "At least I'm going to try. There's a moon, it shouldn't be too dark to see. Coming, Scrawny?"

Scrawny intimated, stretching, that he didn't mind.

The churchyard was even stranger under the moon than by daylight; the mares'-tails threw their zebra-striped shadows everywhere and an owl flew hooting across the path; old Scrawny yakkered after it indignantly to come back and fight fair, but the owl didn't take up his challenge.

"I don't suppose it's really an owl," Emmeline whispered. "Probably one of Queen Belavaun's spies. We must make haste."

Finding the oak tree was not so hard as she had feared, but finding the book was a good deal harder, because under the tree's thick leaves and massive branches no light could penetrate; Emmeline groped and fumbled among the roots until she was quite sure she must have been right round the tree at least three times. At last her right hand slipped into a deep crack; she rummaged about hopefully, her fingers closed on something, but what she pulled out was a small round object, tapered at one end. She stuck it in her coat pocket and went on searching. "The book must be somewhere, Scrawny; unless Queen Belavaun's spy has stolen it.'

At last she found it; tucked away where she could have sworn she had searched a dozen times already.

"Thank goodness! Now we'd better hurry, or there won't be any time for reading after all."

Emmeline was not sorry to leave the churchyard behind; it felt *crowded*, as if King Cunobel's warriors were hiding there, shoulder to shoulder among the bushes, keeping vigilant watch; Sylvan Street outside was empty and lonely in comparison. She scurried into the phone box, clutching Scrawny against her chest.

"Now listen while I read to you about the Druids, Scrawny: they wore long white robes and they liked mistletoe – there's some mistletoe growing on that oak tree, I'm positive! – and they used rings of sacred stones, too. Maybe some of the stones in the churchyard are left over from the Druids."

Scrawny purred agreeingly, and Emmeline looked up the hill, trying to move St Chad's church out of the way and replace it by a grove of sacred trees with aged, white-robed men among them.

Soon it was eleven o'clock: time to hide the book behind the stone and wait for Mrs. Vaughan on the doorstep. Along with his mother came Colin, slouching and bad-tempered.

"Your face is all scratched," he told Emmeline. "You look a sight."

"What have you been up to?" Mrs. Vaughan said sharply.

Emmeline was silent but Colin said, "Reckon it's that mangy old cat she's always lugging about."

"Don't let me see you with a cat round *this* house," Mrs. Vaughan snapped. "Dirty, sneaking things, never know where they've been. If any cat comes in here, I tell you, I'll get Colin to wring its neck!"

Colin smiled; Emmeline's heart turned right over with horror. But she said nothing and crept off upstairs to bed; only, when Scrawny arrived later, rather wet because it had begun to rain, she clutched him convulsively tight; a few tears wouldn't make much difference to the dampness of his fur.

"Humph!" said Mrs. Vaughan, arriving early and unexpectedly in Emmeline's attic. "I thought as much!"

She leaned to slam the window but Scrawny, though

112

startled out of sleep, could still move ten times faster than any human; he was out and over the roof in a flash.

"Look at that!" said Mrs. Vaughan. "Filthy, muddy cat's footprints all over my blankets! Well that's one job you'll do this morning, my young madam – you'll wash those blankets. And you'll have to sleep without blankets till they've dried – I'm not giving you any other. Daresay they're all full of fleas' eggs too."

Emmeline, breakfastless, crouched over the tub in the back wash-house; she did not much mind the job, but her brain was giddy with worry about Scrawny; how could she protect him? Suppose he were to wait for her, as he sometimes did, outside the house. Mrs. Vaughan had declared that she would go after him with the chopper if she set eyes on him; Colin had sworn to hunt him down.

"All right, hop it now," Mrs. Vaughan said, when the blankets satisfied her. "Clear out, don't let me see you again before six. No dinner? Well, I can't help that, can I? You should have finished the washing by dinner-time. Oh, all right, here's a bit of bread and marge, now make yourself scarce. I can't abide kids about the house all day."

Emmeline spent most of the afternoon in a vain hunt for Scrawny. Perhaps he had retired to some hidey-hole for a nap, as he often did at that time of day; but perhaps Colin had caught him already?

"Scrawny, Scrawny," she called softly and despairingly at the mouths of alleys, outside gates, under trees and walls; there was no reply. She went up to the churchyard, but a needle in a hundred haystacks would be easier to find than Scrawny in that wilderness if he did not choose to wake and show himself.

Giving up for the moment Emmeline went in search of Mr. Iachimo, but he was not to be found either; he had never told Emmeline where he lived and was seldom seen by daylight; she thought he probably inhabited one of the condemned houses and was ashamed of it.

It was very cold; a grey, windy afternoon turning gloomily to dusk. Emmeline pushed cold hands deep in her pockets; her fingers met and explored a round, unusual object. Then she remembered the thing she had picked up in the dark under the oak tree. She pulled it out, and found she was holding a tiny flask, made of some dark lustreless metal tarnished with age and crusted with earth. It was not quite empty; when Emmeline shook it she could hear liquid splashing about inside, but very little, not more than a few drops.

"Why," she breathed, just for a moment forgetting her fear in the excitement of this discovery, "it is – it *must* be the Druids' magic drink! But why, why didn't the warriors drink it?"

She tried to get out the stopper; it was made of some hard blackish substance, wood, or leather that had become hard as wood in the course of years.

"Can I help you, my child?" said a gentle voice above her head.

Emmeline nearly jumped out of her skin – but it was only Mr. Iachimo, who had hobbled silently up the street.

"Look – look, Mr. Yakkymo! Look what I found under the big oak in the churchyard! It must be the Druids' magic drink – mustn't it? Made of mallow and vetch and succory, steeped in mead, to give warriors courage. It must be!"

He smiled at her; his face very kind. "Yes, indeed it must!" he said.

But somehow, although he was agreeing with her, for a moment Emmeline had a twinge of queer dread, as if there was nothing – nothing at all – left in the world to hold on to; as if even Mr. Iachimo were not what he seemed but, perhaps, a spy sent by Queen Belavaun to steal the magic flagon.

Then she pushed down her fear, taking a deep breath, and said, "Can you get the stopper out, Mr. Yakkymo?"

"I can try," he said, and brought out a tiny foreign-looking penknife shaped like a fish with which he began prising the fossil-hard black substance in the neck of the bottle. At last it began to crumble.

"Take care – do take care," Emmeline said. "There's only a very little left. Perhaps the defenders did drink most of it. But anyway there's enough left for you, Mr. Yakkymo."

"For me, my child? Why for me?"

"Because you need to be made brave so that you can make people listen to you play your flute."

"Very true," he said thoughtfully. "But do not you need bravery too?"

Emmeline's face clouded. "What good would bravery do me?" she said. "*I'm* all right – it's old Scrawny I'm worried about. Oh, Mr. Yakkymo, Colin and Mrs. Vaughan say they are going to *kill* Scrawny. What can I do?"

"You must tell them they have no right to."

"*That* wouldn't do any good," Emmeline said miserably. "Oh! – You've got it out!"

The stopper had come out, but it had also crumbled away entirely.

"Never mind," Emmeline said. "You can put in a bit of the cotton-wool that you use to clean your flute. What does it smell of, Mr. Yakkymo?"

His face had changed as he sniffed; he looked at her oddly. "Honey and flowers," he said.

Emmeline sniffed too. There was a faint – very faint – aromatic, sweet fragrance.

"Wet your finger, Mr. Yakkymo, and lick it! Please do! It'll help you, I know it will!"

"Shall I?"

"Yes, do, do!"

He placed his finger across the opening, and quickly

turned the bottle upside down and back, then looked at his fingertip. There was the faintest drop of moisture on it.

"Quick – don't waste it," Emmeline said, breathless with anxiety.

He licked his finger.

"Well, does it taste?"

"No taste." But he smiled, and bringing out a wad of cotton tissue, stuffed a piece of it into the mouth of the flask, which he handed to Emmeline.

"This is yours, my child. Guard it well! Now, as to your friend Scrawny – I will go and see Mrs. Vaughan tomorrow, if you can protect him until then."

"Thank you!" she said. "The drink *must* be making you brave!"

Above their heads the clock of St Chad had tolled six.

"I must be off to the West End," Mr. Iachimo said. "And you had better run home to supper. Till tomorrow, then – and a thousand, thousand thanks for your help."

He gave her a deep, foreign bow and limped, much faster than usual, away down the hill.

"Oh, do let it work," Emmeline thought, looking after him.

Then she ran home to Mrs. Vaughan's.

Supper was over; Colin, thank goodness, did not come in, and Mrs. Vaughan wanted to get through and be off; Emmeline bolted down her food, washed the plates, and was dismissed to the streets again.

As she ran up to the churchyard wall, with her fingers tight clenched round the precious little flask, a worrying thought suddenly struck her.

The magic drink had mead in it. Suppose the mead were to give Mr. Iachimo hiccups? But there must be very little mead in such a tiny drop, she consoled herself; the risk could not be great.

When she pulled her book from the hole in the wall a

sound met her ears that made her smile with relief: old Scrawny's mew of greeting, rather creaking and scratchy, as he dragged himself yawning, one leg at a time, from a clump of ivy on top of the wall.

"*There* you are, Scrawny! If you knew how I'd been worrying about you!"

She tucked him under one arm, put the book under the other, and made her way to the telephone box. Scrawny settled on her feet for another nap, and she opened *The History of Kimball's Green*. Only one chapter remained to be read; she turned to it and became absorbed. St Chad's clock ticked solemnly round overhead.

When Emmeline finally closed the book, tears were running down her face.

"Oh, Scrawny – they didn't win! They *lost*! King Cunobel's men were all killed – and the Druids too, defending the stronghold. Every one of them. Oh, how can I bear it? Why did it have to happen, Scrawny?"

Scrawny made no answer, but he laid his chin over her ankle. At that moment the telephone bell rang.

Emmeline stared at the instrument in utter consternation. Scrawny sprang up; the fur along his back slowly raised, and his ears flattened. The bell went on ringing.

"But," whispered Emmeline, staring at the broken black receiver, "it's out of order. It *can't* ring! It's never rung! What shall I do, Scrawny?"

By now, Scrawny had recovered. He sat himself down again and began to wash. Emmeline looked up and down the empty street. Nobody came. The bell went on ringing.

At that same time, down below the hill and some distance off, in Wansea High Street, ambulance attendants were carefully lifting an old man off the pavement and laying him on a stretcher.

117

"Young brutes," said a bystander to a policeman who was taking notes. "It was one of those gangs of young hooligans from up Kimball's Green way; I'd know several of them again if I saw them. They set on him – it's the old street musician who comes up from there too. Seems he was coming home early tonight, and the boys jumped on him – you wouldn't think they'd bother with a poor fellow like him, he can't have much worth stealing."

But the ambulance men were gathering up handfuls of half-crowns and two-shilling pieces which had rolled from Mr. Iachimo's pockets; there were notes as well, a pound, even five- and ten-pound notes. And a broken flute.

"It was certainly worth their while tonight," the policeman said. "He must have done a lot better than usual."

"He was a game old boy – fought back like a lion; marked some of them, I shouldn't wonder. They had to leave him and run for it. Will he be all right?"

"We'll see," said the ambulance man, closing the doors.

"I'd better answer it," Emmeline said at last. She picked up the receiver, trembling as if it might give her a shock.

"Hullo?" she whispered.

And a voice – a faint, hoarse, distant voice – said,

"This is King Cunobel. I cannot speak for long. I am calling to warn you. There is danger on the way – great danger coming towards you and your friend. Take care! Watch well!"

Emmeline's lips parted. She could not speak.

"There is danger – danger!" the voice repeated. Then the line went silent.

Emmeline stared from the silent telephone to the cat at her feet.

"Did you hear it too, Scrawny?"

Scrawny gazed at her impassively, and washed behind his ear.

Then Emmeline heard the sound of running feet. The

warning had been real. She pushed the book into her pocket and was about to pick up Scrawny, but hesitated, with her fingers on the little flask.

"May be I ought to drink it, Scrawny? Better that than have it fall into the enemy's hands. Should I? Yes, I will! Here, you must have a drop too."

She laid a wet finger on Scrawny's nose; out came his pink tongue at once. Then she drained the bottle, picked up Scrawny, opened the door, and ran.

Turning back once more to look she could see a group of dark figures coming after her down the street. She heard someone shout,

"That's her, and she's got the cat too! Come on!"

But beyond, behind and *through* her pursuers, Emmeline caught a glimpse of something else: a high, snow-covered hill, higher than the hill she knew, crowned with great bare trees. And on either side of her, among and in front of the dark houses, as if she were seeing two pictures, one printed on top of the other, were still more trees, and little thatched stone houses. Thin animals with red eyes slunk silently among the huts. Just a glimpse she had, of the two worlds, one behind the other, and then she had reached Mrs. Vaughan's doorstep and turned to face the attackers.

Colin Vaughan was in the lead; his face, bruised, cut, and furious, showed its ugly intention as plainly as a raised club.

"Give me that damn cat. I've had enough from you and your friends. I'm going to wring its neck."

But Emmeline stood at bay; her eyes blazed defiance and so did Scrawny's; he bared his fangs at Colin like a sabre-toothed tiger.

Emmeline said clearly, "Don't you dare lay a finger on me, Colin Vaughan. Just don't you dare touch me!"

He actually flinched, and stepped back half a pace; his gang shuffled back behind him.

At this moment Mrs. Vaughan came up the hill; not at her usual smart pace but slowly, plodding, as if she had no heart in her.

"Clear out, the lot of you," she said angrily. "Poor old Mr. Iachimo's in the Wansea Hospital, thanks to you. Beating up old men! That's all you're good for. Go along, scram, before I set the back of my hand to some of you. Beat it!"

"But we were going to wring the cat's neck. You wanted me to do that," Colin protested.

"Oh, what do I care about the blame cat?" she snapped, turning to climb the steps, and came face to face with Emmeline.

"Well, don't *you* stand there like a lump," Mrs. Vaughan said angrily. "Put the blasted animal down and get to bed!"

"I'm not going to bed," Emmeline said. "I'm not going to live with you any more."

"Oh, indeed? And where are you going then?" said Mrs. Vaughan, completely astonished.

"I'm going to see poor Mr. Yakkymo. And then I'm going to find someone who'll take me and Scrawny, some place where I shall be happy. I'm never coming back to your miserable house again."

"Oh, well, suit yourself," Mrs. Vaughan grunted. "You're not the only one. I've just heard: fifty years in this place and then fourteen days' notice to quit; in two weeks the bulldozers are coming."

She went indoors.

But Emmeline had not listened; clutching Scrawny, brushing past the gang as if they did not exist, she ran for the last time down the dark streets of Kimball's Green.

The Boy Who Read Aloud

ONCE THERE WAS A BOY CALLED SEB WHO WAS unfortunate. His dear mother had died, his father had married again, and the new wife brought in three daughters of her own. Their names were Minna, Hanna and Morwenna, and they were all larger and older than Seb – big, fat, red-haired hateful girls. Minna pinched, Hanna tweaked hair and kicked shins, while Morwenna could pull such terrible faces that she put even the birds in a fright and her mother had forbidden her to do it indoors in case she cracked the cups and plates on the kitchen dresser. The mother was just as bad as her daughters, greedy, unkind, and such a terrible cook that nine months after they were married Seb's father wasted away and died from the food she fed him on. As for Seb, he had to manage on crusts, for that was all he got.

Now Seb had three treasures which his true mother had left him when she died. These were a little silver mug, a little silver spoon, and a book of stories. The book of stories was what he prized most, for when she was alive his true mother had read them aloud to him every day and as soon as he grew old enough to learn his letters he read them back to her while she did the ironing or peeled the potatoes or rolled out the pastry. So, now, when he opened the book, it was as if his true mother were back with him, telling him a story, and for a little he could forget how things had changed with him.

You can guess how hard Seb tried to keep these treasures hidden from his step-sisters. But they were prying, peering, poking girls, and presently Minna came across the silver cup hidden under Seb's mattress.

"You mean little sniveller, keeping this pretty cup hidden away!" she cried. "I am the eldest, it should be mine, and I'll pinch and pinch you till you give it to me!"

"For shame, Seb!" said his step-mother when she heard him crying out at the pinches. "Give the cup to your sister at once!"

So poor little Seb had to give it up.

Then Hanna found the silver spoon hidden under Seb's pillow.

"Let me have it, let me have it, you little spalpeen!" she screeched, when he tried to keep it from her. "Or I'll drag out every hair in your head."

And her mother made Seb give her the little spoon.

Now Seb took particular pains to keep his precious book out of view, hiding it first in one place and then in another, between the bins of corn, under a sitting hen, inside a hollow tree, beneath a loose floorboard. But one evening Morwenna found it tucked up on a rafter, as they were going to bed. Quickly Seb snatched the book from her and darted off to his attic room where he shut himself in, pushing the bed against the door. Morwenna was after him in a flash – though, mind you, it was only pure spite that made her want the book for, big as she was, she could read no more than a gatepost can.

"You'd better give it to me, you little mizzler!" she bawled through the door. "Or I shall make such a fearsome face at you that you'll very likely die of fright."

Seb trembled in his shoes at this threat, but he knew that Morwenna could do nothing till morning, since she was not allowed to pull faces indoors.

Huddling in bed, clutching the book to him, he decided that the only thing for him to do was to run away. He would get up very early, climb out of the window, and slide down the roof.

But where should he go and how should he live?

For a long time, no plan came to him. But at last, remembering the book in his hands, he thought, "Well, there is one thing I can do. I can read. Perhaps somebody in the world would like me to read stories to them."

"In the village," he thought, "by the inn door, there is a board with cards stuck up on it, showing what work is to be had. I will go that way in the morning and see if anybody wants a reader."

So at last he went to sleep, holding the little book tight against his chest.

In the morning he woke and tiptoed out of the house long before anyone else was stirring. (Minna, Morwenna and Hanna were all lazy, heavy sleepers who never clambered from their beds till the sun was half across the sky.)

Seb went quietly through the garden and quietly down the village until he came to the notice-board. On it there were cards telling of jobs for gardeners, jobs for cooks, jobs for postmen, ploughmen and painters. Looking at them all he had begun to think there was nothing for him when up in the top corner he notice a very old, dog-eared card with a bit torn off. It said:

ELDERLY BLIND RETIRED SEA
WOULD LIKE BOY TO READ
ALOUD DAILY

What a strange thing, thought Seb. Fancy reading aloud to the sea! Fancy the sea going blind at all!

But still, he supposed, thinking it over, the sea could get old like anybody else, old and blind and bored. Didn't the emperor Caligula have chats with the sea, and who takes the trouble nowadays even to pass the time of day with his neighbour, let alone have a conversation with the ocean?

There would be no harm, anyway, in going to find out whether the job had been taken already. Seb knew the way to the sea because when his true mother had been alive they had sometimes spent days at the shore. It was about twenty miles but he thought he could walk it in a couple of days. So he started at once.

Now, had Seb but known it, the truth of the matter was this: that card had been up on the board such a long time that it had been torn, and some of the words were missing. It should have read:

ELDERLY BLIND RETIRED SEA CAPTAIN
WOULD LIKE BOY TO READ NEWSPAPER
ALOUD DAILY. APPLY WITHIN

Nobody ever had applied for the job, and in the end the sea captain had grown tired of waiting and had gone off to another town.

But Seb knew nothing of all this, so he started off to walk to the sea, with his treasured book of stories in his pocket.

It was still very early and few folk were about.

As he walked along Seb began to worry in case he had forgotten how to read aloud, because it was now a long time since his true mother had died. "I had better practise a bit," he thought.

When he had gone about five miles and felt in need

of a rest he came to a gate leading into a deserted barn-yard.

"I'll go in here," he thought, "and practise my reading. Because there's no doubt about it at all, it's going to seem very queer reading to the sea till I've grown accustomed to it."

There was an old rusty Rolls-Royce car in the yard, which looked as if it had not been driven since the days when ladies wore long trailing skirts and you could get four ounces of bull's-eyes for a halfpenny. Seb felt rather sorry for the poor thing, so broken-down, forlorn and battered did it seem, and he decided to read to it.

He sat down cross-legged in front of the radiator, took out his book and read a story about the sun-god's flaming chariot, and how once it was borrowed by a boy who had not passed his driving-test, and how he drove the chariot, horses and all, into the side of a hill.

All the time Seb was reading there came no sound or movement from the car. But when he had finished and stood up to go, he was astonished to hear a toot from behind him. He turned himself about fast, wondering if somebody had been hiding in the car all the time. But it was empty, sure enough.

Then he heard a voice, which said,

"Was that a true tale, boy?"

"As to that," said Seb, "I can't tell you."

"Well, true or not," said the voice (it came from the radiator and had a sort of purring rumble to it, like the sound of a very large cat), "true or not, it was the most interesting tale I have ever heard. In fact it was the *only* tale I have heard, and I am greatly obliged to you, boy, for reading it to me. No one else ever thought of doing such a thing. In return I will tell you something. In a well in the corner of the yard hangs a barrel of stolen money; five days ago I saw two thieves come here and lower it down. Wind the handle and you will be able to draw it up."

"Did you ever!" said Seb, and he went to the well in the corner and turned the handle which pulled the rope. Up came a barrel filled to the top with silver coins.

"There's too much here for me," Seb said. "I could never carry it all." So he took enough to fill one pocket (the book was in the other), wound the barrel down into the well again, and went on his way, waving goodbye to the Rolls-Royce car as long as he could see it.

He bought some bread with his money at the next village, and a bottle of milk.

After another five miles' walking he began to feel tired again, so he stepped aside from the road into the garden of an old empty house.

"This would be a good place to read another of my stories," he thought.

So he read aloud a tale of two friends who arranged to meet one night near a hole in a wall. But they were frightened away by a lion and so they missed seeing one another.

When Seb had finished he heard a harsh voice behind him (he was sitting with his back to the house) which said,

"Was that a true tale, boy?"

"As to that," said Seb, "I can't tell you."

"True or not," said the voice, "it has given me something to think about in the long, empty days and nights. I never heard a tale before. So in return I will tell you something useful. Growing in my garden you will find a red flower which, if you pick and eat it, will cure any illness."

"But I haven't got any illness," Seb said. "I am quite well."

"If you eat this flower you will never fall ill, in the whole of your life. But take care not to pick the yellow flower which grows next to it, for that is poisonous and would kill you at once."

Seb wandered through the garden until he found the red and yellow flowers growing side by side.

"'Twould be a pity to pick the red one," he thought, "so pretty it looks growing there. Anyway I daresay somebody will come along who needs it more than I do."

So he thanked the house kindly and went on his way, waving until he was out of sight.

Presently it grew dark, so he ate some more of his bread, drank the milk, and went to sleep under an old thorn tree. Next morning, to thank the tree for watching over him all night, he read aloud a story about a girl who ran away from a suitor and turned herself into a laurel bush.

"Boy," said a rough, prickly voice when he had finished, "is that a true tale?"

"As to that," said Seb, "I don't know."

"True or not," said the voice, "I enjoyed it and it sounds true, so I will tell you something in return. Lodged in my topmost fork is the blue stone of eternal life, which a swallow dropped there a hundred years ago. If you care to climb up you may have it. Carry it in your pocket and you will live for ever."

Seb thanked the tree and climbed up. The stone was very beautiful, dark blue, with gold marks on it and white lines. But, he said to himself, do I really want to live for ever? Why should *I* do so out of all the people in the world?

So he put the stone back in the crotch of the tree. But, unknown to him, as he turned to climb down, he dislodged the stone again and it fell into his pocket.

He went on, waving goodbye to the tree as long as it was in sight, and now he came to the sea itself, with its green waves rolling up on to the sand, each one breaking with a roar.

"Will the sea be able to hear me if I read aloud?" Seb wondered.

Feeling rather foolish, because the sea was so very large and made so much noise, he sat down on the sand. Taking out his book he read first one story and then another. At first it seemed as if nobody heard him, but then he began to hear voices, many voices, saying,

"Hush! Hush!"

And looking up he noticed that all the waves had started to smooth out as if a giant palm had flattened them, so that hardly a ripple stirred as far as he could see. The water creamed and lapped at his feet, like a dog that wants to be patted, and as he waited, not knowing whether to go on or not, a long, thin white hand came out of the green water and turned over the page.

So Seb read another story and then another.

Meanwhile what had happened at home?

When they found Seb had run away the three sisters were very angry, but specially Morwenna.

"Just let him wait till I catch him!" she said. "I'll make such a face at him that his hair turns to knitting needles."

"Oh let him go," said the mother. "What use was he at all, but only a mouth to feed?"

None the less Morwenna and her sisters went off looking for Seb. They asked of this one and that one in the village, who had seen him, and learned that he had taken the road to the sea. So they followed after until they came to the barn-yard, and there they heard a plaintive voice wailing and sighing.

"Oh, won't some kind soul tell me a story?" it sighed. "Alack and mercy and curse it. I have such a terrible craving to hear another tale! Oh, won't somebody take pity on me?"

"Who's been telling you tales?" said Morwenna, seeing it was the old Rolls-Royce car that spoke. "Was it a little runt of a boy with a book he'd no right to sticking out of his breeches pocket? Speak the truth now, and I'll tell you another story."

"Yes, 'twas a boy," the old car said. "He read me from a wondrous book and in return I told him about the silver in the well."

"Silver in the well? Where?" screeched Minna and Hanna. Colliding together in their greed they made a rush for the well-head and wound up the handle. But Minna was so eager to get at the silver and keep her sisters from it that she jumped right on to the barrel when it came up, the rope broke, and down she went. So that was the end of Minna.

"Oh, well, never mind her," said Morwenna. "Come on, let you, for it's plain 'twas this way he went." And she hurried on, taking no notice at all of the poor old car crying out, "My story, my story!"

"Bother your story, you miserable old heap of tin!" she shouted back.

So they came to the empty house, and here again they heard a voice moaning and lamenting.

"Ochone, ochone, why did I ever listen to that boy's tale? Now I've nothing in me but an insatiable thirst to hear another."

"Was it a bit of a young boy with a little black book?" Morwenna said. "Answer me that and I'll tell you a story."

"Ah, it was, and in return for the tale he told me I showed him where to find the red flower that cures you of any sickness."

"Where is it? Where?" And the sisters went ramping through the garden till they found it. But in her haste to snatch it before her sister, Hanna grabbed the yellow flower as well, ate it, and dropped down dead on the very spot.

"Oh, well, she's done for," said Morwenna, and she

hurried on, taking no notice of the old house which wailed, "My story, my story!" behind her.

"Plague take your story, you mouldy old heap of brick," she called back.

So she came to the thorn tree.

"Have you seen a boy?" she asked it. "Did he tell you a story?"

"Indeed he did, and in return I was telling him about the stone of eternal life in my topmost fork."

"Let me lay my hands on that same stone!" said Morwenna, and she made haste to scramble up the tree. But because she was such an awkward, clumsy girl she fell from the top fork in her greedy hurry, and hung head down among the thorns.

"If you'd waited a moment longer," said the tree, "I could have told you that the boy took the stone with him."

"Oh, you villainous old tree!" cried Morwenna, kicking and twisting, and making such faces as turned the birds pale in their tracks. But she was stuck fast, and hangs there to this day.

Meanwhile Seb's step-mother had married again, a man as mean-natured as she was herself. By and by they began to hear tales of a marvellous boy, who sat on the shore and read tales to the sea.

"And the sea's given him great gifts!" said one. "They say he's been shown where the lost treasure of the Spanish galleon lies, with cups of gold and plates of pearl and wine-glasses all carved out of great rubies, and a hundred chests of silver ingots!"

"They say he's been told where every storm is, all over the world, and which way it's heading!" said another.

"They say he can listen to the voice of the sea as if it were an old friend talking to him!" said a third. "And devil a bit of a tide has there been since he began reading aloud, and a great inconvenience it is to the navigation in all realms of the world!"

"Can that boy be Seb?" wondered the step-mother and her husband. They resolved to go and see for themselves. So they harnessed up the pony-cart and made their way to the sea.

Sure enough, there on the sand was Seb, reading away from his little book. So many times he'd been through it now, he and the sea just about knew it by heart, between them.

"Why, Seb!" says his step-mother, sugar-sweet. "We've been in such anxiety about you, child, wondering where you'd got to. Sure you'll be catching your mortal end of cold, sitting out on this great wet beach. Come home, come home, dear, for there's a grand cup of cocoa waiting for you, and a loaf with honey."

"That's very kind of you ma'am," Seb says back, all polite. "But if my sisters are there I'd just as lief not, if it's all the same to you."

"Oh, they've left," she says quickly. "So come along, dear, because the pony's beginning to fidget."

And without waiting for yea or nay she and her husband hustled Seb into the pony-cart and drove quickly home. Didn't they give him a time, then, as soon as they got in, pinching, poking and slapping one minute, buttering him up with sweet talk the next, as they tried to find out his secrets.

"Where's the sunken Spanish galleon? Where's the plates of pearl and glasses of ruby and the hundred chests of silver ingots?"

"I'm not remembering," says Seb.

"Didn't the sea tell you?"

"Sure the sea told me one thing and another, but I was paying no heed to tales of ruby glasses and silver ingots. What do I care about silver ingots?"

"You little wretch!" she screamed. "You'd better remember, before I shake the eyes out of your head!"

"But I do remember one thing the sea told me," he says.

"What was that?"

He'd got his head turned, listening, towards the window, and he said, "The sea promised to come and help me if ever I was in trouble. And it's coming now."

Sure enough, the very next minute, every single wall of the house burst in, and the roof collapsed like an eggshell when you hit it with a spoon. There was enough sea in the garden to fill the whole Atlantic and have enough left over for the Pacific too. A great green wave lifted Seb on its shoulder and carried him out, through the garden and away, away, over the fields and hills, back to his new home among the conches and coral of the ocean bed.

As for the step-mother and her husband, they were never seen again.

But Seb is seen, it's said; sometimes at one great library, sometimes at another, you'll catch a glimpse of him, taking out longer and longer books to read aloud to his friend the sea. And so long as he keeps the blue stone in his pocket, so long he'll go on reading, and hearing wonderful secrets in return, and so long the tides will go on standing still while they listen.

Is this a true tale, you ask?

As to that, I can't tell . . .

Moonshine in the Mustard Pot

DEBORAH HAD BEEN ANXIOUS ABOUT WHAT SHE would find to do while staying with Granny. "Shall I take toys?" she asked, and her father said, "It's a very small house. Better not take much, there'd be nowhere to put them."

At home, in spite of having her own room crammed with toys, Deborah was bored as often as not, and would trail in search of her mother, yawning. "What shall I do, Mum?" And her mother, quick as lightning, always found her a job: tidy the spoon-and-fork drawer, polish the silver teapot, weed the moss out of the front steps. Not bad things in themselves, but jobs done to fill a gap are like going on your favourite walk with somebody who walks at the wrong pace; there's no satisfaction in them. Deborah never seemed to learn this, though; sooner or later she would be wandering back again saying, "I'm bored; what shall I do?"

Granny's house, in a little street in York, certainly was

tiny. The first thing Deborah noticed about it was that it sat flat on the ground: no front steps to climb (or weed). Somehow, inside, you could feel the earth, right there under the floor; it was a bit like going out in very thin-soled slippers. Her father said, "I hope I've brought enough warm clothes for her; I wasn't sure what to pack." Deborah's mother was sick; that was why she was here. "Well, if the weather gets cold, the child can wear my woollies," Granny said. "She's almost as big as I am."

It was true, Granny was small, suited to her house, thin and straight as a candle in her cotton-print pinafore over two layers of jerseys. Her hair, fine and soft and white as smoke, she wore pinned back in a bun; and her face was white as well, so pale that Deborah feared at first she must be ill too, but no ill person could possibly be as energetic as Granny. "It's just old age," she explained about the paleness later. But the black eyes in this white face sparkled like two live coals; they were never still for a single second.

The minute Deborah's father had gone, Granny showed her over the house. There were four rooms and a pantry. The doors were so narrow that you could only just carry a chair through them. The stairs, equally narrow, led straight out of the kitchen, through another tiny door. "Suppose you wanted to get a big piece of furniture up?" said Deborah. "Wouldn't have room to put it anywhere if I did," said Granny. "Besides, I don't like big furniture, I like things I can move myself. The biggest load isn't the best."

Indeed, all her things were small and light – stools, low narrow beds, tiny velvet nursing chairs. "Bought at auctions," said Granny with satisfaction. "Never paid more than a pound for anything yet. And I make sure I can lift it before I bid." She had painted and upholstered everything herself: clear soft blues, apple-green, warm brick-red, white, rose-pink, purple, indigo, chocolate-brown.

The whole house sang and flashed with colour. "How did you paint the ceilings, Granny?" "With a brush tied to a mop handle, of course. Never believe in getting in a man for jobs you can do yourself. Take days and make the fiend's own mess and charge double, the robbers. Now: I've just bought this little chest for the bathroom, I thought you might like to help me paint it."

"Oh, yes!" said Deborah. "What colour?"

The bathroom was brand-new, Granny's pride. "Your Uncle Chris made it for me when he was home from India for a month. Didn't tell the Council. What the eye doesn't see, the heart doesn't grieve over. Oh, he's a clever one, that Chris." About the size of a kitchen table, the bathroom was tucked in a corner of Granny's bedroom. "Before, I had to go all the way to the wash-house." The wash-house was in the tiny garden, out at the back, across a brick-paved yard and also a narrow lane, which was a public right-of-way. "Not very convenient when you want to brush your teeth," said Deborah. "Oh, I did *that* in the kitchen sink." "But what about in the winter when it snows?" "Well, you get used to anything." But Deborah was glad Uncle Chris had made the bathroom. It was lined with dark-blue tiles and had a white basin and toilet seat, so they decided to paint the chest scarlet, and it took them till lunch-time. "And after lunch, while it dries," said Granny, "I'll show you my allotment, where I grow my vegetables."

"Not your back garden?"

"No, that's for sitting in."

The back garden, past the wash-house, and about the same size as the kitchen, had grass and four apple trees, covered with young uncurling leaves and coral buds. "Apples off them lasted me all winter," said Granny. "Coxes, Laxtons, Bramleys, and Beauty of Bath." Deborah had never heard these names and now learned them in

135

a jingle, "Cox and Laxton, left of the path, on the right Bramley and Beauty of Bath."

Granny fetched her bicycle out of the wash-house. It was painted apple-green (the same paint as the kitchen dresser) and was so ancient that the back wheel was protected by a skirt-guard of strings threaded from holes in the rear mudguard to the hub. A square hamper was strapped on the carrier. "For vegetables," explained Granny. She added a cushion on top of this and sat Deborah on top of the cushion; so they rode through the city of York to Granny's allotment, which lay out on the far side. Granny pedalled along at a spanking pace and the traffic kept respectfully out of her way.

"Granny," yelled Deborah through the mixed sun and wind and shadow of their headlong course, "can you explain something Dad said?"

"What was that, child?"

"He said, 'I hope Deb will be all right with her. Mother takes her life in her hands twenty times a day.'"

Granny swept the bike up to a hawthorn hedge covered with white blossom and a gate which led to the allotments.

"That's the way life ought to be taken," she said. "If you have your life in your hands, then you can steer it, can't you? I wouldn't give a brass button for the sort of life that's just left lying around, like wet washing. Now, we'll do the hoeing and weeding first, then I'll introduce you to the bees." Hoeing and weeding was not at all dull, as Deborah had expected it would be, because in among her vegetables Granny had scarlet anemones and dark-blue grape hyacinths and dark velvet-brown wallflowers and clumps of primroses; there was always something beautiful to look at and smell. "I like them and the bees like them," said Granny. "Nothing but vegetables makes a dull garden."

Also, while they hoed, Granny taught Deborah some of what she called her gardenwork poems: Bonnie Kilmeny gaed up the glen, Where the pools are bright and deep, Loveliest of trees the cherry now, No man knows Through what wild centuries Roves back the rose. "I have different ones for doing housework, of course, and different again for sewing and going to sleep. Everybody ought to have plenty of different sets of poems stowed away."

Deborah had never thought of poems as something you could *have*, like flowers or stamps or coloured stones. "Of course you can," said Granny. "And the best of it is, that everybody can have them at the same time. And they cost no more than moonshine in the mustard pot."

"Moonshine in the mustard pot – what's that, Granny?"

"Why, nothing at all."

Granny was full of interesting proverbs. "If that was a bear, it would have bit you," she said when you were looking for something and it was right under your nose. "I'd rather have stags led by a lion than lions led by a stag. He that would live for ever must eat sage in May. Ask a kite for a feather, she'll tell you she has only enough to fly with."

"Now you can come and meet the bees, but you must put on a hat first."

Secretly, Deborah was rather nervous of the bees, who lived in three square white hives by the hedge, but they seemed to be wholly busy helping themselves to nectar from the hawthorn blossoms. "This is their hard-work time," said Granny. "Well, all times are busy for bees, once the daffodils begin. Of *course* they must get to know you. Don't you know that you have to tell bees everything?"

"What happens if you don't?"

"They pine and grieve and sing a sad song. And the honey tastes bitter. Or there is none. Besides," said Granny as they put on old panama hats draped with white veiling that made them look like Tibetan monks from Mount Everest, "your name, Deborah, *means* a bee, didn't

137

you know? So that's a special reason for saying good afternoon to them."

She lifted off the tops of the hives like box-lids and Deborah, peering down through the drifts of her veil, saw the black and gold bees, more than any multiplication table could calculate, in their tireless to-and-fro. The combs, pale caskets of wax, were built between glass panels so that Granny could see how the honey was getting on. It glowed light and dark gold through the rind of wax, and the bees made a continuous murmur, a blend of all their different humming notes, with one steady note in the centre.

"Perhaps that's the Queen Bee's note?" said Deborah.

On the bike ride home (they kept on their hats and veils for the ride and were the wonder of York) Granny taught Deborah a bees' poem – "Heavy with blozzomz be The Rozes that growzez In the thickets of Zee."

After tea Deborah helped Granny water and feed all her plants, of which she had about fifty, ten to each windowsill. She talked to them all the time she was attending to them, scolding and praising, telling them news of the plants in the other rooms and the garden. "They grow better if you do that," she explained.

"Do you say poetry to them too?"

"You can do," said Granny, "but plants seem to like real news best. Sometimes I read the paper aloud to them. They do like music, it's true. And of course you have to listen to them as well."

"Listen?"

"In case they've got any grievances. Terrible ones for sulking, some plants can be."

When the plants were done, there was the starling to be given his lesson.

"When he first came to live here I could hardly abide him," said Granny. "Squawk, squawk. Not one decent sensible thing to say for himself. But Mr. Jones (who's the music teacher at the Comprehensive and plays the piano in Chapel on Sundays), he lent me a book of tunes you can teach birds. Hundred years ago, everybody was doing it. Now it's all television, nobody has time."

The starling, Jack, who had a lame leg, had been rescued by Granny from a cat and had decided to take up residence in her house. He came and went as he chose, through a hinged pane in the kitchen window, but spent most of his time sitting among the willow-pattern china on the green dresser. He was as glossy himself as a lustre mug. "I will say for him, he's clean as a Quaker," said Granny. "I've never known him clarty the place but once, and then the curtains were drawn and he couldn't find his way out. Here's the book, do you want to teach him a tune?"

The book, which looked quite old, was called *100 Prettie Tunes to teach Canarays or Other Cage Birdes*. But Deborah was obliged to confess that she could not read music.

"Can you not, child? Oh well, I'll soon teach you that." And in half an hour she had. "See, it goes up and down along the stave – that one is *God Save the Queen*, Queen Anne it would have been then I daresay – so you can see how it works – and this note here, like a ball of wool on a knitting-needle, that's C – " she sang it in her thin, clear old voice. "But how do you know?" said Deborah. "Well, if you don't know you can find out from the tuning-fork," said Granny and took it out of a stone marmalade jar on the dresser, a thick Y of blue metal, "but you'll soon find you remember the note." Deborah found this was true. They began teaching Jack the first line of *Lillibullero* but quite soon he became tired and stuck his head under his wing. "You'd better go off to bed too, child," said Granny. "Oh, but I don't go to bed nearly as early as this at home," said Deborah. "No, but at home I daresay you don't get up so early," said Granny. "I'm always up at six and through the housework before breakfast, so as to have it out of the way for the day."

Deborah ate her supper in front of the kitchen fire: cup of cocoa, piece of dripping-toast, and the crusty end of the loaf spread thick with globby home-made yellow plum jam.

"Now," said Granny, "you must choose your bedroom. The back one's bigger, and has the sun in the morning, and looks over the garden, but then you have to come through my room to get to the bathroom. Or, if you like, you can have my room, and then you're right beside the bathroom – but then *I* shall have to come past *you* – and I warn you, old people are always getting up in the night. After seventy you sleep with one eye open."

Deborah thought she would have the back room; she didn't want to turn Granny out of her bed. Granny gave her a small torch in case she needed to find her way to the bathroom in the dark. Also an apple.

"Eat an apple going to bed, make the doctor beg his bread."

Perhaps because of the apple, or the cocoa, or the strange bed, or because she had learned so many new things during the previous day that her mind was buzzing with them, like all three bee-hives put together – Deborah woke after she had been asleep about four hours, and sat straight up in bed. Perhaps, after all, it was the moon that had woken her – a bent square of light lay, half on the white wall, half on the blue-painted floor. There seemed no need for her torch, after all, but Deborah took it just in case Granny's room was darker. She slipped out of bed on to her little braided rag rug (made long ago by Granny who had promised to show Deborah how) and tiptoed across the shiny blue floor into the other room. That was quite light too, with reflected moonlight from the windows of the houses across the street. There lay Granny, a small breathing shape, flat in her bed. But the minute

Deborah set foot in her room she sat bolt upright, throwing off the covers. Her straight white hair, free from its knot, hung round her face like a child's. Her eyes were fast shut.

"Who are you? And where are you from?" she said sharply. Her voice was different from her daytime voice – higher and clearer too; a younger person's voice.

Deborah's heart battered against her ribs, like Jack the starling looking for his way out through the curtains.

"It's Deborah, G-Granny," she stammered. "I'm Deborah!"

Granny turned her impatient, sightless face towards the door. "No, who *are* you?" she snapped. "Who *are* you, I said – and where are you *from*?"

"But I'm Deb – your grand-daughter Deborah. From – from home. From London."

"Who *are* you?" Granny repeated for the third time. "Where are you *from*?"

Deborah was so terribly daunted and abashed by this that she retreated on tiptoe from the doorway, back across her moonlit floor, and then jumped into bed and pulled the bedclothes tight round her chin. She was half afraid that Granny would come after her. Nothing of the kind had ever happened to her before. She felt terribly queer – as if she had found herself, by mistake, inside the egg of some strange bird who was shouting Trespassers will be Prosecuted in her ear. Or a mermaid's egg – do mermaids have eggs?

Luckily she had not wanted to go to the bathroom too desperately; before she knew it, she had slipped back into sleep.

In the morning, Granny was so exactly the way she had been yesterday – which seemed so just and precisely Granny-ish that Deborah could not imagine her ever having been different – she was so neat and active, so brisk and talkative, nipping about with a mop and duster while the kettle sang, and the bacon frizzled – that Deborah plucked up courage, and while they were upstairs, making the beds, told what had happened in the night.

"You sat up in bed, Granny, as straight as a stick, and you said it in *such* a fierce tone that I was really frightened."

Granny couldn't help laughing at the story – in fact she laughed so much that she had to sit down on Deborah's blue bedroom chair – but when she had recovered she said. "*That* won't do, will it now? We certainly can't have you frightened like that."

"Why do you suppose you didn't believe me when I said I was Deborah?"

"I daresay because it seemed too simple."

"How do you mean, Granny?"

"Well when you're asleep you're much more than just plain Deborah, aren't you? You might be a princess, or a fish, or a tree, or a horse, or the moon, or a whole lot of things one after the other – you're everything that you ever dreamed you were, all baked together in a pie of sleep."

"But *you* were the one who was asleep, Granny – I was awake!"

"That's what I mean," said Granny. "If you're explaining to someone who's asleep, you've got to put it *all* in – not just the top layer. Do you see?"

"I'm not sure," said Deborah.

"Well, of course, the first thing is not to be scared, if it should happen again. Just give me an answer. And if it isn't the right one, first time, go on trying till it is. Or walk past. After all, I'm only your old Granny!"

"But suppose *you're* a fish, or a tree, or the moon?"

"Sit down and eat your breakfast, child – the bacon's getting cold. Cold bacon hot again, that love I never."

After breakfast they sides-to-middled some worn sheets

– Granny let Deborah tear the old flimsy cotton which gave with a scrumptious purring rip, like wood splitting but softer. Then the torn edges had to be hemmed and the outer sides joined together; Deborah turned the handle of the sewing-machine while Granny guided the cotton under the bright foot and the rapid-thudding needle that flashed up and down. Then they changed over, Granny turned the wheel and Deborah learned to steer the material; it was more difficult than she had expected and she made some wild swerves before she mastered the knack, but, as Granny said, it all helped to strengthen the sheet and was good practice.

Then they added a bit more on to the patchwork quilt which was, Granny said, the ninth she had made; it was already single-bed size but needed to be double, since it was intended for a wedding present. The pieces were six-sided, the colours mostly dark reds and pale greens and cream colour, but each corner contained a circle made up of all kinds of patterned bits, and in these Deborah recognised pieces left over from several dresses that Granny had made and sent her in the past.

Then they whitewashed the inside of the wash-house, using big brushes and buckets of distemper and getting so splashed that they had to have baths afterwards. Then they bicycled down to the shops, singing *Pop Goes the Weasel*, and bought half a pound of rice, which cost considerably more than twopence, and a tin of treacle, and Granny taught Deborah how to make a treacle tart. And then they ate it.

After lunch they went to the allotment and planted young leeks and sowed peas and two kinds of beans. "You'll have to come back to help me eat them," said Granny. "I don't want to go away from here, ever," said Deborah. On the ride back they went round by way of York Minster for Deborah to see it; the arched ceilings inside reminded her of Granny's patchwork quilt, except that they were creamy white, but they were covered with the same kind of patterns; and the windows were *exactly* like the inside of Granny's house; they gave just the same feeling of somebody's having thought very hard, deciding which were their favourite colours, and then put every single one of them in.

That night Deborah went to sleep almost before her head hit the pillow (Jack the starling had learned another six notes of *Lillibullero* but it had been hard work); then the moonlight woke her, four or five hours later, shining like a TV screen on the wall opposite her face. She crept across her room and was half-way to the bathroom door when, as before, Granny woke and sat bolt upright in bed.

"Who's that? Who are you?"

"I'm a bicycle," Deborah said, guessing. Granny moved her head a little, frowning in her sleep, as if this *might* be the right answer, but not all of it. "I'm the wind, I'm a streetlight, I'm a one-way street, I'm a zebra-crossing."

At each of these things, Granny nodded. "Where are you from?" she said.

"I'm – I'm from the other side of town," said Deborah, and made her escape into the bathroom. When she came out again, Granny was lying down fast asleep, and never stirred.

"There you are, you see!" she said triumphantly next morning. "I told you it was perfectly simple. All you have to do is say the right thing!"

That day they made new curtains for the kitchen (Granny had bought the material ten years ago at a jumble sale and had been saving it for just this use – it was plain black-and-white stripes with, just here and there, a bunch of green grapes printed on the cotton); they sponged the shiny indoor plants, sowed some broccoli and got ready a cold frame for vegetable marrows. They told each other stories. They bought a small, undressed doll at an auction (along with a stepladder, a jam cauldron, and five large earthenware crocks) and began planning its wardrobe. Deborah learned how to make shepherd's pie. They picked big bunches of grape hyacinths and narcissi, which smelt sweet as honey all over the house.

And that night, when Granny said, "Who are you?" Deborah said, "I'm a needle, I'm a spoon. I'm a length of cotton. I'm a ladder, I'm a bird, I'm a window."

"Where are you from?"

"I'm from all around you, Granny?"

Instantly Granny lay down, perfectly satisfied, it seemed, with these answers.

During the next month of nights they played this game many times in Granny's sleep. It was like fishing, Deborah thought – except that she was not quite sure who was the fish and who the fisher. Granny asked the question and Deborah threw out her answer like a line; sometimes it was right, sometimes wrong. If it was wrong, Granny would not have it. "I'm an apple, Granny." "No, you are *not! Who* are you, and where are you from?" Some nights Deborah got it right at once, sometimes she had to feel her way slowly, guess by guess, cold, warm, warmer, until she hit the right answer. "I'm a line, a rope, a fish, a trout, an eel!" "And where are you from?" "From – from Newfoundland!" And where she got that answer from, goodness knows; but it seemed to satisfy Granny.

Of course, Deborah did not get up every night; sometimes, tired from all they had done and said and learned and thought, she slept clean through the silent hours of dark. But she often had a curious feeling on those nights, even more than after the ones when she had woken, that Granny had been asking questions and she had been answering them, without the need for words.

At last a letter came. Deborah's mother was better. And then her father came to take her home.

Deborah did not want to go. She wanted to stay so badly that it seemed probable no one but Granny could have persuaded her to get into the car with her father. "You'll be able to show your mother how well you can make a shepherd's pie and a treacle tart. And I'm going to give you these plants to look after for me, and you must write to me every single week and tell me how they are getting on."

Loaded with all the things she had made – the pair of trousers, the doll with two sets of clothes, the pot of lemon curd, the cake, the Japanese garden made from stones and moss in a foil pie-pan, the pincushion stuffed with dried coffee-grounds, the clove orange – Deborah went home. "Why can't everybody be like Granny?" she wept and her father, driving the car, said, "It's just as well everybody isn't, or there wouldn't be room to move in the world with all the things that got made and everybody bustling about," and he swerved his car to avoid an old lady who was bicycling along with a full basket.

In fact Deborah settled down at home again not too badly. She had all her new skills to practise, and she kept up the habit of learning a new poem every day, and she wrote to Granny, with pictures, about the growth of the plants and about her new baby brother, and sent patchwork pieces, and sometimes a poem that she had written herself. Granny always answered right away, on a postcard. 'Pieces v. useful. Glad to hear about the plants. Jack learned *Danny Boy*. Strawb. jam turned out well. Saving pot for you. Too busy to write more at present. G.'

The cards were always gorgeously coloured. Granny got them from a bookshop near the Minster, they were reproductions of pictures that had taken her fancy, and presently Deborah had half a wall full of them – battlescenes, flowers, landscapes, ships, angels, breakfast tables.

And then one day Deborah's father had a telegram:

Your mother injured in street accident in York hospital please come.

"I always said she'd end up in trouble, riding that crazy old bicycle," he said, distractedly throwing socks and razor and pyjamas into a bag.

Deborah got out her own bag and began packing it. "No, no, dear, *you* can't go," said her mother. "It wouldn't be at all suitable. Children are only in the way when people are ill; it wouldn't do at all."

But Deborah was so absolutely ferociously determined – "Granny would *want* me. After all, I know how she does things – I'd know *everything* she wanted – " that in the end, somehow, without anyone actually having said yes, you can go, she was there in the car, driving to York with her father. "We'll go straight to the hospital," he said. "But you won't be allowed in to see her, I'm sure, so don't expect it."

"Why not?"

"Children never are allowed to visit sick people in hospitals."

"Why not?"

He didn't really know. "I suppose they'd bother the other patients."

"I wouldn't!"

"Well, anyway . . ."

At the hospital they talked to a matron. It seemed the accident hadn't been Granny's fault: two cars had collided and one had bounced back on to Granny who was coming up behind it on her bike. "I'm afraid she's very ill indeed," said the matron. "She may not know you." And there was absolutely no question of Deborah's being allowed in. She was told to wait in a dull empty room with nothing but a flat green bench and a smell of old flowers. Her father went with the matron and Deborah sat wretchedly, kicking her heels against the legs of the bench and trying to say over one of the poems she had

147

learned. "Where the bee sucks, there suck I, In a cowslip's bell I lie . . ." But this seemed no place for poems.

The worst of it was, she began to be certain that she could hear Granny's voice. So sure was she that she moved out of the waiting-room and along a wide, huge, shiny corridor with doors all along each side. She listened, she walked a little farther, she listened again.

She came to a door that was not quite shut, and pushed it open a bit. And then she could definitely hear Granny's voice inside, with all its old impatience, saying,

"No – who are you? Who *are* you?"

She heard her father's voice. "It's John, Mother. Don't you know me?" Granny's voice had been clear, but his sounded all choked up with worry and embarrassment.

Deborah put her head round the door. There were several people by a bed, doctors, she supposed, and nurses in white, and her father sitting on a chair. And Granny, trying to push herself up in the bed – at least it must be Granny because the white hair was certainly hers, but the face was mostly bandaged – and a nurse was trying to persuade her to lie down again.

"No, but who *are* you?" cried out Granny, as if she could hardly bear all this stupidity, and Deborah, running to the bedside, said, quickly, before anybody could stop her,

"Hullo, Granny! It's me – I'm a wing, I'm a flying leaf, no, I'm a bit of thistledown, I'm something high up and light, I'm a bird – *no* – I'm a *bee*, Granny! I'm Deborah! I'm a bee!"

Granny turned her head towards Deborah's voice and listened keenly. Then she slowly settled herself back into a curled-up lying position, facing Deborah. A nurse tucked the clothes round, but she pushed them sharply off again, as if they bothered her.

"Deborah," she said, "That's it! You're Deborah. And do you know what you must do?"

"What, Granny?"

"You have to go and tell the bees, child . . . tell them . . ."

"Yes, I'll tell them, Granny," said Deborah. Tears were running down her cheeks, which was silly, because of *course* the bees must be told; anybody knew that was the first thing that must be done after an accident or any important happening.

A nurse led her out of the room – there was a lot going on – and she was put in a different place to wait: someone's office. But Deborah was thinking about the bees. Really they should be told at once; she slid down off her chair and walked to the end of the corridor, where she found a fire door and an outside flight of steps. She and Granny had passed the hospital once on one of their bicycle trips; she was pretty sure that she could find her way from there to the allotments.

The broad beans they had sown now dangled heavy pods, lumpy as Christmas stockings; some of the peas had pods, others were still in blossom. Marigolds and bachelors' buttons flashed among the rows of green. But the sun was gone by now; dew was falling. The sky was a pale oyster-green. All but the most far-wandering bees had returned to their hives for the night.

Deborah knelt in the cold, dewy grass by the middle hive. She said,

"It's about Granny. I think you ought to know—"

Inside the bees seemed to be listening. Their slumbrous murmur had dwindled to a sigh that was hardly louder than her own breathing. And then she heard – or did she imagine it? – a tiny voice that might have been from the hives or from somewhere deep inside her own head, a voice imperiously demanding.

"But who are *you?*"

"I'm Deborah," she whispered. And then she lay face down on the wet grass and cried her heart out. It was there that her father, scolding, anxious, harassed, sad, finally found her.

"Did Granny die then?" said Deborah.

She was quiet now, calmer than her father, who could only nod.

"Well, I expect it was best," Deborah said, after a minute. "She would think it was better than not being able to ride her bike or dig in her garden or climb ladders, or any of the things she always did. Can you get someone to move her hives to Putney? Are there bee-movers?"

"Move them to *Putney*? Are you crazy? People don't keep bees in Putney!"

"Why not? Our garden's just as big as Granny's allotment. And there's all Putney Heath too. We've got to look after Granny's bees; besides, she left them to me; they're mine now. And you have to take care of bees; you can't just leave them to starve."

"I don't know *what* your mother will say . . ."

But he knew she would get her way; as she had over the trip to York. On the way to London, while Deborah, curled in the back seat, taught lame Jack to whistle the first four bars of *Cherry Ripe*, her father, driving the car, thought to himself, We've got another of them in the family now. She's going to be exactly the same.

The Man Who Pinched God's Letter

HIS NAME WAS FRED ACORN, AND IN HIS HEY-
day he had been a postman. This was in a little grey
town called Incaster Magna, which clung to the side of a
green grassy hill, somewhere in Wales. Down at the
bottom of the hill was a river in a valley, and round
the corner of the hill, farther up the valley, was a much
smaller place called Outcaster Parva. We shall come to
that by and by.

During the years that Fred was a postman he was as
happy as it was possible for him to be. Fred was a strange-
looking little fellow; one of his legs was a couple of inches
longer than the other, so that he rocked as he walked
along. And his back was a bit hunched, and he wasn't
very tall. And his ears stood out on either side of his head
like pink butterflies' wings. And his hair was a bright
ginger colour. So that altogether, when you saw him first,
it was a bit of a shock, and no girl had ever felt inclined
to go to the pictures with him. Which was a pity, because

the two blue eyes that looked out from under his ginger thatch were friendly and sad, and he had a very affection- ate heart.

Because one of his legs was shorter than the other, the pedals of his postman's bicycle were specially adapted, one of them built up extra thick, so that he would whizz about on it at top speed, delivering letters. The bicycle was painted bright red, with the letters E.R. and a crown in black on the middle bar, to show that it belonged to the Post Office and not to Fred personally. But that did not prevent him loving it very much, and he always kept it in tiptop condition, oiling it and cleaning it, washing the red parts, polishing the shiny parts, and making a cover for the saddle out of an old black beret. And, twice a day, he went darting about, through the streets of grey houses, over the bridge, past and round the large village green of Incaster Magna, delivering the mail: first-class post first thing in the morning, starting at half past six, and second-class post in the afternoon. Fred looked rather like a small red ladybird taking their letters to the people of Incaster Magna. (He did not deliver to Outcaster Parva, which was eight miles away; and anyway there were only five houses, so the people in that village thought them- selves lucky to get one post a day, which was delivered at teatime by mail-van.)

At twelve o'clock midday Fred went home for his dinner, and his old mother always had it ready for him, piping hot: a pot of stew with carrots, or some thick soup, or fried fish and chips, or sausages and mashed potato.

But presently Fred's old mother became *very* old, and then she died, and then life was very lonely for Fred. It wasn't so bad during the daytime, as he shot about on his bike, shouting "Good morning" or "Good afternoon" to people as he poked letters and parcels into their letter- boxes; but in the evenings he was very lonely indeed with nobody to talk to, nobody to have a bright fire lit and waiting for him to come home to, nobody to have the stew ready for him. After his mother's death, Fred lived on boiled eggs and sausages, and he began to look very thin and sad; even his pink ears no longer seemed to stick out like butterflies, but hung down sorrowfully like autumn leaves. Nobody ever asked Fred out to supper, for the other people in the town all looked down on him – all but one.

And, now that he was all alone in the world – for he had no brothers or sisters, no aunts, uncles, grandparents, nieces, nephews, or cousins – another thing began to worry Fred that had never worried him before.

This was not his looks – bless you, he was used to *them*, and worried no more about what he saw when he looked in the glass than a craggy hill does about its reflection in the lake down below. No – what upset Fred and began to stick in his mind like a miserable splinter was the fact that although he was delivering letters and cards, parcels and packets, all day and every day, not one of them was ever addressed to *him*. For he had not a friend in the world to write to him. And sometimes he would be seized with a terrible burning envy, or a bitter grieving sadness, as he pushed some interesting letter in a blue-and-red airmail envelope, all covered with foreign stamps, through somebody's letter-box or maybe a coloured postcard showing lakes or snowy mountains. And when he had to ring the doorbell and hand in a heavy, exciting parcel, carefully tied up with plenty of brown paper and a good lot of string, and maybe a bit of sealingwax as well – then sometimes poor Fred's heart would almost burst with sorrowfulness, remembering that nobody had ever sent *him* such a parcel – and very likely never would. For not a soul in the world knew when Fred's birthday came, now that his mother was dead. When his birthday *did* come – it was on the first of May – he was sometimes tempted to send himself a card or a greetings telegram in a golden

153

envelope, just so that he would have *something* to open. But it would not have been very exciting, because he would have known what was going to be inside it. So in the end he never did.

But because of this envy of other people's letters, Fred became more and more tempted to do a thing which led to a lot of trouble. And finally he did it. He stole someone else's letter. For he thought, even a letter that was addressed to somebody else would be better than no letter at all.

There was a woman in the town called Mrs. Prout, who had no end of aunts, cousins, and nieces, and she was always writing to them. Mrs. Prout was not a pleasant person – she wrote very spiteful gossiping letters about her neighbours; she spent almost all her time doing this; but because she wrote so many letters, she received a great many in return; and Fred thought, out of so many she'll never miss *one.* So in the end he gave way to temptation. One day, quite early, about seven, when he had to push half a dozen letters through Mrs. Prout's letter-slot, he kept one of them back, and slipped it into his pocket.

But as Fred's ill-luck would have it, Mrs. Prout, in her curlers and dressing-gown, was just peeking through her front curtains at that moment, to see what kind of a day it was; and she saw Fred put the letter in his pocket.

All day, as Fred rode about the town on his red bike, his heart felt as light as a dandelion-puff when he thought about the envelope in his pocket. It was very fat. What would there be inside? A long interesting letter, perhaps, or some photographs – Fred was very partial to looking at photographs; or an invitation to a party – or a recipe for Christmas pudding – he could hardly wait to get home and find out what it was.

And meantime, Mrs. Prout, quick as lightning, had sorted through her mail, and was round complaining to the Post Office that she had not received her usual weekly letter from her niece Ella. She did not directly say that she had seen Fred take the letter; that was not Mrs. Prout's way; she just said that Ella *always* wrote on a Tuesday, she *always* had the letter on a Wednesday, and there was something funny going on; carelessness, no doubt, on the part of Fred the postman; and she strongly recommended that Fred should be asked about it.

And what about Fred? He had gone home at last, given his dear bicycle rather less than its usual careful polish, rushed inside, and slit open the envelope.

What was his disappointment to discover that all it contained was an enormously complicated knitting pattern, pages and pages of it. Knit twenty together, slip two, twenty plain, twenty purl, cast on, cast off, knot some more together, slip some, knot some, drip some, drop some – Fred could make neither head nor tail of it, although he puzzled over it for hours. He felt most terribly let down as he glumly fried himself a couple of sausages, leaving them all pale and damp because he was now very hungry indeed and couldn't be bothered to do them properly.

And then, while he was eating them, his conscience began to attack him. Perhaps Mrs. Prout was anxiously waiting for that knitting pattern, which would be very useful to *her*, and was absolutely no good at all to him? He had better take it round to her, and explain, and apologise. And so, very sadly and unwillingly, he put on his red postman's raincoat, uncrumpled the envelope – which he had screwed into a ball in his first disappointment – and went round to Mrs. Prout's house.

"Oh, I'm very sorry, ma'am," he said nervously when she opened the door – "Here's this letter of yours which I – I accidentally kept, and opened in error – I'm ever so sorry and I hope you haven't been waiting for it."

Mrs. Prout wasn't a bit appeased by his nervousness and apologies, but instantly flew into a fearful passion.

"I don't believe a word of what you say, Fred Acorn! You only brought the letter back because I've been round complaining at the Post Office. How could you confuse the name *Prout* with the name *Acorn*, answer me that? You didn't keep that letter in error – everybody in the town knows that you never get a letter, so how *could* it have been yours, pray? You are a disgrace to the Royal Mail Service and I am going to see that you are hounded out of it – you deserve to have that red postman's raincoat dragged from your back!"

And she snatched the knitting pattern from him and slammed the door in his face.

Well, Mrs. Prout was as good as her word. She was a big, forceful woman with a power of going on and on about something till everybody was quite tired out, and she went on and on about poor Fred, and how he had only taken her envelope because he thought it had money inside – which was not the case at all – and nobody's mail was safe from him and how did they know what else he might not have stolen? So that, although several people pointed out that so far as was known, not so much as a postcard had been stolen during all the years that Fred had carried the mail, in the end Mrs. Prout had her way, and Fred was dismissed from his job. He had to hand in his red raincoat and, what was much worse, his beautiful red bike.

And the only job he could get was that of street-cleaner, which carried no bicycle with it, only a wheelbarrow. Poor Fred had to limp around the streets, from six in the morning to five in the evening every day, with a broom and dustpan, sweeping up all the toffee papers and cigarette butts and lemonade-can ring-tops, and sales tickets that people dropped – and many nastier things also.

It was much more tiring work than being a postman, and very depressing. Instead of delivering things to people that would cheer them up, all he did was clear up the mess they left behind. And there was never an end to it – by the time he had got to one side of the town, the other side was all littered over again with gum packets and chocolate wrappers. Poor Fred was just about as miserable as he could be, and he was angry too; for he thought: I honestly took her letter back and said I was sorry. What good did that do? I might as well have kept the letter.

A new young postman called Martin Gully had been appointed; he was a shiftless young fellow who took no pride in his work, never polished the bike, allowed the letters to get wet if it rained, and got through the deliveries as fast as he could. He went to breakfast in the middle of the morning delivery-round, so that people had to wait till quite late for their first-class mail. And instead of pushing the letters right into people's letter-boxes, he used to leave the corners sticking out, getting wet and dirty; or he would poke letters half under front doors, again leaving a bit sticking out which might get trodden on by dogs or by people in a hurry.

Fred used to notice these corners of letters, when he went on his rounds with broom and pan and wheelbarrow, sweeping along the pavements and gutters. *I* wouldn't have done that, he used to think. And sometimes, if he was in a generous mood, he would poke the letters right through, out of sight. But one day when he was doing this, Mrs. Prout happened to pass by.

"You leave those letters alone, Fred Acorn!" she screeched at him. "I know what you're up to! You're a-feeling of the envelopes to see if there's any five-pound notes inside! You're a disgrace to the town, that's what you are, and in my opinion you ought to be kicked out of Incaster."

Now this made Fred so angry that he thought, Blow the old trout. I might be hung for a sheep as for a lamb. I really will take a letter! And so, when he came across another corner sticking temptingly out of a letter-box, he glanced up and down the street to make sure the coast was clear, and then quickly flipped the letter out and into the pocket of his roadman's cape.

All day as he swept the streets – and it was a miserable, rainy day, only Fred was out in it, clearing up the Coke cans and cigarette packets and old newspapers – all day his heart was warmed and cheered by the thought of the letter in his pocket. All day he wondered what could be in it. And that night he opened it with trembling hands – but first he put some sausages on to grill under a low heat, so that they could be cooking while he read his letter.

'Dear Daddy,' the letter said – it was in a very round childish handwriting that was almost print – 'Dear Daddy I am very unhappy at school. I wish you had not sent me to this boarding-school for everybody is very unkind. They all laugh at me because I do not have a case to carry my books in like the others but only an old cloth bag. I know you have said twice that you are not going to waste money on a case because the bag will do, but please please Daddy do please change your mind. If I had a case the others would stop laughing at me, I really do need one. If you could only send me £5, I would be so happy I would polish your shoes every day for a year. Your loving daughter Tessa.'

This letter made Fred feel very sad. It was addressed to Mr. Moffat, who was the Mayor of Incaster. Mr. Moffat was a very stingy man who grudged spending every penny. He ate margarine instead of butter, and dressed his children in second-hand clothes from an old-clothes stall, and sent them to a cheap school, run by a friend of his, where they went for half-price.

'She'll never get that case,' thought Fred, and he felt very sorry for little Tessa. He knew what it was to be laughed at.

And then a happy thought struck him. Why shouldn't he, Fred, send the five pounds? He had plenty of money saved up, all his postman's wages and his street-sweeping money too, for though that wasn't much, there never seemed to be anything he wanted to buy, except food, and he didn't eat a lot. So he put a five-pound note in an envelope and addressed it to Miss Tessa Moffat, Sunnybank School, Cloud Hill. How amazed and pleased she'll be, he thought, as he posted his letter. Of course it was rather sad that she would never know the money came from Fred, so he would never get a letter of thanks from her, but never mind; just the thought of Tessa's pleasure in her new case kept him cheerful for days as he swept up the toffee-wrappers.

And he kept a sharp look-out for Mr. Moffat in the streets, hoping to surprise an expression of puzzlement on his face – for no doubt Tessa would think the five pounds came from her father and write to thank him for it – but in fact Mr. Moffat was such a sour, bracket-faced glum-looking man that Fred could never be sure whether he was looking puzzled or not.

Well, as I say, thinking about Tessa kept Fred cheerful for quite a while. But then this cheerfulness began to wear thin – and he felt again a terrible craving to take another letter. There were all those corners that young Martin left poking out so temptingly from people's front doors – surely just *one* more wouldn't be missed? Winter had come now, dark till half past eight in the morning, so it was only too easy to take another without being spotted.

Fred took another.

It was addressed to Tom Whilliwell, Esq.

'Oh my darling,' (Fred read that evening, after he had put the sausages on to grill), 'Oh my darling, Father says that I must never speak to you again. He says we are too young to think of marriage and anyway you are only the blacksmith's son, even if you *are* going away to college, and that I must put you right out of my head. Oh Tom, I am so sad about this, but Father is keeping me locked up in my room and Mother will only let me have bread and water to eat until I promise not to see you anymore, so what can I do? I will always love you but I have to give in as I can't stand bread and water. I will never forget you. Will you do one thing for me? Stand on the bridge below our house every evening at nine for the three days before you go away to college and I will be looking out of my bedroom window and sending you my silent love. Your despairing Janet. P.S. You had better wear a sack on your head when you stand on the bridge so Father doesn't know it is you.'

Well, what could Fred do?

He could have told Tom Whilliwell about the letter, but on the whole he thought it better not to. In Fred's opinion, Tom would be happier going off to college than trying to marry Janet Prout. Fred guessed it must be Janet who had written the letter because the Prouts' house was by the bridge and he had seen Janet sitting on the parapet of the bridge sometimes, talking to Tom. Janet was a pale, sulky girl, with her mother's spiteful disposition, and, taking everything together, Fred thought that Tom was lucky to have got away from her. But still, the poor thing ought to have some answer to her sad request; so, for two weeks, Fred put a sack on his head and went and stood on the bridge every night in the streaming rain. He was not sure, you see, which day was the one on which Tom went off to college, so it seemed better to be on the safe side and do it for quite a few days.

At the end of two weeks Tom was not seen about the streets any more, so it was to be presumed that he had gone; and Janet was looking much more cheerful and had started going out with young Sid Pulling whose father kept the hay and feed store. And Fred had a terrible cold from standing in the rain. But still, on the whole, he felt quite cheerful because at least he was doing things for people and had plenty to think about.

And then ... after a while, he began to have a craving to take another letter.

He kept the urge at bay for quite a long time.

He thought, No, it's stealing. I shouldn't take people's letters, It worked out all right twice, but that was only luck.

If only I could think of somebody to write to, he thought, then someone would write back to me. But he could think of no one to write to.

Just the same, he managed to struggle against the temptation for six months.

At the end of that time, Janet Prout got married to Sid Pulling. There was a big wedding in the church, with masses of confetti and flowers. Afterwards, Fred was kept busy for hours, sweeping up all the confetti from the churchyard grass and the path leading to the church, and even inside the church porch.

When he was sweeping out the church porch, what did Fred see?

He saw a letter stuck in the letter-basket on the inside of the church door.

It was addressed to God.

Oh, Fred went through terrible temptation then!

He thought, Come on Fred, pull yourself together. If it is wrong to take a person's letter, it must be a thousand times worse to take one that is addressed to God.

But then he thought, After all, God knows everything. So he must know what is inside that letter already – he doesn't have to read it. And I might just as well take it, because I *don't* know.

He thought, Perhaps the person who wrote that letter is in trouble, and I might be able to help them, the way I helped Janet and Tom and Tessa Moffat. It could do no harm just to look at the letter. If I can't help the person, I can always put it back and let God take care of it.

So, in the end he took the letter.

What he didn't know was that Mrs. Prout was inside the church, collecting the flowers that had been used as decorations for the wedding because she was too mean to leave them there for everyone to enjoy but was going to put them in her sitting-room. She looked out from the dark back of the church and saw Fred take the letter and go off with it.

First she carried the flowers home, then she rushed to the police-station.

"That Fred Acorn is at it again!" she screeched. "He pinched a letter out of the church! It probably had money in it! You'll have to arrest him."

Very unwillingly the local police superintendent, Mr. Griffin, went round with her to Fred's cottage, where they found Fred looking very pale and worried.

"Mrs. Prout has made an accusation," said Superintendent Griffin. "She says you took a letter from the church porch. Is that true?"

"Yes it is," said Fred sadly.

"What was in the letter?"

"That letter is a private matter between me and God and whoever wrote it," said Fred.

"Never mind that! You just hand it over, so that we can inform whoever wrote it, and see if they want to prosecute."

"You won't be able to do that," said Fred.

"Why not?"

"Because it isn't signed."

Well they went on and on at him, they called in the magistrate, Mr. Muchness, and, in the end, Fred had to hand over the letter. And he was right, the letter did them no good at all. For it was printed in block letters. And it said.

162

"Dear God, I'm in dreadful, dreadful trouble. Only you can help me. I know you've got lots of things to worry about, God, and I hate to take up your time, but I've no one else to turn to. Only one person in this town has ever given me so much as a smile, and that's Fred the postman, and *he* wouldn't be able to help me in the trouble I'm in, which is really dangerous and dreadful. So, please, God, will you do something – anything you like, I leave it to you to get me out of this. I would really be grateful. You know who I am, so I don't need to sign, but will only put, Yours faithfully."

Well, Mr. Muchness and Superintendent Griffin and Mrs. Prout didn't know what to make of that.

"Someone who's no better than they should be, *I'*d say," sniffed Mrs. Prout.

"Some poor nut," said the superintendent.

"We certainly can't arrest Fred for taking *that*," said Mr. Muchness.

But Mrs. Prout went on and on so, about how Fred was a danger to the community, that in the end Mr. Muchness and Mr. Moffat agreed to demote him to the grade of assistant road-sweeper, and he was sent away to the much smaller village of Outcaster Parva, to sweep the streets there. Since there wasn't a spare cottage in Outcaster, Fred had to live in an old disused laundry, eating his meals off a huge flat pressing-machine, heating his bath water in a laundry copper, and making his toast and boiling his kettle for tea on a little black coal-stove which was intended for heating up flat-irons. It was rather a strange place to use for a dwelling, but Fred quite enjoyed it, for it gave him lots of new things to think about.

There was only one street to sweep in Outcaster, and that was only fifty yards long. And instead of a big hand-some village green, like the one at Incaster, there was a tiny little green about the size of a kitchen table, which was walked over so much that it should have been called a brown, rather than a green. But all around the edge of the village were big, beautiful mountains, and the families who lived in its five houses, ten people to a house, were a friendly lot, all fifty of them, so Fred soon found that he was having a much happier time than he had since his mother died – he was invited out to supper almost every night.

But what he liked best of all in Outcaster were the dogs.

For its size, Outcaster had an amazing lot of dogs – more per head of population than any other town in the British Isles. There were seventy-one, most of them Welsh collies. They didn't fight, but got on with each other well enough – of course they were nearly all related – but they suffered badly from not having enough to do. And as Fred himself had very little to do, once he had swept the fifty yards of street, he soon fell into the habit of taking the dogs for walks. There were always half a dozen – or twelve – or eighteen – sitting about on the little patch of brown, rather bored, with their tongues hanging out, waiting for something to happen, hoping that someone would be going somewhere, for they didn't have the initiative to go off on their own.

Fred used to take them down to a big field that belonged to no one in particular, and there he would throw sticks for them. At first he had to work extremely hard to supply them all with sticks, but once they had become used to this game it worked out really profitably for Fred, since all the dogs of the village would come running to him with sticks in their mouths as soon as he put his head outside the laundry door. He didn't need to collect sticks for his fire from November to March.

So in many ways Fred was happy. But in one way he was not, and you will have guessed what it was.

He was worried to death about the person who had written that letter to God.

Sometimes he thought, Well, God must have known about the person, so my having taken the letter won't have made any difference; I expect he has helped the person by now.

But sometimes Fred thought, Supposing God overlooked the letter because of its having been taken away and put in a file at the police-station?

Suppose that person is still in terrible trouble? I wish I knew who it was, he thought; it must be someone that I have smiled at, one time or another, but there are quite a few of those. If only I was still working there, riding or walking about the streets of Incaster, I'd be able to find out who was in trouble by looking at people's faces. I ought to do something about it, he thought, for perhaps that person is my responsibility; perhaps God *meant* me to take that letter out of the church porch and do something about it?

His thoughts went round and round like this for several weeks. And in the end he decided to walk down to Incaster one Monday (which was his day off); stroll about the streets there and see if he couldn't spot the person who had written the letter. It could do no harm.

So he set off to walk the eight miles down the valley.

You can guess what happened.

The fifteen dogs who were sitting on the village brown instantly got up and followed Fred. And – since dogs have a kind of telepathy of their own and can pass messages to one another quick as radio – in no time at all, the rest of the fifty-six dogs who were scattered about the valley, rabbiting or ratting or helping their master with the sheep – had got the message too, left what they were doing, and came galloping across country to follow Fred. So after he had walked a mile or so the whole seventy-one were following him, and it was a handsome sight to see them all flowing along the narrow road like a black-and-white river.

Though by the end of the eight miles some had become tired and were lagging quite a way behind.

When Fred reached Incaster, there seemed to be nobody about the streets.

He walked on till he came to the middle of the village. And that was where all the people were, dead silent, round the edge of the green.

And in the middle of the green was a big bonfire piled up, but not lit yet.

That's funny, thought Fred, for it's not Guy Fawkes Day.

Then he saw that there was a woman standing in the middle of the pile of wood, with her arms tied behind her.

That's Emma Birdcage, thought Fred. What's she doing in the middle of the bonfire?

Emma Birdcage was a very plain girl, with one blue eye and one brown, who kept an old-clothes stall down by the bridge. Mrs. Prout said it was an eyesore and a disgrace to the town, and should not be allowed, but she couldn't prevent it, for Emma's family had been doing it for as long as records went back, and had a right to use the spot. But Emma was the last of the family, and an orphan, so it looked as if the right might die out with her.

She had a very bad stammer, as well as the odd eyes, and the children used to tease her on their way to school.

"Yah, boo, Em-m-ma-ma-ma-ma-ma-ma B-b-b-b-b-b-birdcage!"

One particularly nasty boy, Henry Moffat, used to tip over her stall so that all the clothes went into the mud, if he could do it and get away in time. The last time Fred had seen Emma, Henry had just done this, and was racing off, shouting,

"Yah, b-b-b-b-b-boo!"

Emma had shaken her fist after him and called,

166

"You'll b-b-b-b-be s-s-s-s-sorry for that s-s-s-some day, Henry M-m-m-m-offat!"

Then Fred had helped her pick up all her old clothes.

Now, standing on the green, Fred asked the man next him (it was Superintendent Griffin), "What's happening?"

"She's being burned for a witch," Superintendent Griffin said.

"For a *witch*? *Why*?"

"She was heard uttering threatening words against Henry Moffat. And the very next month he ran in front of a bus and got squashed flat. Since then there's been lots of other accusations."

Indeed Mr. Muchness the magistrate was reading them out.

"The accused was seen to look at young Tom Whilliwell and subsequent to that he failed all his exams. She was also seen to look at Mrs. Griffin who only three weeks later trod on a bit of orange peel and broke her ankle."

"She made my hen lay addled eggs!" shouted an old lady from the back of the crowd.

"She overlooked my roof so that twenty tiles came off in the gale last Thursday!" somebody else called out.

"She looked at my cat and it had seventeen kittens. What can I do with seventeen kittens?"

"She stood on the bridge for fourteen nights with her head wrapped in a sack looking at my house!" screeched Mrs. Prout. "Why should she do that unless she was trying to put a curse on my family – the spiteful thing?"

Well, Fred began to feel very worried indeed for Emma Birdcage. Because, although he thought probably all the accusations against her were just as silly and groundless as Mrs. Prout's, he could see that the crowd was in a very nasty mood.

But just at that moment all the seventy-one dogs from Outcaster Parva arrived in a flowing black-and-white stream. They were panting, and rather tired; that was why

167

they had fallen behind Fred. But when they saw the big pile of sticks in the middle of the green, all their hundred and forty-two eyes lit up with joy and their bushy tails began to wag, and they bounded forward with but one thought in their seventy-one heads. In two minutes flat there wasn't a bit of wood left on the bonfire; the dogs of Outcaster, each one carrying as many sticks as he could manage, were speeding off on their way back to Fred's laundry.

"Ladies and gentlemen, it is quite plain that we have been privileged to witness a miracle," announced Mr. Muchness, greatly relieved, for he wasn't a bad man at heart. "If the dumb animals declare Miss Birdcage innocent, then innocent she must certainly be."

(The dogs of Outcaster were *not* dumb, but it is impossible to bark while carrying a stick in your mouth.)

"I have much pleasure in declaring that Miss Birdcage is *not* a witch, and in liberating her herewith," said Mr. Muchness, and he cut through the cords that tied Emma to a stake in the middle of where the bonfire had been piled.

Some of the people in the crowd were quite disappointed, and looked it, Mrs. Prout for one. But Emma, glancing nervously round, was relieved to meet the beaming smile of Fred Acorn. He walked up to her and said,

"Was it you who left a letter in the church porch?"

"Y-y-y-y-y-yes," said Emma.

"Do you like dogs, Emma?" said Fred, thinking how uncommon, and how pretty, it was to have one blue eye and one brown.

"Y-y-y-y-y-yes I do," she said.

"That's a good thing! Will you marry me, Emma?" he said.

"Y-y-y-y-y-yes I will!" she said.

So they were married, and Emma ran the laundry, using

sticks supplied by the dogs of Outcaster Parva, where everybody was so fond of Fred and Emma that they could have gone out to supper for three hundred and sixty-five nights in the year, if they had chosen to. But sometimes they preferred to stay at home.

Crusader's Toby

SAND WAS WHAT THE KNIGHTS CAME FOR, AND sand there was, plenty of it. North of Swaycliffe the dunes stretched away, acres and acres of them, like the sandy breakers of an inland sea, crested with shaggy tufts of grass – long, swooping curves of sand, over which the gulls and curlews flew in parallel swoops as if they were playing on a switchback of air.

"There's enough sand here to bury the Pyramids," Toby Knight said once, and his father said, "You might as well throw in the Taj Mahal and the Empire State Building while you're at it."

In between the dunes and the North Sea lay the beach itself, flat, white, empty sand, as empty and shining as the moon.

The curious thing was that neither of Toby's parents actually made much use of the sand.

To the right of the village – which was only eight houses, a Post Office, and a pub – the little Sway river ran out, noiselessly fast, clear as pale brown ink in its sandy channel, pouring down past the huge width of the beach, into the waiting sea. And here, day-long every day, Mr. Knight stood fishing on a comma-shaped spit of sand, around which the silent hurrying river had to curl its way. Sometimes he caught trout, sometimes he caught sea-fish, sometimes he caught nothing at all, but there he stayed, like a motionless speck in the vast bright emptiness of the beach.

And Toby's mother, meanwhile, was busy writing a book, she took her portable typewriter every day and climbed up to the little ruined church on the cliff, and wrote there.

The cliff was actually a grassy headland across on the other side of the Sway river; Mrs. Knight had to walk a quarter of a mile inland up the river-bank and go over the bridge, and up a steep sandy path to reach it. Mostly Toby went with her and carried her typewriter. He liked to pay a daily visit to the crusader in the church. While his mother settled herself in the sun, leaning against a bit of flying-buttress, sitting on one chunk of Norman masonry and with her typewriter balanced on another, Toby went inside the airy roofless shell of sea-whitened stone to visit Sir Bertrand de Swaye, who lay gazing calmly towards the east, with his legs crossed and his hand on the hilt of his sword. He looked comfortable enough, except that his feet were tipped up higher than his head because the ground underneath his tomb had subsided. In fact the whole church was falling into the sea, piece by piece; Sir Bertrand's wife and five children had already disappeared into the sea several years before.

"Isn't the church rather a dangerous place for Mum to go and do her writing?" Toby asked his father once, but Mr. Knight said no. "It's only in the winter that the storms are bad enough to loosen the cliff and make bits of it slide into the sea. Anyway I did make her promise to sit

171

at the landward end of the church. If she sits there I can see her when I'm fishing and we can wave to one another."

The church certainly still looked solid enough, with its round arches all decorated in zigzag dogtooth, like the ends of crackers, and its eight massive circular pillars holding up nothing but sky.

The following spring, though, when they came back, two of the pillars had gone, fallen into the sea, and Sir Bertrand was tipped even more head-down, though he still appeared quite at ease, gazing towards Jerusalem, with his hand on his sword.

The best thing about Sir Bertrand, of course, was his dog, who, curiously enough, was also named Toby. This Toby was not at all like the usual crusaders' dogs who lie looking rather meek and suppressed under their masters' feet; he was too big for that, to start with. He lay on a kind of step at the end of Sir Bertrand's tomb, lower than his master, but with his head raised vigilantly high so that Sir Bertrand, looking past his own armoured toes, could probably just see Toby's upraised muzzle.

Old Mr. Brooman, who lived in the village, said that Toby might be a kind of Afghan hound. "Well, he could ha' been, stands to reason. Sir Bertrand got him when he was out in the Holy Land, they say. It's all overland from there to Afghanistan. The Arabs and Persians had Salukis; it's common sense that they must all ha' been related once."

Mr. Brooman lived in a little cobble-built cottage at the end of the short village street, right by the beach. He was retired, his wife dead, his children long since scattered about the world; one son was in South Africa, a daughter in New Zealand. He knew a lot about dogs; that was how Toby first met him, during their first summer at Swaycliffe, when Harriet, Toby's Jack Russell terrier, developed a bad limp and was very sorry for herself. There was no vet in the village but someone suggested that Mr. Brooman might be able to help. And so he had: he was so very kind to Harriet, carefully examining her foot, finding the splinter that was the cause of the trouble, soaking it out, disinfecting the wound and putting on it some ointment of his own invention which healed it overnight, that Harriet instantly fell in love with him. After that, each time they came back to Swaycliffe, the very first thing she did was to gallop along to Mr. Brooman's house, throw herself down in front of him and roll over and over, waving her paws in the air.

Mr. Brooman had had various dogs in the past. His last one had been an Alsatian called Minnie. When Minnie died, he told Toby, he had resolved to have no more dogs. "She was the finish. I knew I could never love any dog better than Minnie, so it was best not to have another. Besides, I'm getting on myself; I wouldn't like for to die and leave a dog lonely. No, that wouldn't do. A human being's got distractions; if someone dies, or goes off and leaves you lonely, there's things you can do to cheer yourself: you can read, you can study, you can do carpentry. But a dog can't do any of those things."

Mr. Brooman did a lot of carpentry; one summer he made a vaulting-horse for Toby so that he could practise athletics out on the empty beach; and he made a strong little table for Toby's mother and carried it up to the church for her, so that she could type more comfortably.

"'Tis all made from bits of ship's teak, washed up on the sands, so that'll take no harm from the weather, ma'am; you can just leave it up there, rain or shine."

Mr. Brooman himself visited the church almost every evening; had done for years; it was he who had given the crusader's dog the name Toby.

"I always did think it suited him, some'ow. Funny you should have the same name, my boy. That's what's known as a coincidence. Yes, I've bin a-visiting this-ere old Toby for donkey's years; him an' me's had many a gossip. Wonderful bit of carving that is, when you think what a long time he's been here. Seven 'undred years old, that dog is."

Crusader's Toby was a big dog, tall and rangy like a greyhound, but stronger-looking. His coat was smooth but wavy, and his ears, cocked high and intelligently, were fringed inside like the petals of a chrysanthemum. As for his tail, one could see that it had been tremendously plumed, with long swags hanging below it all the way from tip to base, like the underside of an ostrich feather. Some of the plumes had broken off or worn away, unfortunately, but there were still enough left to show. He had a long, keen intelligent nose, big eyes well set in a broad forehead, and big strong feet.

"Good for running in all that sand," Mr. Brooman said. "Wonderful clever those crusaders' dogs were – they could sniff out a Turk from a Christian, it's said."

There were several legends about Crusader's Toby: he had saved his master's life three times over, once in battle against the Saracens, once from assassins sent by the Old Man of the Mountains to waylay him on the way back from the Holy Land, and once within sight of home when his ship was wrecked off the mouth of the Sway, and Toby had swum through the dangerous undertow, supporting his wounded master's head on his own powerful shoulders.

"That was why Sir Bertrand wanted his memorial carved separate, because he set such store by the dog, and he had it done while he was still alive, to make sure it was done proper. In fact there's some as say Sir Bertrand carved it hisself. He was a clever man. He writ a little book, too, all in Latin, about his adventures on the crusades, and it's still in the museum in York. That came out o' the castle that was here once; it was a Norman castle, up there on the headland by the church. But that fell into the sea two 'undred year back."

Toby resolved to go and see Sir Bertrand's book in the museum one day, but York was a long way off. "It's a pity it couldn't be kept here in the village," he said.

"Ah, it is," said old Mr. Brooman. "I don't hold wi' taking things away from where they belong. Things what comes from the village ought to stay in the village."

Mr. Brooman was a native of Swaycliffe, born and bred, though it was true he had travelled a long way from home in his time.

"In the army I was, see; had to go where I was sent. I been in India and in Australia too; and in the Mediterranean. Gibraltar, and then Malta; lots o' crusaders' stuff there. And in Hong-Kong I was, for a while."

Mr. Brooman had also, when he was young, been a long-distance runner. It was hard to imagine this now; he was bent and red-faced, with broken veins in his cheeks, and a ragged white moustache; the front part of his head was bald, a thin fringe of white hair curved round the back. And he was very lame indeed with rheumatism and arthritis, never walked without the help of his thick stick. But while he was still in the army he had been an Olympic runner, had carried a blazing torch in the relay from Athens up across Europe in 1936, and had won a gold medal, which he kept on his mantelshelf alongside Minnie's photograph.

During the Easter holidays, when Toby was running and racing out on the sands with Harriet, who went wild with joy every time she saw the great shining bare flatness of the beach, Mr. Brooman would often come limping out and sit on the cobbled sea-wall and shout advice.

"Don't clench your fists up so and tighten your chest, boy! You want to run easy, like as if your whole body was in one piece; you don't want to waste any little bit of energy on anything but the running itself, see? Mind you,"

175

he added kindly, "you shape well; you'll be a sprinter, I can see that; I'd fancy you at a hundred yards."

And in the summer, when Toby came back and said that he had won the junior hundred yards at school, Mr. Brooman said, "Well there. What did I tell you?"

That was the summer Mr. Brooman made the vaulting-horse, and spent long days out on the sand, teaching Toby to do long-fly and short-fly and something called High-and-Over.

In the evenings they went for walks along the beach, north or south; Mr. Brooman limping lopsidedly but rapidly along, Toby hunting for shells and beach treasures, Harriet racing backwards and forwards across their track, now up on the dunes, now right down at the edge of the sea, which, when the tide was out, seemed about a mile away. The sun sinking behind the land dyed the crests of the dunes all red and ragged; and when it was down out of sight there would be a spreading luminous pink after-glow, turning the whole sky a brilliant peach-colour. It was possible to walk north along the coast for five miles before you came to the next town, Calnmouth, but Toby and Mr. Brooman didn't often get as far as that, because, after the sun went down, dusk fell quickly, and then Mr. Brooman would say that his leg was getting tired.

At Easter, when they came back after a winter's absence, Toby noticed that the familiar dunes had completely changed their shape: mountains had piled up where he remembered valleys; a favourite little hidden dell of his where he had been accustomed to go and read on long, hot peaceful afternoons, was now a wide-open shell-backed plateau with a strange twisted tree, smooth and grey from long soaking in the sea, half-buried in the middle of it.

"Ah, it was a terrible winter for storms," said old Mr. Brooman – who had not changed at all since last year. "Sometimes the wind blew for ten-fifteen days at a stretch;

all the coast's changed along here an' there's a great bit out o' the beach up Calnmouth way and they've had to build a plank bridge across. You'll find changes up at the church, too."

Toby saw what Mr. Brooman meant as soon as he had run across the bridge and up the cliff path: two more of the round columns had fallen, and were to be seen, in bits, down below on the beach, half-buried in sand. Sadder still, Sir Bertrand de Swaye had disappeared too; only Toby remained, still with his head raised, gazing alertly towards the distant east, as if he wondered where his master had gone.

Poor Toby, thought the human Toby, remembering what Mr. Brooman had said: "I wouldn't like for to die and leave a dog lonely." It seemed hard that he should have lost his master after they had been so long together.

That evening, when they went for their first walk along the wet, shining beach, pink with sunset reflections, Mr. Brooman told Toby a queer thing.

Harriet, mad with happiness at so much space after her confinement in London all winter long, was racing in crazy circles, down to the sea, up to the dunes, tearing back to Toby to spatter him with sand, then off again into the far distance to tease a feeding flock of gulls or sandpipers, dashing with a volley of barks among them to drive them into the air.

"Now, you watch, quiet-like," said Mr. Brooman. "I don't *know* as it'll work, for I've never done it when there was someone else along, but watch and see."

He pulled out his dog-whistle. This was a small silver gadget which he had often shown Toby. You could blow it like an ordinary whistle, but you could also twist the mouthpiece around, so that the sound it produced was too high for human ears, and could be heard by dogs alone.

They were walking on the beach south of the Sway river

mouth, below the headland; one or two bits of broken Norman column lay near the cliff. Toby had already searched all over the sands for Sir Bertrand himself and had found no sign of him; the winter seas must have broken him up, or the undertow had dragged him out and buried him deep.

Above, on the grassy height, the frail bonelike ruins of the church were outlined in black against a pale-pink sky.

"Now then," said Mr. Brooman, and blew his silent whistle.

Harriet heard it at once.

She came racing towards them from far away on the sea's edge as if she had been pulled back on the end of a long elastic string.

But then, when she had nearly returned to Mr. Brooman and Toby, she began behaving in an odd and unexpected manner. Instead of dashing up against them and covering them with sand in her usual way, she began barking and bouncing about, crouching right down on her elbows and then shooting up in the air, twisting sideways, sometimes rolling over and over, somersaulting and panting, with yards of her tongue out of her mouth as if she were laughing.

"How queer! She looks just as if she's playing with another dog – that's the way she carries on with some of her friends in London," Toby said, puzzled.

"Ah. That's it," said Mr. Brooman. He put the whistle back in his pocket.

Now Harriet was off again, on a long slant back to the sea. But she ran with her head cocked to the left, taking sudden sideways swerves and snatches, as if another dog ran beside her and she was playfully bumping up against him, butting him with her head or shoulder, taking a teasing nip out of his ear.

"It's *crazy*," said Toby. "Mr. Brooman – do you think—?"

What he wanted to suggest seemed so ridiculous that he hesitated, but Mr. Brooman said it for him.

"Toby from up above's come down for a run and she's a-playing with him."

"But—"

"He wakes up, now, you see, when I blows the old whistle. He'll be glad to have company. There's no dogs in the village since Mrs. Grimes at the Post Office lost her Blackie. Old Toby likes a bit of company, you can see that."

"But why," said Toby the boy, watching Harriet, who looked as if she were being rolled over and over by a large invisible paw, "why didn't he ever come down before?"

"Well, he didn't need to, did he? He had his master alongside. So long as they was together he was pleased to stay there. But now it's different. He's hunting for his master, see? Times I've been out with him, on the shore, I've felt him running along, close by the water's edge, a-looking and a-looking to see if he can't make out where has his master got to. Sometimes," said Mr. Brooman, looking around the huge empty beach to make sure no one could hear what he was going to say, "sometimes I've almost been sure I could *see* his footprints by the edge of the water where the sand's all wet and soft – or the splashes he was a-throwing up when he went in the sea. And then he'll come along close arter me, I can almost hear him, pad, pad, right be'ind, and I can hear him thinking, You're a yuman, why can't *you* tell me where he is?"

Toby looked at Mr. Brooman with some doubt. Could the old man be getting a bit cracked from living alone?

But then Harriet came trotting up, tired for the moment, covered with sand, ready to fall in alongside the humans and go at their pace. She had no attention to spare for them, though; she was engrossed in conversation with someone bigger and taller and invisible who was lolloping at an easy pace beside her.

"*Do* dogs have ghosts?" Toby said.

Mr. Brooman thought for a while.

"The way I figure it is this," he said finally. "What is there in you that lasts? It's your soul, ennit? call it that. The body part of you dries out and turns into earth, even the bones do that, give 'em long enough, arter you die. But there's some bit of you that's different, that makes you different from any other person, that sends invisible streamers out like a jellyfish, and they hooks on to things round about while you're still alive. Call that your soul. And that'll still be there after you've died, hooked on to all those things round about that you was fond of while you was alive. See what I mean?"

"You think dogs do that too?"

"Why not? Special if a dog gets to be very fond of his master. Then they hook together, like. I tell you what I think," said Mr. Brooman, glancing back at the black shell of the roofless church silhouetted against the pink sky on the headland behind them. "I think that Sir Bertrand did carve that there statue of Toby hisself. It must ha' taken him a long, long time, it was done so faithful. And while he was a-doing it, a bit of Toby's soul must ha' got knitted into the stone, like, an' it's still there. Arter all, they say that painters put their soul into their pictures, don't they? You put your soul into anything you're really keen on."

"Well then," said Toby, "is it Toby's soul, or Sir Bertrand's?"

"Now you foxed me there," said Mr. Brooman. "Tell you the truth, I don't rightly know. Maybe it's both. Maybe when you get a friendship like that, they gets kind of woven together."

Toby glanced again to his right, at Harriet so happy with her new friend. Having got her breath, she was beginning to bounce and gambol again, and next moment she set off on another half-mile sprint, down to the edge of the sea, and into the water, which as a rule she was reluctant to enter unless somebody went with her.

Were there two sets of splashes or only one?

That night when they got back to the house Harriet flung herself down on the hearth-rug and slept like a worn-out dog, not even stirring and twitching with dreams as she usually did. And the moment she woke next morning she dashed outside, looking alertly about as if she expected somebody; she seemed rather puzzled and crest-fallen at the emptiness of the salty, sunny village street.

"I suppose you'll have to wait till this evening, Harriet," Toby told her. "Till Mr. Brooman blows his whistle. But we can go up to the church and have a look at old stone Toby, if you like."

They walked up to the church with Mrs. Knight when she went to do her daily chapter. There lay stone Toby, basking in the April sunshine, but Harriet was not interested in him. The Toby she expected must be somewhere locked inside the stone, or else already down below searching for his master on the sunswept wind-swept beach.

Just in case he was somewhere inside, Toby sat down for a moment with his arm round stone Toby's neck, and murmured into the fringed clever uplifted ear:

"Good boy then, good old boy! Don't you worry, Toby, I'm sure he's waiting for you, down there in the sea. And Lady Swaye and the children will be there too. You'll have to learn to be a water-dog, Toby."

Motionless, apparently deaf to this consolation, stone Toby went on gazing vigilantly towards the east. But Harriet, jealous and impatient, barked and pranced from side to side, and tugged at her master's sleeve until he got up and followed her down the steep and slithery sand path which led on over the headland and back to the beach. Ghost-Toby did not join them there; it seemed that wherever he was, he would only come out to play when summoned by Mr. Brooman's whistle. But that never failed. Dusk after dusk the four of them went along at their varying paces over the wet sand, live dog and ghost-dog racing ahead, Mr. Brooman limping, helped by his stick, telling stories of Malta and Gibraltar, of the dogs of Hong-Kong and the plains of Yugoslavia where he had carried the Olympic torch, while Toby the boy listened and watched Harriet's antics, and sometimes raced ahead, alongside of her and her unseen companion, practising for the four-hundred-and-forty yards, which was his next ambition.

When the Knights came back in the summer, Toby with a silver cup to show off proudly to Mr. Brooman, stone Toby was still up there on the headland. And as in the spring, he joined them invisibly on their walks in the long twilit evenings.

"Sometimes, nowadays," confided Mr. Brooman, "he'll come right along the village street, right up to the 'ouse with me. But I never yet got him to come inside. 'E always stops outside the door."

It was a happy summer. The long salty sunlit days stretched in a peaceful shining chain, one after another, each exactly like the one before, and yet all as different as the shells on the beach; time seemed to have slowed down. Toby's father fished, and his mother wrote, and stone Toby drowsed in the sun all day, up on his headland, waiting for Sir Bertrand, and came down in the evenings to race and play.

"Well, well," said Mr. Brooman rather sadly when September came, and it was time for the Knights to leave, "I'll miss you, young Toby, and Harriet, when the nights draw in and the winds get a-blowing. It seems a long time to spring. I'm not getting any younger, and that's the truth."

Looking carefully at Mr. Brooman, Toby saw that it *was*

the truth. Somehow, unnoticed by him, the old man seemed to have shrunk in the course of the summer; the skin hung more loosely on his face, and his limp was more pronounced.

"It's good that you've got Crusader's Toby to keep you company. Maybe when it gets to be real winter you'll be able to persuade him into your house."

"Ah; maybe I will," said Mr. Brooman thoughtfully, and Toby felt a sudden queer pang of anxiety – was it for the old man or for stone Toby up there on his headland? Would they be able to look after each other through the storms of the coming winter?

"I'll try to get Mum and Dad to come down at Christmas," he said. "I've often asked them and Dad did promise that some year we might."

"Ah, you do that! Swaycliffe's grand in winter, when the sea piles up and roars for days on end, and the sky gets black as ink and the beach is all white with the snow. It's worth seeing, that is."

By hard pleading, Toby did manage to convince his parents that they should come back to Swaycliffe in the winter holidays. All the time they were packing the car with food and warm clothes and extra bedding, Toby was on edge with expectation. During the drive down on Christmas Eve he longed for the sight and smell of the sea, all winter-wild, and for the company of Mr. Brooman and Crusader's Toby. A gale had been lashing the north-sea coast all the week before Christmas. Would Toby be all right? Would he still be there, up in the church?

As soon as they had arrived and unpacked the car, Toby ran along the snowy lane to Mr. Brooman's. But the house was dark, shut and locked. Full of worry, he went on to the Post Office to ask Mrs. Grimes if the old man had gone away.

"Ah, dear, then you hadn't heard?" she said, giving her

eyes a wipe. "Well, to be sure, it was only ten days ago, I daresay you wouldn't have. Poor old gentleman."

"What happened, Mrs. Grimes? Did he get ill?"

"No, 'twasn't like that. It was all along of that there crusader's dog up in the church."

"What happened?" Toby asked again, anxiously.

"Well, Mr. Brooman was very upset, dreadful upset he was, on account of the Historical Monuments Department, or some such, sent an inspector along and then they decided as how the old dog shouldn't be left here an' allowed to fall into the sea like all the rest o' the bits from the church, but was to be took off and put into York Museum. Oh, he argued about it terrible, did Mr. Brooman, an' ast the vicar and even writ to the Council, but they wouldn't take no notice of him, said it was best that the dog should be preserved because it was a uncommon example of twelfth-century work."

"Oh my goodness." Toby's heart sank dreadfully. He could imagine how Mr. Brooman must have felt. "Did – did they take the dog away?"

"Well, they was all set to. A couple of chaps come out with hammers and chisels and a council van, an' they took the old dog off his base and put him in a crate an' fetched it down here to the village. 'Twas a desprit cold arternoon, snow and wind, an' it must ha' been a sharp old job prying that heavy stone thing loose, up there on the headland. So when they was done they went into the Old Ship for a quick warm-up. And you'll never guess what Mr. Brooman did."

"What did he do?" Toby asked, though he thought he *could* guess.

"Why, he must ha' fetched out his old garden barrer – for bits of it was washed up along the shore next day – an' (no one knows how he done it, all on his own, wi'out help) he must ha' got that crate out o' the van an' into his wheelbarrow and wheeled it down to the sea – wheeled it right *into* the sea. And Doctor Motkin reckons that musta give him a heart-failure – for he'd had one or two bad turns with his heart already, this last two-three months – anyway, he never come back." She wiped her eyes again. "Washed up, he was, next morning, half a mile down the shore. But they say his face was ever so peaceful. Maybe he was glad to go. Arter all, 'tis a long time since his missis died, poor old soul,"

"What about Tob – what about the dog? Did they find him?"

"Never a trace. There's a big undertow here, you know – special when summat's heavy – it must ha' gone right down deep. The Ancient Monuments people were mad about it; terrible put out they were. But there was naught that anyone could do."

No there wasn't, thought Toby, and he felt proud for old Mr. Brooman, battling his way down to the sea through snow and gale. He thought of the old man's voice saying, "Things that come from the village ought to stay here."

He thanked Mrs. Grimes and went out into the street.

He knew that he ought to go home and help his mother – who would be wondering where in the world he had got to – unpack and make the beds and decorate the Christmas tree. But he hadn't the heart to do that, quite yet.

He turned into the biting wind, followed by Harriet, who was rather subdued, and walked along the short snowy street to the beach.

Dusk was falling. As far as the eye could see the beach curved away to right and left, an unbroken sweep of white. And the sea mumbled and muttered, inky black, far out, with a pale frill of foam at its edge. Nobody, nothing was stirring. Even the birds were silent.

But out on that windswept emptiness Harriet's spirits suddenly picked up, and she went bounding off, lifting

185

her feet ridiculously high, with a rocking curvetting motion, like a painted dog. Down to the water's edge she galloped, and splashed in.

Toby raced after her, as fast as he could go – faster – much faster – swallowing great gulps of burning cold air. And as he ran, the sorrow for Mr. Brooman's death fell away behind him, and a feeling of freedom and triumph streamed through him – as if he had been joined by the happy spirits of Crusader's Toby and Mr. Brooman, old no longer but light and strong as on the day when he had raced with the Olympic torch across the plains of Yugoslavia.

The Cat-Flap and the Apple-Pie

IT WAS THE LAST DAY OF THE SUMMER HOLIDAYS. Apples lay about all over the grass. A burnt patch on the lawn showed where the boys had had a bonfire the week before, and cooked sausages. Wet sandy swimming trunks hung on the clothes-line, and several dozen sea-shells were strewn over the front path, where somebody had dropped them and somebody else had kicked them.

The Crask family were having breakfast. Tim Crask had already eaten his, and was cramming bread and cheese into his anorak pockets.

"I'm going down to Beezeley's farm to drive the tractor," he said. "Shan't be back till suppertime."

"It's illegal to drive a tractor at your age," said Mr. Crask with his head in the newspaper. He had been saying this all through the holidays.

"I'm driving it in a field, not on the road," said Tim, as he had all through the holidays.

"Mind you get back in time to put your things together for school," said Mrs. Crask. "Have you done your holiday work?"

Tim took no notice of this.

"There's a horrible draught coming from the back door," said Mr. Crask. "Can somebody shut it?"

"Mishkin's outside."

"For heaven's sake! Can't that kitten learn to miaow, if he wants to come in?"

"Nobody hears him. And that big fat black tom of the Kingsleys chases him – he hasn't got *time* to miaow."

"Well, leave the scullery window open."

"Then the Kingsleys' cat comes in and beats him up in here."

"I wish we'd never *got* that cat," Mr. Crask said from inside his paper.

The phone rang.

"Answer it, will you, Tim, there's a love, as you're standing up," said Mrs. Crask, who was washing twenty jampots preparatory to making blackberry-and-apple jelly.

Tim scowled, but answered the phone, which was in the hall.

"It's Aunt Daphne, wanting to speak to Dad," he said, returning with an expressionless face.

Mr. Crask went into the hall.

"Hullo, Daphne," they heard him say. "Oh – are you? Yes, that would be perfectly okay. No, we aren't – good to see you all. What time will you get here? Yes, yes, we're all here – school starts tomorrow. Fine – see you, then."

Mr. Crask's telephone conversations never lasted long. He came back into the kitchen, having hardly stopped reading his paper, which he carried with him, and sat down again.

"Daphne and Bob and the girls are coming to lunch," he announced, looking over the top of the newspaper for a moment.

"*What?*" shrieked his wife.

George's face assumed an expression of settled despair. Tim walked quietly out of the house, mounted his bike, and rode off.

"*Tim!* Come back!"

No good. Tim was already out of earshot.

"You *asked* them to *lunch* – when you know I've got all the boys' school clothes to go through – and I was going to make blackberry jelly—"

"They asked themselves. They said they were driving by this way. What else could I do?"

"*I* shan't talk to those horrible girls," George said. "All they can do is brag about their school and how well they did in their O-levels."

"You certainly *will* talk to them," said his father. "It's very rude not to. – What will you give them for lunch, Ann?"

Mrs. Crask looked distraught.

"George, do you think you could cycle down to the butcher and get some steak-and-kidney? Then I suppose I could make a stew."

"Stew! That's not very festive."

"I don't feel very festive," said Mrs. Crask flatly.

"Yes, I'll go," said George, who liked stew. "Then I can get a cat-flap at Moxon's, and put it in the back door."

"*I'm* not paying for any cat-flap," said Mr. Crask.

"I've got enough money myself. From potato lifting," said George.

"Well don't come running to *me* when you've made a mess of it," said his father. George didn't answer that one.

Breakfast was over. Mr. Crask strolled out to finish reading his paper in the garden, as the weather was so fine and warm. Mrs. Crask looked round the house, which was a total mess. A lot of left-over picnic things had been dumped in the hall. The dining room had been used for a game of Progressive Pingpong, with obstacles piled up round the table to make it harder for the players to run from one end to the other. The sitting room had a lot of deckchairs in it because it had come on to rain suddenly last night and it was quicker to bring the chairs in than take them all the way down to the shed.

"We'll have to tidy the house," Mrs. Crask said to George when he came back with the meat and the cat-flap.

"I want to fix this in the back door. Look," said George, as Mishkin, the marmalade kitten, shot across the lawn, pursued by the fat black tom from next door. George rushed out and aimed a swipe at the black tom with a cricket bat, but missed him and chopped the heads off a clump of marigolds. Mishkin came indoors wailing and wanting to be picked up and petted. One of his ears was covered in blood. George took the cat-flap out of its wrappings.

"Tidy the house *first*, before you start on the cat-flap," his mother said.

George gloomily helped her.

"It's unfair that Tim gets out of this," he said.

It was unfair, and his mother knew it.

"Life is unfair," she said. "It's unfair that I have to make lunch for the Bewdleys when I want to get on with my jam."

"I *hate* those girls," said George. "Susan wears lipstick. *Lipstick!* Ugh."

"What are you going to give them for afters?" Mr. Crask shouted from the front garden.

"They can have bread and cheese and fruit, as we've done all holidays."

"They most certainly can *not!* Why don't you make them an apple tart? Daphne loves your orange-flavoured apple tarts. Yes," said Mr. Crask, "make them an apple tart."

"Oh, *fudge*," muttered Mrs. Crask.

Dashing about, she and George tidied the dining room

and the sitting room, hurling everything into the cupboard under the stairs. The stew was prepared, and put on to simmer. George scrubbed a lot of potatoes, ready for baking.

Then he got a fretsaw and cut an oblong out of the back door, the same size as the cat-flap that he had bought. The job was hideously difficult, because the back door was made of hard, weathered boards, very likely fifty years old. Also, his mother kept interrupting him.

"George, could you go and pick me some parsley and thyme. George, could you be a love and take this basket and get some runner beans, enough for seven people."

"It's like eating walking-sticks," grumbled George, returning with the basket of enormous, tough, stringy beans. As he shut the back door the fat black tom from the next house jumped in through the hole he had just sawed. "*Get out!*" said George, furiously swatting it with the basket. Beans flew about the kitchen.

Mrs. Crask let out a sudden shriek.

"*Now* what's the matter, Mum?"

"I put the orange for the apple tart into the oven to soften up, and forgot all about it. Now it's gone all brown and hard."

"Pour boiling water on it," suggested George, looking at the pie-dish of cut-up orange pieces; they had turned mahogany-brown.

"But that would dilute the orange flavour," objected his mother.

"Pour on some orange squash then."

"No – I know – I'll soak them in sherry."

"*That's* not orange flavour."

"No, but it's fairly like. And doesn't taste so phoney as orange squash. And then I'll put them back in the oven, just for a minute or two, to soften up again. *Don't let me forget they're in the oven.* Oh, George, could you be an *angel* and go and pick up some windfall apples. Enough to make a pie."

While George was picking up the apples the phone rang.

"Could you answer it, Andrew," called Mrs. Crask to her husband. "My hands are all covered in pastry."

"*Never* get a *minute* to read the *paper*," grumbled Mr. Crask, coming into the hall. He snatched up the receiver. "Yes, who is it? Oh, Daphne, you again – what is it now?"

George, returning with the apples, met his mother's eyes.

"Perhaps they can't come after all," she whispered hopefully.

"Oh, Andrew dear," said his sister at the other end, "look, it seems the girls invited their friend Felicity for the day. Will it be all right if we bring her along too?"

"Oh, sure. Two or three, four or five, what's the difference?" said Mr. Crask heartily. "See you then. 'Bye."

"The girls are bringing that friend of theirs too," he shouted through the kitchen door. "Lord, this room's a mess! I hope you tidy it up before they come."

He returned to his paper.

"Oh, *not* that *awful Felicity*!" said George, aghast. "I cannot *stand* it! Well, I'm certainly not going to talk to *her.*"

"George, you must. I'm sorry, but you must. Oh *damn* – my bits of orange!"

Mrs. Crask leapt to the oven.

The orange pulp had now cooked to a dark-brown goo, but the slices of peel were still as tough as oak bark.

"If *I* were you, I should just use the goo, and throw away the peel," said George.

"There won't be enough goo to flavour the pie, without the peel."

"Well, mash it all up with the little mixer then. I'll do that if you like," said George, who was rather fond of using the little mixer. It was a single electric prong with a tiny fierce windmill at its tip; and you had to be very careful when using it, for if the windmill part came above the surface of whatever you were mixing, splashes shot all over the room.

Indeed, it proved to be a mistake to use it on the baked cut-up orange. The blades of the windmill kept encountering bits of orange-peel, and the kitchen was soon generously spattered with dark-brown gooey splashes.

"Stop, *stop*!" shouted Mrs. Crask. "You are wasting all my orange on the walls."

"Well, you'd better put it in the big blender then," advised George.

"There's hardly any left," said Mrs. Crask, looking into the bottom of the dish.

"Add some more sherry to it."

Even so, Mrs. Crask had to keep tilting the big blender from side to side, or the blades went round uselessly, without finding anything to mince up.

"All this for an apple-pie for those brutes to eat!" said George, and he went back to work on his cat-flap. The flap came in two parts, a frame, which fitted into the hole he had cut, and a hinged door, which slotted into the frame. At this point George realised that he had put the frame in upside down. While he was reversing it, the fat black tom from next door chased Mishkin through the hole. Mishkin fled screaming and knocked over the pot of glue that George had been using. George grabbed a ratchet screwdriver and aimed a swipe at the black tom, just missing him. As he had picked up the screwdriver by the blade part, he cut his hand quite deeply, but did not notice this until he began to wonder where all the blood on the floor was coming from.

Mishkin sat up on top of the broom cupboard, wailing. The phone rang again.

"Someone *else* will have to get it *this* time," said Mr. Crask. "I'm just going for some cigarettes. *Good God*, what a mess," he said, looking at the floor inside the back door, which was covered with glue, sawdust, wood splinters, blood, and tools. "I hope you'll have the kindness to get that cleared up before they come."

George answered the phone; covering the receiver with blood and glue.

"Oh, hullo, Aunt Daphne. Yes. I see. You want to get here at twelve, for an early lunch, because the girls want to go on to the beach afterwards. Yes. Okay. Goodbye," said George tonelessly, and he said to his mother, who was peering into the blender, "They want to get here at twelve for an early lunch."

His mother did not reply.

"What are you going to give them for starters?" said Mr. Crask from the doorway.

"Andrew! Daphne is your *sister*! The Bewdleys do *not* rate *hors-d'oeuvres*."

"Well, I'd have thought you could give them *something*. Stuffed tomatoes or *something*," said Mr. Crask as he went up the front path, kicking the heap of shells out of his way.

George washed his hands, stuck a plaster on the worst of the cuts, and slotted the cat-flap into its frame.

Mrs. Crask cut up the windfall apples and put them into a pie-dish.

The sky clouded over and a light rain started to fall.

"They won't want to go to the beach in this," said Mrs. Crask, looking out.

"Oh, heavens! We'll have them for the whole afternoon!" groaned George.

There was a sudden outburst of screeching and caterwauling from the garden. The fat black tom shot through George's new cat-flap, pursued by the tough tabby from three houses along.

The house seemed full of cats. They went skittering upstairs.

"Where's Mishkin?" said Mrs. Crask.

Mishkin was outside the cat-flap, wailing pitifully. He did not know how to use it.

"Look, you dumb oaf, you do it like this," George told him. "Put your nose under the flap and *tip* it *up*."

He demonstrated over and over, he held Mishkin up to the flap, he pushed him through, he pulled him through. Mishkin still totally failed to grasp the principle.

"Try cutting a slit in a cork and sticking it on the side of the flap to hold it open," suggested Mrs. Crask. "I've heard that helps. Oh, *heavens*, my stew!"

She snatched it off the stove.

"Has it dried up?"

"A bit. Not too bad."

"Put some orange squash in it," suggested George, slicing a cork with a razor-blade. The fat black tom bolted past him, making its getaway, and he cut his thumb.

Mishkin sat inside the cat-flap and wailed.

"I'm fed up!" said George suddenly. "I'm going to turn into a tree."

He went out on to the damp front lawn. From his trouser pocket he took a small tube of water. He poured some of the water on to his shoes.

"George!" shouted his mother through the window. "Don't be silly!"

George took no notice.

He stood motionless on the grass, with his arms out sideways, hands curved upwards to catch the rain.

The telephone rang.

Mrs. Crask put her stew back on the stove and went to answer it.

"Oh – hullo Daphne. Yes indeed, and how are you? *What?* You think you won't come after all? Oh – to lunch. The girls want to go to a Wimpy Bar? *I* see. But you'd like to come to tea instead? Yes. Yes, of course. No – no – not the least bit in the world."

Slowly Mrs. Crask put the receiver down. A tremendous racket of screeches and caterwauling came from the garden. Mrs. Crask looked out of the kitchen window. A new tree, a well-grown young cherry, was to be seen in the middle of the front lawn. Mishkin had run up it, and was crouched in the fork, defying his pursuers.

"George!!!"

George did not answer.

"Where's that little tube?" said Mrs. Crask.

When Mr. Crask came home with his cigarettes the house was quite silent. Rain fell steadily. The stew bubbled gently on top of the stove. A delicious-looking orange-flavoured apple-pie stood cooling on the kitchen table.

And two new trees were growing on the front lawn.

Mrs. Nutti's Fireplace

MARK, WHO WISHED TO GET RID OF THE SPACE-gun his great-uncle had sent him, and acquire something more useful, had brought home a copy of *Exchange and Mart.*

" 'Princess-type boiler fireplace exchanged for gent's bicycle,' " he read aloud consideringly.

"But we don't want a fireplace," Harriet pointed out. "And we haven't a bicycle."

"Or there's five gross jazz-coloured balloons, a tiger's head, and two whale teeth. Offered in exchange for go-kart or griffin's eggs."

"The balloons would be nice." Harriet swallowed her last bite of cake – they were having Friday tea – and came to hang over his shoulder. "If we had a go-kart."

" 'Sale or exchange road-breaker tools interested arc welder, spray plant, w.h.y. Buyer collects.' I do wonder w.h.y.? They seem queer things to collect."

" 'Pocket Gym, judo suit, height increaser, neck developer, strength course, weights and Dynamic Tension course.' *That* seems a bargain. Only three pounds."

"No height increasers in this family, thanks," said Mr. Armitage, without looking up from his evening paper. "Or weight increasers. Kindly remember the house is three hundred years old."

" 'A hundredweight of green garnishing in 10-inch sections, de-rinder and sausage-spooling machinery'; they might come in handy for Christmas decorations," Harriet said thoughtfully.

" 'One million toys at 65p per 100, including Woo-Woos, Jumping Shrimp, et cetera.' "

"Mother wouldn't like the Jumping Shrimp."

"I would not," agreed Mrs. Armitage, pouring herself another cup of tea.

"*Gosh!* '7 in. span baboon spider with $\frac{1}{2}$ in. fangs, £5.' "

"*No.*"

"I don't really want it," Harriet said hastily. "But – listen – '$2\frac{1}{2}$-year-old Himalayan bears, only £42' – oh, Mother, *they'd* be lovely. 'Or would exchange griffin's eggs.' What a pity we haven't any of those. Lots of people seem to want them."

"*Forty-two pounds?* You can't be serious. Besides, it would be too warm for Himalayan bears here."

" 'Various rattlesnakes, 6 ft Mangrove snake, £8.' "

"Shall we get away from this section?" Mr. Armitage suggested, lowering his paper. "Anyway, isn't it time for your music lesson, Mark?'

"Yes, in just a minute. Here's something that might interest Mr. Johansen," Mark said. " 'Would exchange room in town for room in country; pleasant outlook required. View by appointment.' Mr. Johansen was saying only last week that he wished he had a bedsit in London so that he could go to concerts and not always have to miss the last movement to catch the ten-fifteen. I'll take this along to show him."

"Bring it back, though," said Harriet, who did not want to lose track of the Himalayan bears.

Mark was very fond of Mr. Johansen his music teacher, a sad, gentle man who, as well as teaching the piano and violin, had for many years run a dogs' weekend guest house. Lately, however, he had given up the dogs because he said he was growing too old to exercise them properly. When young, he had been in love with a German princess who had been lost to him by an unfortunate bit of amateur magic. He had never married. Everybody in the village liked him very much.

"Look, Mr. Johansen," said Mark, before settling down to his five-finger exercises. "You were saying only the other day that it was a pity not to use your spare room; here's somebody who wants to exchange a room in town for one in the country. Don't you think that would do for you?"

"Ach, so?" Mr. Johansen carefully scanned the advertisement. "Why yes, ziss might certainly be useful. I wvonder wvere ziss room is? I will write off to ze box number." He made a note of it.

A week passed. Harriet, who had developed a passionate wish for a Himalayan bear, was hardly seen; she spent every evening making very beautiful dolls' furniture out of egg-shells, plastic egg-boxes, yoghurt pots, snail shells, and shampoo containers; when she had a hamper full of furniture she hoped to sell it all to a London toyshop for the price of a bear. She had not mentioned this plan to Mrs. Armitage, who thought that a cat and a unicorn were sufficient pets for one family.

"Candleberry's lovely to ride on," Harriet said to Mark, "but you can't bring him indoors. And Walrus is always out catching mice. A bear would be cosy."

Mark was in the middle of his lesson with Mr. Johansen the following week when there came a brisk peal at the front-door bell. The music master opened the door and let in an uncommon-looking old lady, very short, very wrinkled, rather like a tortoise with a disagreeable expression, wearing rimless glasses and a raincoat and sou'-wester which might have been made of alligator-skin. She limped, and walked with a stick, and carried a carpetbag which seemed to be quite heavy.

"Answer to advertisement," she said in a businesslike manner. "Name, Mrs. Nutti. Room in town exchange room in country. Which room? This one?"

She stumped into the music-room. Mark twirled round on his music-stool to look at her.

"No, no. Upstairs," said Mr. Johansen. "Ziss way, if you please."

"Good. Upstairs better. Much better. Better outlook. Air fresher. Burglars not so likely. Can't do with burglars – Well, show way, then!"

Mr. Johansen went ahead, she followed, Mark came too.

The music teacher's house was really a bungalow, and the spare room was really an attic-loft, with sloping ceilings. But it had big dormer windows with a pleasant view of fields and woods; Mr. Johansen had painted the walls (or ceiling) sky blue, so that you could imagine you were out on the roof, rather than inside a room; there was blue linoleum on the floor, an old-fashioned bed with brass knobs and a patchwork quilt, and an even older-fashioned wash-stand with a jug and basin covered in pink roses.

"Very nice," said Mrs. Nutti looking round. "Very nice view. Take it for three months. Beginning now."

"But wait," objected Mark, seeing that Mr. Johansen was rather dazed by this rapid dealing. "*He* hasn't seen *your* room yet. And shouldn't you exchange references or something? I'm sure people always do that."

"References?" snapped Mrs. Nutti. "No point. Not exchanging references – exchanging rooms! You'll find my room satisfactory. Excellent room. Show now."

She snapped her fingers. Mark and Mr. Johansen both

lost their balance, as people do in a fairground trick room with a tilting floor, and fell heavily.

Mark thought as he fell,

"That's funny, I'd have said there was lino on this floor, not carpet."

"Donnerwetter!" gasped Mr. Johansen (Mark had fallen on top of him). They clambered to their feet, rather embarrassed.

"It is zose heavy lorries," the music master began explaining apologetically. "Zey do shake ze house so when zey pass; but it is not so very often—"

Then he stopped, staring about him in bewilderment, for Mrs. Nutti was nowhere to be seen.

Nor, for that matter, was the brass-headed bed, the patchwork quilt, the wash-stand with jug and roses, the blue ceiling—

"Gosh," said Mark. He crossed to one of two high, lattice casement windows, treading noiselessly on the thick carpet, which was intricately patterned in red, blue, rose-colour, black, and gold. '*Gosh*, Mr. Johansen, do come and look out."

The music master joined him at the window and they gazed together into a city filled with dusk, whose lights were beginning to twinkle out under a deep-blue, clear sky with a few matching stars. Below them, a street ran downhill to a wide river or canal; a number of slender towers, crowned with onion-shaped domes, rose in every direction; there were masts of ships on the water and the cries of gulls could be heard.

Immediately below there was a small cobbled square and, on the opposite side of it, a café with tables set under a big leafy tree which had lights strung from its branches. A group of men with odd instruments – long curving pipes, bulb-shaped drums, outsize jews' harps – were playing a plaintive tune, while another man went round among the tables, holding out a wooden bowl.

201

"I do not understand," muttered Mr. Johansen. "Wvat has happened? Wvere are we? Wvere is Mrs. Nutti? *Wvere is my room?*"

"Why, don't you see, sir," said Mark who, more accustomed to this kind of thing, was beginning to guess what had happened. "This must be Mrs. Nutti's room that she said she'd show you. I thought she meant in London but of course in the advertisement it didn't actually say London it just said 'room in town' – I wonder what town this is?"

"But – ach, himmel – zen wvere is *my* room?"

"Well, I suppose Mrs. Nutti has got it. This seems quite a nice room, though, don't you think?"

Mr. Johansen gazed about it rather wildly, pushing long thin hands through his white hair until the strands were all standing on end and he looked like a gibbon.

Mrs. Nutti's room was furnished in a much more stately way than the humble attic bedroom. For a start, there was a massive four-poster bed with crimson damask hangings. The walls, also, were covered with some kind of damask, which made the room rather dark. Two tall black polished cabinets on claw feet stood against the wall facing the windows. A lamp in a boat-shaped gilt container hung suspended by a chain from the ceiling and threw a dim light. A velvet curtain, held back by a tasselled cord, partly covered the doorway; a small organ stood to the right of the door. Strangest of all, opposite the doorway there was a fireplace with a large heavy pair of polished metal and irons and a massive white marble mantelpiece which appeared to have suffered from some accident. The right side of the mantel was supported by a large carved marble heraldic beast with a collar round its neck, but the beast that should have supported the left-hand side was missing; it had apparently been dragged out of the wall, like a decoration from an iced cake, leaving nothing but a jagged hole.

"*That's* a bit of a mess," Mark said. "I do think Mrs. Nutti should have put it right for you before she lent you her room. It's rather a shame; the monster on the other is awfully nice. A kind of furry eagle."

"A griffin," corrected Mr. Johansen absently. "Ze legs, you see, are zose of a lion. Head, zat of an eagle, also wvings, But wvere *is* zis Mrs. Nutti?"

"Wherever she is, she's left her carpet-bag behind," said Mark, picking it off the floor. "Blimey, what a weight. Hey, Mrs. Nutti? Are you downstairs?"

He put the bag down again, walked through the open door, and stuck his head back through again to say, "She really has done a neat job, Mr. Johansen, it's still your landing outside."

Bemusedly, Mr. Johansen followed him out and discovered that, as Mark had said, the transformation of the loft-room went no farther than the door; outside were Mr. Johansen's tidy bare landing, his coconut-matted stairs, and his prints of Alpine flora.

They went down, expecting to find Mrs. Nutti in the music-room. But she had gone.

"Back to wherever she came from, I suppose," Mark said.

"Taking my room wizz her," Mr. Johansen murmured plaintively.

"But really, sir, hers is quite a nice room, don't you think? And it has a smashing view. I know it's not London, which was what you wanted, but maybe they have concerts in this town too. Where do you suppose it is?"

"How should I know?" said poor Mr. Johansen, twisting his hair some more.

"Do let's go back upstairs and have another look."

But by the time they had gone back, full dark had fallen on the town outside the window of the new room, and not much could be seen except a wide prospect of twinkling lights. They could hear music from across the square, and smell delicious smells of herbs and grilled meat.

"We'll have to come back in daylight," Mark suggested. "Tell you one thing, though, this place must be east of England; it gets dark sooner."

"Zat is so," agreed Mr. Johansen. "In any case, I suppose zose towers are minarets; zis town is perhaps in Turkey or Persia."

"What's Turkish music like, is it nice? Shall we have a wander round the streets and ask where the place is?"

Mr. Johansen was somewhat hesitant about this; it took Mark a while to persuade him.

But now they came up against a difficulty: they could see the town, but there seemed to be no way of getting into it. If they went downstairs and out through Mr. Johansen's front door, they merely found themselves in his ordinary garden, walking between neat rows of Canterbury bells towards the commonplace village street.

"We'll have to jump out of the window," Mark said.

But it was a very much higher drop from Mrs. Nutti's window – and on to a cobbled street at that – than from Mr. Johansen's attic. Mr. Johansen demurred.

"Never should I be able to face your dear Muzzer if you wvere to break your leg. Besides, how should we get back?"

Mark had not considered this problem.

"I'll bring our fruit-ladder from home tomorrow morning," he said. "Perhaps I'd better be off now; Mother gets worried if I'm more than three-quarters of an hour late for supper, and thinks I've fallen in a river or something."

Harriet was greatly interested in the story of Mr. Johansen's room-exchange.

"I wonder *why* Mrs. Nutti wanted to swap?" she pondered, and made Mark tell her over and over the few not particularly enlightening things the old lady had said.

"She seemed worried about burglars? And part of the

fireplace was missing? Perhaps burglars had gone off with it?"

"You'd hardly think anyone would pinch half a fireplace," Mark objected. "Still, it was gone, that's true. Maybe she wanted to make sure no one could go off with the other half."

"What was in the carpet-bag she left behind? Did you look? Do you think she left it by mistake or on purpose?"

"I didn't look. It was jolly heavy, whatever it was. Maybe she got fed up with carrying it about."

"When you go down tomorrow I'm coming too," Harriet said firmly.

"Good, then you can help carry the ladder."

Taking the ladder was a waste of time, however, as they soon discovered. They leaned it up against the front of the house, so that its narrow top was wedged firmly against what appeared to be the window of Mr. Johansen's attic.

Then they rang the door-bell and the music master let them in.

"Is the room still there, sir? Has Mrs. Nutti been back? Did she fetch her bag? Can you still see the city?"

"Ja – ja – ze room is still zere, and ze bag also. But Frau Nutti has not returned. You wvish to see it?" he asked Harriet kindly.

"Oh yes, please!"

Mark and Harriet ran eagerly upstairs, Mr. Johansen following more slowly.

"There!" said Mark with pride, pointing to the view.

"Coo!" breathed Harriet, taking it all in.

It was blazing daylight now, and obviously hot, hot weather, most unlike the grey chilly June day they had left behind downstairs. Dogs lay panting in the shade under the big tree. Men in caps like chopped-off cones sat sipping coffee and cool drinks. Boats with coloured sails plied to and fro across the river.

"What a gorgeous place," said Harriet. "Do let's go down. *Oh* – where's the ladder?"

"Not there," said Mark sadly.

"What a swindle. I've an idea though – next time we come we'll bring a rope. Then we can tie it to the window-catch and climb down."

Mark cheered up at this practical plan. "It's bad luck about your concerts, though, sir; still, I suppose it's only for three months."

"Is no matter. I can listen to zose men across ze square; zeir music is most uncommon. Also I have ze organ to play on."

He sat down at the little organ, fiddled around with bellows and pedals, and suddenly produced a short, sweet, powerful snatch of melody.

"Oh, do go on!" cried Harriet, as he stopped.

But he, looking round, said, "Wvat wvas zat noise?"

A kind of crack or tap had come from the other side of the four-poster. Harriet ran round.

"It sounded like an electric bulb going. Oh, is this Mrs. Nutti's bag? Heavens, it's heavy – whatever can there be in it?"

Harriet parted the flaps of the bag, which was not fastened, and began lifting out masses of empty paper bags, crumpled old magazines, newspapers, tissues, paper napkins, and other wadding.

"What a lot of junk. There's something hard and heavy right at the bottom though – quite big, too. Oh, it's an egg."

Mr. Johansen got up from the organ-stool and came to look over their shoulders at the contents of the carpet-bag.

An egg it certainly was, and no common egg either. It was a good deal bigger than a rugby ball; it might just have fitted into the oval kind of washing-up bowl. It was plain white, but veined over with faint greenish-blue lines. Egg-shaped.

"How queer that Mrs. Nutti should have forgotten about it—" Harriet was beginning, when the sound came from the egg again – crack!

"It's hatching!"

At this, Mr. Johansen suddenly became very upset.

"No, no, zis I cannot have. Zis is too much! Her room, yes, I do not object, provided she take goot care of my room, I wvill do ze same for hers. But to have care of an egg, no, no, zat is ze outside, das tut mir zehr leid, I am not an incubator! Ze doggies I haf give up, because I can no longer take sufficient care—"

"I'll hatch it, I'll look after it!" said Harriet eagerly. "I've hatched lots of owls' eggs, I'll put it in our airing-cupboard, I'll really look after it carefully, Mr. Johansen. I'm sure Mother won't mind. Oh, do you suppose it could be a roc?"

"Not big enough," said Mark.

Mr. Johansen looked doubtful and distressed. "Suppose Frau Nutti come back? It is, after all, her egg?"

"Then you tell her to come up the road to us," Mark said, "My sister really knows a lot about eggs, sir, she's an expert chick-raiser."

"In zat case, best to get it home before it hatches quite out, nicht wahr?"

This proved a difficult task. The carpet-bag was so heavy that it took them all their united strength to get it down the stairs.

"And you say Mrs. Nutti was a little old lady?" said Harriet, scarlet with effort. "How can she ever have carried it all the way from—"

"All the way from wherever she came from?"

"Well we certainly can't carry it from here to home. Mr. Johansen, could we possibly borrow your wheelbarrow?"

"Jawohl, yes indeed," said Mr. Johansen, only too glad

to be rid of the responsibility of the egg before it hatched. They balanced the fruit-ladder across the barrow and put the carpet-bag on top of the ladder, and so set off for home. Mr. Johansen watched them anxiously until they were out of sight; then he started upstairs, going slowly at first but faster and faster. He entered Mrs. Nutti's room, sat down at the organ, and was soon lost, deaf, and regardless of anything but the beautiful music he was making.

When Harriet and Mark reached the Armitage house and unloaded the carpet-bag, they were disconcerted to find that the egg's weight had bent the ladder into a V like a hockey-stick.

"Oh, dear," Harriet said. "I'm afraid Father's not going to be very pleased."

Luckily their parents were out, so they were able to manhandle the egg upstairs without interference. A cast-iron cannon ball would not have been much harder to deal with.

"What kind of bird can it possibly be?" panted Harriet.

Mark had a theory, but he wasn't going to commit himself just yet.

"Maybe it comes from some planet where the atmosphere is less dense. Anyway, whatever it is, it seemed to enjoy Mr. Johansen's music. Perhaps we ought to play to it, to help it hatch."

"No organ, though; it'll have to be satisfied with recorders."

The egg took longer to hatch than they had expected; perhaps the recorder music was not so stimulating. A couple of weeks went by. Occasional cracking noises came from the airing-cupboard, but Harriet had carefully swathed the egg in winter blankets, so that it was not visible; Mrs. Armitage said absently, "I do hope the immersion heater isn't going to blow up again," but she was busy making strawberry jam and did not investigate the noises. "Why have you children taken to playing your recorders on the upstairs landing all day long? Can't you find anything better to do?"

"Rehearsing for the fête," Harriet said promptly.

"It seems a funny place to rehearse."

"Well, it's warm, you see – just by the airing-cupboard."

At last the egg burst.

"Good god, what's that?" said Mr. Armitage, rushing in from the garden, where he had been thinning out lettuces.

"Oh my gracious, do you think someone's planted a bomb on us?" exclaimed his wife, dropping a pot of jam on the kitchen floor.

"More likely something those children have been up to," said their loving father.

Mark and Harriet had been eating their elevenses – apples and cheese – in the playroom.

At the tremendous bang they looked at each other with instantaneous comprehension of what had happened, and raced upstairs.

"Heavens! The smell!" gasped Harriet.

It was very strong.

"Sulphur," said Mark knowledgeably.

There was a good deal of mess about, too. The airing-cupboard door was a splintered wreck, and the floor and walls for some distance round were splashed with yellow goo, like egg-yolk, only more so. Several windows were cracked.

A tangle of damp and soggy blankets and towels on the upstairs landing made it difficult to get to the airing-cupboard.

Mr. and Mrs. Armitage arrived.

"What *happened?*" cried Mrs. Armitage.

"Harriet put an egg to hatch in the airing-cupboard," Mark explained.

"An egg? what kind of an egg, would you be so kind as to explain?"

"Well, we don't know yet – somebody left it with Mr. Johansen, you see, and he didn't feel quite equal to the worry—"

"Oh, delightful," said Mr. Armitage. "So he just passed it on to us. Mr. Johansen is an excellent music teacher but I really—"

"Listen!" said Harriet.

From the sodden mass of household linen still inside the cupboard came a plaintive sound.

It was a little like the call of a curlew – a kind of thin, bubbling, rising, sorrowful cry.

"It's the chick!" exclaimed Harriet joyfully, and she began pulling out pillowcases and tablecloths. Out with them came the lower half of Mrs. Nutti's egg, and, still crouched in it, filling it and bulging over the broken edges, they saw a bedraggled, crumpled, damp, dejected creature that seemed all bony joints and big eyes and limp horny claws.

"Well – it's rather a poppet," Harriet said, after a pause.

Mr. Armitage stared at it and made a thoughtful comment. "I'm not one for rash statements, but I don't think I *ever*, in all by born days, laid eyes on an uglier, scrawnier, soggier, more repulsive-looking chick. In the north country they'd call it a bare golly. What's it supposed to be, tell me that?"

"And for this hideous monster," wailed Mrs. Armitage, "all our sheets and blankets and tablecloths and the best monogrammed towels have to be ruined?"

"Honestly, Ma, don't worry," Harriet said. "Mark and I will take everything down to the coin-op dry-clean after lunch, I promise. I must just give the chick a rinse first, and set him on the playroom radiator to dry. You'll see, when he's cleaned up and fluffed out he'll look quite different."

"He can look a whole lot different and still be as ugly as sin," prophesied Mr. Armitage.

"And what's he going to eat?" demanded Mrs. Armitage, as Harriet lifted up the chick, egg-shell and all, and carried him away, staggering under his weight, to the playroom, calling to Mark over her shoulder as she did so to fetch a bucket of warm water and some soapless shampoo.

While they were cleaning and disinfecting the sheets and blankets at the laundromat (it took three trips and the whole afternoon and all their next month's allowance) Mark said to Harriet,

"Now do you know what the chick is?"

"No, but he's a very queer shape, I must say. His back end isn't a bit like a bird, and he's got a funny straggly tail with a tassel at the end. How big do you think he's likely to grow?"

"I should think he's about a fifth of his full size now."

"How do you reckon that?"

"I think he's a griffin-chick."

"A griffin?" said Harriet, dismayed. "Are you sure?"

"Well, he's just like the one carved on Mrs. Nutti's mantelpiece."

"Oh my goodness," Harriet said sadly. "If only we'd known when he was in the egg, we could have exchanged him for a Himalayan bear."

"No we couldn't," said Mark primly. "He's not ours to swap. He's Mrs. Nutti's. I suppose she sent him to the country to hatch out."

"Well, *I* think it was very neglectful of her to go off and just *leave* him."

When they finally tottered home with the last piles of clean laundry ("Honestly," grumbled Mark, "we shall have biceps like boa-constrictors after all the lifting we've done lately,"), Harriet's disappointment over the loss of the Himalayan bear was greatly reduced.

"Oh, I say!" she exclaimed, lifting a fold of newspaper in the laundry basket which they had left propped against the warm radiator. "Do look! He's dried off and he's *furry!*"

At the sound of her voice the griffin-chick woke up, sleepily uncurled, and staggered out from among the crumpled newspapers.

His appearance was now quite different. The dark damp tendrils all over his back, sides, hind legs and tail were fluffed out into soft, thick grey fur, like that of a short-haired Persian cat. His stumpy little wings and head were covered with pale grey eiderdown. His beak, brown before, had turned red, and it was wide open.

"Gleep. Gleep. Thrackle, thrackle, thrackle. Gleep. GLEEP!"

"Oh, heavens, he's starving! Just a minute, Furry, hang on a tick, and we'll get you something to eat. Do you suppose he'll eat bread-and-milk?"

"We can try," said Mark.

Bread-and-milk went down splendidly, when dolloped into the gaping red beak with a dessert-spoon. One basinful was not enough. Nor were two. Nor were seven. But after the ninth bowlful the baby griffin gave a great happy yawn, closed his beak and eyes simultaneously, clambered on to the lap of Harriet, who was kneeling on the floor beside him, tucked his head under a wing (from where it immediately slipped out again as the wing was not nearly big enough to cover it) and fell asleep.

After about three minutes, Harriet said,

"It's like having a cart-horse on one's lap. I'll have to shift him."

Struggling like a coal-heaver she shifted the chick on to the hearthrug. He did not even blink.

Harriet and Mark sat thoughtfully regarding their new acquisition.

"He's going to be expensive to feed," Mark said.

This proved an understatement.

After three weeks Mrs. Armitage said, "Look, I don't

212

want to seem mean, and I must admit your Furry does look better now he isn't so bony and goose-pimply but – thirty-six bowls of bread-and-milk a day!"

"Yes, it is a lot," agreed Harriet sadly.

"Maybe Mr. Johansen could contribute towards his support?"

"Oh, no, he's awfully hard up," Mark said. "I'll pay for the bread and Harriet can pay for the milk. I've some money saved from apple-picking."

"That still leaves the sugar and raisins."

Harriet decided that she would have to dispose of her dolls' furniture.

Unfortunately that was the day when Furry, tired of his newspaper nest, looked round for somewhere new to roost, and noticed the wicker hamper in which Harriet stored her finished products. He flapped his little wings, jumped up on top, turned round two or three times, digging his claws into the wicker, until he was comfortable, stuck his head under his wing (where it now fitted better; his wings were growing fast) and went to sleep. Slowly the hamper sagged beneath his weight; by the time Harriet found him it was completely flattened, like a wafer-ice that has been left in the sun.

"Oh, *Furry*! *Look* what you've done!"

"Gleep," replied the baby griffin mournfully, stretching out first one hind leg and then the other.

He was hungry again.

"It's no use blaming him," Harriet said, inspecting her ruined work. "He just doesn't know his own weight."

The next night was a chilly one, and in the middle of it Furry, becoming fretful and shivery and lonesome, clambered on to Harriet's bed for warmth and company. Harriet, fast asleep, began to have strange dreams of avalanches and earthquakes; by the morning three legs of her bed had buckled under Furry's weight; Furry and

213

Harriet were huddled in a heap down at the south-west corner.

"It's queer," said Mark, "considering how fast he's putting on weight, that he doesn't grow very much bigger."

"He's more condensed than we are," Harriet said.

"Condensed!" said Mrs. Armitage. "From now on, that creature has got to live out of doors. Any day now he'll go right through the floorboards. And your father says the same."

"Oh Mother!"

"It's no use looking at *me* like that. Look at the playroom floor! It's sagging, and dented all over with claw-marks; it looks like Southend beach."

"I suppose he'll have to roost in the woodshed," Harriet said sadly.

They fetched a load of hay and made him a snug nest. While he was investigating it, and burying himself up to his beak, they crept indoors and went to bed, feeling like the parents of Hansel and Gretel.

Next morning Furry was up on the woodshed roof, gleeping anxiously. The woodshed had tilted over at a forty-five degree angle.

"Oh, Furry! How did you ever get up there?"

"He must have flown," said Mark.

"But he can't fly!"

"He was bound to start soon; his wings are nearly full-grown. And proper feathers are sprouting all over them, and on his head too."

If Furry had flown up to the roof of the shed, however, he showed no signs of remembering how to set about flying down again. He teetered about on the sloping roof, gleeping more and more desperately. At last, just in time, he managed to fly a few hasty, panic-stricken flaps, and coasted to earth as the shed collapsed behind him.

"You *clever* baby," said Harriet, giving him a hug to show that nobody blamed him.

"Thrackle, thrackle. Gleep, cooroocooroo, gleep." Furry leaned lovingly against Harriet. She managed to leap aside just before he flattened her; he now weighed as much as a well-nourished grizzly.

Harriet and Mark were extremely busy. In order to earn Furry's keep they had taken jobs, delivering papers, selling petrol at the garage, and washing up at the Two-Door Café, but they were in a constant state of anxiety all the time as to what he might be doing while they were away from home.

"Do you think we ought to mention to Mr. Johansen that it's rather difficult with Furry?" Harriet suggested one day. "It isn't that I'm not *fond* of him—"

"It's rather difficult to get him to pay attention these days; Mr. Johansen, I mean."

Indeed, the music master seemed to be in a dream most of the time.

"Never haf I played such an instrument, never!" he declared. When he was not playing Mrs. Nutti's organ he was leaning out of the spare-room window, gazing at the view, listening to the music across the square, rapt in a kind of trance. Mark was a little worried about him.

"Honestly, sir, don't you think you ought to get out for a bit of fresh air sometimes?"

"But you see I have ze feeling zat from zis window I might some day see my lost Sophie."

"But even if you did, we still don't know how to get into the town."

Their experiment with rope had proved a failure. The rope had simply disappeared, as fast as they paid it out of the window. Nor was it possible to attract the attention of the people down below and persuade them to fetch a ladder (which had been another of Harriet's suggestions). Neither shouts nor waves had the slightest effect. And Mr. Johansen had vetoed any notion of either Mark or Harriet climbing out.

"For you might disappear like ze rope, and zen what should I tell your dear Muzzer?"

"So even if you did see your lost Sophie from the window it wouldn't do you much good; it would be more of a worry than anything else," Mark said with ruthless practicality.

"Ach – who knows – who knows?" sighed Mr. Johansen.

Several more weeks passed. Furry, measured by Mark, was now nearly as big as the marble griffin under the mantelpiece.

Then, one evening, when Mark was in the midst of his piano lesson, Harriet burst in.

"Oh – Mr. Johansen – I'm terribly sorry to interrupt – but it's Furry! He's flown up on top of the water-tower, and he's dreadfully scared and gleeping away like mad, and I'm so afraid he might damage the tower – *do* come, Mark, and see if you can talk him down, you're the one he trusts most. I've brought a pail of bread-and-milk."

They ran outside, Mr. Johansen following. It was the first time he had been out for days.

The village water-tower stood a couple of fields away from the music master's bungalow. It was a large metal cylinder supported on four metal legs which looked slender to support the weight of goodness knows how many thousand gallons of water, but were apparently equal to the job. It did not, however, seem likely that they were equal to supporting a full-grown griffin as well, particularly since he was running back and forth on top of the cylinder, gleeping distractedly, opening and shutting his wings, leaning to look over the edge, and then jumping back with a tremendous clatter and scrape of toenails on galvanized iron.

"*Furry!*" shouted Mark. "Keep calm! Keep calm!"

"Gleep! Thrackle, thrackle, thrackle."

"Shut your wings and stand still," ordered Mark.

With his eyes starting out as he looked at the awful drop below him, the griffin obeyed.

"Now, Harriet, swing the bucket of bread-and-milk round a bit, so the smell rises up."

Harriet did so. Some bread-and-milk slopped out on the grass. The sweet and haunting fragrance steamed up through the evening air.

"Gleeeeeep!"

A famished wail came from the top of the water-tower.

"You're very silly!" Harriet shouted scoldingly. "If you hadn't got yourself up there you could be eating this nice bread-and-milk now."

"Furry," called Mark, "watch me. Are you watching?"

Silence from up above. Then a faint thrackle.

"Right! Now, open your wings."

Mark had his arms by his sides; he now raised them to shoulder height.

Furry, after a moment or two, hesitantly did the same.

"Now, lower them again. Do as I do. Just keep raising and lowering."

Following Mark's example, Furry did this half a dozen times. The tower shook a bit.

"Right, faster and faster. Faster still! Now – *jump*! KEEP FLAPPING!'

Furry jumped, and forgot to flap; he started falling like a stone.

"Gleep!"

"*Flap*, you fool!"

The onlookers leapt away, just in time, Furry began flapping again and, when he was within eight feet of the ground, suddenly soared upwards once more.

"*Don't* land on the tower again. Flap with *both* wings – not just one. You're going ROUND AND ROUND," Mark shouted, cupping hands about his mouth. "That's better. Don't flap so fast. Slower! Like this!"

He demonstrated.

217

Furry hurtled past, eyes tight shut, claws clenched, wings nothing but a blur. Then back again. It was like the progress of a balloon with the string taken off.

"Make your strokes *slower*."

"It's as bad as learning to swim," Harriet said. "People get quick and frantic in just the same way. Still, he is doing better now. Just so long as he doesn't hit the tower. Or Mr. Johansen's roof."

Several times Furry had only just cleared the bungalow. At last, more or less in control, he flapped himself down to Mr. Johansen's front garden, shaving off all the front hedge on his way, and flattening a bed of Canterbury bells.

Mark and Harriet arrived at top speed, with the half-full bucket slopping between them, and set it down on the path. Furry, gleeping between mouthfuls, began frantically gobbling.

At this rather distracted moment, Mrs. Nutti arrived.

"What's this, then, what's this?" she snapped angrily, taking in the scene at a glance. "Who let him out? Should be *upstairs*, in room, not in garden. Burglars, burglars might come, might see him."

"Out?" said Harriet. "He's too heavy to keep indoors these days."

"All wrong – very bad," said Mrs. Nutti furiously. "Why did I take room in country? To keep him out of way of griffin collectors. Town full of them. Come along, you!" she bawled at Furry. Before Mark or Harriet could protest she had snapped a collar on his neck and dragged him indoors, up Mr. Johansen's staircase.

They ran after her.

"Hey, stop!" shouted Mark. "What are you doing with him?"

Arriving in the spare room, they found Mrs. Nutti struggling to push Furry into the ragged hole under the mantelpiece.

"You don't mean," gasped Harriet, outraged, "that you intend him to spend the rest of his life *there*, holding up that shelf?"

"Why else leave egg here to hatch?" panted Mrs. Nutti angrily, dragging on the collar.

But Furry, reared on freedom and bread-and-milk, was too strong for Mrs. Nutti.

With a loud snap the collar parted as he strained away from her, and he shot across the room, breaking one of the bedposts like a stick of celery. The window splintered as he struck it, and then he was out and away, flapping strongly up into the blue, blue star-sprinkled sky over the foreign city.

One gleep came back to them, then a joyful burst of the full, glorious song of an adult griffin.

Then he dwindled to a speck and was gone.

"There!" said Harriet. "That just serves you right, Mrs. Nutti. Why, you hadn't even looked after him and you expected him to hold up your fireplace!"

She was almost crying with indignation.

Mrs. Nutti spoke to no one. With her lips angrily compressed she snatched up the carpet-bag, cast a furious look round the room, and marched out, pulling the room together behind her as one might drag along a counterpane.

By the time they heard the front door slam, they were back in Mr. Johansen's attic, with its brass bedstead and patchwork quilt.

Mr. Johansen walked slowly to the window and looked out, at the trampled garden and the empty bread-and-milk bucket, which still lay on the path.

"I suppose we'll never see Furry again," Mark said, clearing his throat.

"Or I, my Sophie," sighed Mr. Johansen.

"Oh, I don't know," Harriet said. "I wouldn't be surprised if Furry found his way back sometime. He's awfully fond of us. And I'm *sure* you'll find your Sophie some day, Mr. Johansen. I really am sure you will."

"We'll start looking for another room in town for you right away!" Mark called back, as they walked out through the battered gate.

"It really is lucky Furry didn't hit the water-tower," Harriet said. "I should think it would have taken years of pocket-money to pay for *that* damage. Now – as soon as we've fixed up the airing-cupboard door—"

"—And the fruit-ladder—"

"And the woodshed and the legs of my bed and Mr. Johansen's front gate – I can start saving up for a Himalayan bear."

The Midnight Rose

THERE'S A VILLAGE CALLED WISH WINTERGREEN IN the county of Somerset, just where the Mendip hills slide down into the marshes. Not a large village – only forty houses, or thereabouts, set round in a square, but with all that's needed – one church, one pub, one school, bank, butcher, baker, builder, plumber (who also does TV repairs), chemist, jail, fish-and-chip shop, court-house, post office; outside the square of houses, and their long green gardens full of apple trees and roses and cabbages, there are eighty-nine green mounds, set round in a ring. How big are the mounds? About as high as a double-decker bus. The children roll down them in summertime, and toboggan down them in winter. What's under them? Nobody knows. Canon Godliman, grandfather to the present vicar, started digging into one of them a hundred years ago; he was struck dumb for a month; then he couldn't stop talking, night or day, for another month. His wife couldn't decide which was worse. What did he talk about? All kinds of queer things – unicorn teams, the city of Neksheb, the evil spirit of the north who plays his gloomy strains in Swedish waters, the three frivolous battles of Britain, Roman soldiers who carried bundles of nettles to keep them warm, Doll money, and the wake of Teanley Night. No one could make head or tail of such stuff. At the end of the second month he died, worn out; but he was eighty-nine, so it might have happened anyway.

One day, in the gloomy month of January, this tale begins. The village was very quiet that day. Wish Wintergreen is a quiet place at all times, the natives don't talk a lot, but that day it was extra quiet. Christmas had long gone by, but spring was nowhere yet in sight. Not a soul in the road or on the green. In the village school the teacher, Miss Clerihand, was saying: "Well, children. We all know what's going on in the court-house today, and we can't help thinking about it. So there's no use trying to do sums or spelling. We'll do history instead. Barbie, where was the land of Dilmun?"

"On the edge of the world, miss."

"What was there, Paul?"

"A beautiful garden, with cucumbers and apples and grapes in it."

"What else, Sammy?"

"In that garden, the wolf snatches not the lamb,
The lion kills not."

"What else, Tom?"

"In that garden, the wolf snatches not the lamb,
The sick man says not 'I am sick.' "

"What else, Ted?"

"In that garden the old woman says not 'I am an old woman,'
The old man says not 'I am an old man.' "

"Who lived there, Cecily?"

"Our great-grandmother Eve."

"What was her other name, Harold?"

222

"Ninmu, the lady who makes green things grow."

"Who came to the land of Dilmun, Ellen?"

"A gipsy, one of the wandering tribe of the Tchingani."

"His name, Sarah?"

"Duke Michael."

"What did he do, Paul?"

"Told the lady Eve's fortune. Said she would have two beautiful babies."

"What did she give him, Chris?"

"A basket of earth with a root in it."

"Where did he go, Sammy?"

"In a boat, down one of the four rivers flowing out of the land of Dilmun."

"And where then, Tom?"

"Half around the world to Somerset, the Land of Summer."

"What did he do there, Barbie?"

"Built himself an island and planted a garden."

"And in the middle of it," chorused all the children, "he put the basket of earth and the root."

"What happened then?"

"He grew old and died."

"What did he say before he died?"

"Ten thousand years from today, on a night midway between winter and spring, the rose shall blossom at midnight," all the children said.

"Who will be there to behold it?"

"Whoever is there to behold it, they shall remember the beginnings of the world, and shall also see forward to the ending of the world. And in their power shall it be to make that ending a ruin or a victory."

"Good," said Miss Clerihand. "What became of Dilmun, Sammy?"

"It was swept away in the Great Flood."

"Where to, Tom?"

"It floated off into space."

"Where is it now, Barbie?"

"Become one of Saturn's moons."

"Right. And when is the night that the rose shall blossom?"

"Between now and St Valentine's Day!" they all shouted.

"And where will it blossom?"

"Here! Right here! In our own village."

"Right," said Miss Clerihand again. "And we don't want any strangers coming here to dig up the rose and take it away to the Science Museum or the National History Museum, do we?"

"No, *that* we don't!"

"Good," said the teacher once more. "You know your history well. I think we'll take a break now and play Up Jenkins. Joe," she said to one boy, who had not answered any of the questions, but sat quiet and pale in the back row, "Joe, you may go outside if you like, for a breath of air."

Joe nodded without reply, slid from his seat, put on his duffel jacket, and ran outside. His face was marked by the tracks of two tears which had rolled down in spite of all his efforts to keep them in.

When he left the classroom, Joe walked out of the school porch and crossed the village green, where a great dead elm stood and a new young oak had been planted. He stood listening outside the grey stone court-house, where some cars were parked. No sound came from inside, and he did not dare go in. So instead he walked very slowly, kicking the frosty ground, to the high-arched bridge over the Wintergreen brook, which ran very clear, deep, and rapid here, over white pebbles, with watercress growing in clumps.

Joe sat on the parapet of the bridge, his shoulders hunched, his face downcast, chewing on a stem of watercress and listening to the silence.

Presently along rolled a Landrover, which looked as if

it had been driven over mountains and through deserts and maybe through the Red Sea as well – every inch of it was rusty, there were shreds of palm leaves and coconut fibre and seals' whiskers sticking out of the cracks, and in the dust on panels and windscreen rude remarks had been scrawled in dozens of foreign languages.

The vehicle slowed to a halt beside Joe and the motor stopped as if it meant never to start again. The driver jumped out.

"Where's everybody?" he asked. He was a tall, bronzed man, with a harsh, beak-nosed face, and sparkling black eyes, and bushy black eyebrows; his hair must have been black once, too, but had turned white as snow, what remained of it; Joe noticed that a curved metal plate had been patched over part of his bald crown. And down his left cheek ran a great dried scar.

"Where's everybody?" he asked again.

"Indoors," said Joe shortly, "watching the trial on TV."

"What trial?"

"The one that's going on in there," and Joe jerked his head towards the court-house.

"Why don't they watch it live?"

"They'd sooner stop at home."

"Who's being tried? And for what?"

Joe paused and swallowed, began to speak and stopped. At last he said, "The man who dug up the trowel."

"What trowel?" The stranger's deep eyes flashed.

But Joe said, "How did your head get hurt, mister?"

"In a fight," answered the man absently, "in the Valley of Gehenna. But a Persian doctor put this silver plate in for me, to replace the missing piece of bone."

"Must be hot when the sun shines on it, mister?"

"Then I wear a hood. The silver plating picks up sounds and echoes very well," said the traveller, tapping his head with the car key which he held; the silver surface gave out a faint ringing sound, like a glass tapped with a fork.

The stranger asked again: "What trowel did the man dig up?"

"An old wooden one. Ten thousand years old, the professor from the London Museum says it is."

"Why should they try a man for digging up a wooden trowel?"

"Because he won't give it to the museum people. He buried it again, just where he found it. And he won't tell them where that is. So they say he'll be sentenced to prison for ten years for disobeying a Court Order and refusing to hand over important historical objects."

"When will the trial end?"

"Today or tomorrow. Or the next day."

"Who is this man?"

Slowly and reluctantly the boy said, "He's my father."

"What's his name?"

"Joe Mathinwell." The boy nodded towards a small builder's yard with a painted sign over the gate: 'Joseph Mathinwell, builder, plumber & undertaker'.

"Where *did* he dig up the trowel?" asked the traveller inquisitively, but Joe, turning to give him a clear steady look out of slightly red-rimmed eyes, answered, "If he had told me, do you think I would tell *you*?"

"No," said the traveller. "No, I can see that you would not. It is plain that you are a brave, trustworthy boy."

Joe made no reply to that.

The stranger walked across to the shop of Mrs. Honeysett, Baker & Confectioner, went in, and bought a rock cake. The old lady observed that when he put his hand down to the tray with buns in it, the rock cake jumped right up into his hand.

"Do you know," asked the traveller, "whereabouts in this village the Midnight Rose is expected to bloom?"

Mrs. Honeysett shook her head. "Reckon the only fellow who could answer that question is Joe Mathinwell, father of that poor little mite out there. Ah, and his mum dead two years past, of the jaundice, and his dad liable for a ten-year sentence! But I've told Joe I'll keep the lad and look after him, if things fall out according."

The traveller left her shop and went into that of Mr. Chitterley the butcher, where he bought a slice of ham. As he moved towards the cash desk a large china pig that stood above it fell to the floor and was smashed to pieces.

"Can you tell me," asked the stranger, "whereabouts in this village the Midnight Rose will bloom?"

"No I can't," snapped the butcher, looking with annoyance at his shattered pig. "And if I could, I wouldn't. We can keep a secret in these parts, mister."

The traveller went into the Somerset and West Country bank, where he cashed a traveller's cheque. As he wrote his name a great looking-glass on the wall behind the counter fell down and cracked clean across. And the big crystal chandelier that hung in the middle of the ceiling let out a faint secret hum, which was echoed, even more faintly, by the silver plate on the traveller's head.

"Can you tell me," he asked, handing in his cheque, "where the Midnight Rose will bloom?"

"Certainly not," was the manager's short answer, as he counted out pound notes. "That is not the kind of information we are required to divulge to customers. *Good* day to you."

The traveller went on to the chemist, Mr. Powdermaker, where he bought fivepence worth of powdered ginger, to the TV repair shop, fish bar, post office, and to the church (where he looked up rather warily at the stone griffins and dolphins which grinned down at him from the corners of the tower). At each place he asked the same question, and everywhere received the same answer.

The vicar was more polite about it than his parishioners.

"Really, my dear sir, it's impossible to say where Joe Mathinwell might have dug up the trowel. Mr. Mathinwell is such a very busy man. Why, in this past week he has laid two new floorboards in the school, repaired a piece of paving in the south aisle of the church, cleaned out Mrs. Honeysett's drains, unblocked Mr. Chitterley's slaughterhouse outlet, renewed the wiring at the bank, installed damp-proofing in the pub cellars, dug out a cavity for Mr. Powdermaker's new boiler, laid a cement floor in Farmer Fothergill's pigsties, repaired Mr. Porbeagle's basement stairs, and mended a crack in the post office counter. So you see he might have come across the trowel in any one of those places."

"And where he found the trowel, there the rose is, d'you reckon?" eagerly asked the traveller.

The vicar at once began to look extremely absent-minded.

"Ah well, maybe, maybe, who can say?" he replied guardedly. "I know, myself, when I am gardening, that I tend to drop my tools in all kinds of odd places, not necessarily just where I have been working. But now excuse me, excuse me, my dear sir, I must go and write a sermon this very minute," and he hurried away, his shabby coat tails flying.

The traveller ended up at the pub, The Rose Revived, where he was able to obtain a room for the night. But Mrs. Bickerstaff the landlady was not able to give him lunch. "I've my hands that full with cooking a meal for the lawyers and the judge," she explained. "Not but what I wouldn't object to drop a spoonful of arsenic in that old Tartar's Windsor soup! But business is business. I can make you a sandwich, though, sir."

"A sandwich will be enough. How long is the trial expected to continue?"

"Another two-three days, maybe. 'Tis to be hoped as the rose'll bloom before sentence is passed, and then Joe Mathinwell, poor soul, won't need to hold his tongue no longer."

"Do you know where the rose will bloom, Mrs. Bickerstaff?"

"Ah," she replied, "that'd be telling, wouldn't it?"

After he had eaten his sandwich, the stranger went into the court-room to hear the trial of Joseph Mathinwell taking its course. But the arguments back and forth between the lawyers were very dull; they seemed to be about what grounds the government had for considering that it had a claim to the trowel which Mr. Mathinwell had dug up, and why Mr. Mathinwell ought to have obeyed the Court Order to produce the trowel. Nothing about where he had found it.

Mr. Mathinwell himself sat calm and quiet. He was a thin pale man with a tussock of darkish hair on the top of his head. He kept his eyes steadily on his joined hands, and never looked up at the stranger sitting in the public benches. The old judge brooded at his high desk: Jeffreys, his name was, Mrs. Bickerstaff had told the traveller, Lord Roderick Jeffreys, descended from that same wicked old Judge Jeffreys who had conducted the Bloody Assizes in the neighbouring county of Dorset; and had the same kind of reputation, took pride in sentencing offenders to the maximum penalty. He looked like that too: bitter mouth shut like a rat-trap and deep-sunk eyes like holes out of which something nasty might suddenly pop.

By the afternoon's end matters were no farther advanced, and the judge stumped out to his Bentley and had himself driven away to Mendip Magna, where there was a three-star hotel.

School was over for the day; children were catapulting from the grey stone building and across the bridge over the Wintergreen brook; the stranger began asking them questions.

"Do any of you know where this Midnight Rose is expected to bloom? In the post office, maybe? Or the laundrette?"

229

Laughing and chattering they surrounded him.

"My dad says it'll be in the British Legion Hall!" "No – in Farmer Tillinghast's barn!" "No – down the Youth Club!" "Not there, glue-brain – at the wishing-well! You come with me, mister – I'll show you!" "No, mister – you come with *me*!" "With me!" "With me!"

This way and that they dragged him. Deciding that the wishing-well sounded the likeliest site, he pulled himself from a dozen hands and followed Cissy Featherstone, who had promised to conduct him to it.

Meanwhile young Joe Mathinwell had been allowed a few words with his father by the kindly Serjeant of the Court, who at other times was Fred Nightingale the sexton.

"Only five minutes, now, mind!"

They were in the front office of the little jail, which had two cells, one for males, one for females. This was the first time in living memory that it had been used.

"Dad!" said young Joe urgently. "There's a stranger in the village and he's asking around everybody and all over for where the rose is going to bloom!"

"Is he a newspaper reporter? Is he offering money?"

"I didn't hear, but he asked Mrs. Honeysett, and Sam Chitterley, and Mr. Moneypenny, and Mr. Powdermaker and Mr. Godliman and lots of others."

"So? Did they tell?" asked Joe's father with a keen look.

"I reckon not. So now he's asking the kids."

"Well," said Mr. Mathinwell, "I reckon they won't tell him either."

"Who d'you think he is, Dad?"

"Oh," said Joe's father wearily, "who can tell? Best take no chances. Maybe he's one o' them scientific foundations wishful to get hold of the rose and *measure* it. Or a film company a-wanting to film it."

"Would that be so wrong, Dad?"

"There's things," said Joe Mathinwell, "ought to be kept

230

private and quiet. Remember what it says in the good book: 'And after the fire, a still, small voice.' Do you think that still small voice would 'a' been heard if there'd been thousands of folk camping and shuffling around, and dozens of TV cameras? 'He that contemneth small things shall fall,' it do say in Ecclesiasticus. Don't *you* do that, Joe."

"No, Dad, but—"

"Time's up, Joe, son," called Fred Nightingale, keeping watch at the street door.

"Joe," said his father quickly, "that rose oughta be watered. See to it, will ye?"

"Yes, Dad," said Joe, gulping. "How much water?"

"Not too much. Just a liddle – just as much as it asks for."

The Mathinwell garden had the best roses and the biggest cabbages in Wintergreen; Joseph, his neighbours said, could talk to green things through the tips of his fingers.

"What kind of water, Dad?" said Joe urgently.

But Mr. Nightingale firmly shooed the boy out.

"Mrs. Honeysett taking good care of 'ee?" called Joseph senior with anxious love in his voice.

"Yes, Dad . . ." Then Joe was out on the frosty, twilit green, his eyes brimming with tears, and his mind with worry.

The stranger had now returned from the wishing-well, and the various other false goals offered him by the village children (the way to the wishing-well had been a particularly long and slippery track along the side of a cowy valley); he was not angry at being fooled, but he looked thoughtful. He began to walk towards Joe, who broke into a desperate scamper, nipped through Mrs. Honeysett's side gate, along to the back of her garden between the bee hives, through Mr. Porbeagle's allotment, and so out among the great grassy mounds that encircled the village.

(The Sleepers, they were called, no one knew why.) Icy, frosty dusk was really thickening now; the mounds had turned dove grey and did look very much like curled-up sleeping beasts.

"Don't let him find me," Joe whispered to them as he ran dodging among them; by and by he was fairly certain that he had shaken off the stranger's pursuit, but in order to make even more certain he took the road to Chew Malreward and walked along it for a couple of miles, then circled back by a bridlepath. The moon climbed up, and then slid behind a bank of black cloud; but before it did so, a wink of something bright in the hedge-bank caught Joe's eye: bright, a small circle of light, it was, and he put his hand into a tussock and pulled out a wineglass, with a round bowl and a stem the length of his two middle fingers placed end to end.

"Well, there's a queer thing!" muttered Joe. "Who could have been drinking wine out here in the middle of no-man's-land? And left his glass behind? Folk on a picnic last summer? Reckon I'll never know."

The glass was neither chipped nor cracked nor broken; when he had cleaned out a few sodden leaves with a swatch of grass, it gleamed sharp as crystal. Mrs. Honeysett would be pleased to have it, Joe thought, and checked a stab of pain, remembering the row of dusty tumblers unused on the shelf in his own home, locked now and shuttered.

Still, coming on the glass like that had someway lightened his spirits; he felt hope rise in him as he trudged along, clasping the stem of the glass, holding it in front of him as if it were a flagstaff. Hope of what? He hardly knew.

When the rain began, first a few drops, then a drenching downpour, he held the glass even more carefully upright, for a question had slid into his mind: would there be enough rain, before he reached the village, to fill the glass right up to its brim? Perhaps there might, he thought; just perhaps. Heaven knows *he* was wet right through his duffel jacket to his skin, and his boots scrunched with water as he walked. One good thing, in such weather as this, most probably the stranger would have given up his prying and his prowling, and would be shut away snug in the bar parlour of The Rose Revived.

By the time that Joe made his way over the humpbacked bridge, the glass was brim full. Not another drop of rain would it hold. Maybe it doesn't matter about the stranger after all, Joe thought joyfully; and so he went straight to the school, let himself in by the little back door, which was never locked, and watered the rose.

At ten minutes to midnight Lord Roderick Jeffreys's limousine softly re-entered Wish Wintergreen; it glided over the hump-backed bridge and came to a stop in the shadows by the church. The night was wild now; huge gusts of wind roared and rollicked; as the chauffeur got out and stepped to open the car door for his master, a massive stone griffin dislodged itself from the cornice of the church and came crashing down on to the car roof, trapping the man inside, who yelled with agony.

"Saunders, Saunders! Get me out of here! I think my leg's broken! Get me out!"

"I can't, sir," gasped the driver, wrestling with the smashed door-lock.

"Well then phone the police! Phone for an ambulance! Ring somebody's doorbell. Knock somebody up! Bang on their doors!"

The chauffeur rang and knocked at house after house, but nobody seemed to hear his calls and tattoos. Either the inhabitants of Wish Wintergreen were a set of uncommonly sound sleepers – or else none of them was at home. Not even at the jail could Saunders raise any response.

And the phone-box on the green was, as usual, out of order.

Doggedly, finding nothing better to do, the chauffeur began walking along the road to Mendip Magna.

And the wind began to drop.

In the village school, all was dark and silent. Not a shoe squeaked, not a corset creaked, not a bracelet clinked. Yet the whole population of the village was there, packed in tight and soundless, like mice in a burrow, intently watching: children breathless, kneeling, squatting and crouching in front, while their parents stood in a circle behind them. Fred Nightingale was there, and Joseph Mathinwell, his hands resting on the shoulders of his son Joe in front of him. All their eyes were fixed on one thing, the rose that was slowly growing out of a crack between two floorboards in the centre of the room.

It was a white rose; that they all remembered afterwards. But that was the only point on which their recollections did agree. About all else, their memories were at variance. Size? Big enough to fill the whole room. Or tiny, no larger than a clenched fist; but every single petal clear and distinctly visible, though you could see clean through, like a print on a photographic negative. The flower cast a shadow of light, as other objects cast a shadow of darkness. Scent? The whole school was imbued with its shadow and its fragrance. Fragrance of what? Apples, cucumber, lilac, violets? No, none of those things. Like nothing in the world, but never to be forgotten. The leaves, in their tracery of delicate outline, of an equal beauty with the flower.

Now, as the flower itself opened wider and wider, the watchers found that their hearts almost stopped beating from terror. Terror? Why? Because how much longer could it continue to grow and expand its petals? How many more seconds had they left to marvel at this wonder? They clasped each other's hands, they held their breath. For all in the room five seconds, ten seconds, seemed to lengthen into a millennium of time. Then the church clock struck the first note of midnight, and, as it did so, swifter than a patch of sunlight leaving a cornfield, the rose was gone. Nothing remained but a faint fragrance.

Nobody spoke. *Think* they might, but their thoughts were locked inside them. Quiet as leaves, the villagers dispersed, each to his own home, children stumbling dreamily, clasping the hands of parents, lovers arm in arm, old and young, friends, grandchildren and grandparents lost in recollection.

Only Joseph Mathinwell paused by the jail door a moment to exchange a few quiet words with the stranger, who had been there too, at the back of the group, as was proper for an outsider.

"You'll be taking it back then – the root, and the trowel? And the basket of earth? To where it came from?" Joseph sighed.

"Yes," the stranger answered him. "It should never have been brought away. For thousands of years I and my fathers before me have searched. The duty was laid on us. Now the search is over; restitution will be made. The gap will be filled. Farewell then, my friend, Joseph Mathinwell."

"Farewell, Duke Michael."

The prisoner turned and walked back into the jail; Fred Nightingale locked him in.

The trial of Joseph Mathinwell had to be adjourned because of the injuries to Judge Jeffreys, who had two broken legs. But before a new judge was summoned, the prisoner had agreed to reveal where he had found the wooden trowel. It had been under the floor of the village school, he said. When officials from the London museum visited the school, however, it became plain that someone had been there before them. One cubic metre of earth, approximately, had been removed from beneath the floorboards. Mathinwell obviously could not have done it, for he had been in jail; nobody else in the village could throw any light on the matter. The prisoner was duly released, and went about his business. The school smelt faintly of roses, and does to this day.

The inhabitants of Wish Wintergreen, never a chatty lot at any time, walk about even quieter these days, with a solemn, happy, inward, recollected look about them. Sometimes, at night, they may glance up at the planet Saturn, in a friendly recognising way, as if they looked over the hedge at the garden next door. They do not speak about these things. They are used to keeping secrets. But if anything at all hopeful is to happen in the world, there may be a good chance that it will have its beginnings in the village of Wish Wintergreen.

> *In that garden, the raven utters no cry,*
> *The lion kills not.*
> *In that garden, the wolf snatches not the lamb,*
> *The sick man says not "I am sick"* . . .

Book **1** in the FELIX TRILOGY

GO SADDLE THE SEA

*A*ction-packed adventure, high-tension drama and heroic swashbuckling!
Join dashing hero Felix Brooke as he boldly embarks upon the journey of a lifetime...
Here's a taster to tempt you!

'Ye've run yourself into a real nest of adders, here, lad,' Sammy whispered.

'I know they are smugglers,' I began protesting. 'That was why the fee was low. But I could take care of my — '

'They are worse than smugglers, lad – they are Comprachicos,' he breathed into my ear.

'Compra — c-comprachicos?'

At first I thought I could not have heard him aright. Then I could not believe him. The I *did* believe him – Sam would not make up such a tale – and, despite myself, my teeth began to chatter.

THE FELIX TRILOGY by Joan Aiken from Red Fox

Go Saddle the Sea	£3.99	ISBN 0 09 953771 0
Bridle the Wind	£3.99	ISBN 0 09 953781 8
The Teeth of the Gale	£3.99	ISBN 0 09 953791 5

Book **2** in the FELIX TRILOGY

BRIDLE THE WIND

*If you're an adventure addict then you'll love
BRIDLE THE WIND – it's un-put-downable!*

Here's a taste of what's in store...

*Shipwrecked, imprisoned and then haunted by a ghoulish
premonition – brave Felix may be down on his luck but
he'll never, ever give up...*

'*Oh*, but I don't want to die!'

And then, a second time, putting the fear of death, such
as I had not felt, even through the shipwreck, into my own
heart, '*Oh – but – I don't – want – to – die!*'

Petrified, I stared all around me. From where could the
voice possibly come?

Trembling uncontrollably, I looked upward, and now,
just for a moment, it seemed to my dazed senses that I
could see something - some *body* - suspended from one of
the arching boughs overhead, that I could see a thin form
swinging, dangling at the end of a rope not three feet
above me... It faded, melted, and was gone.

THE FELIX TRILOGY by Joan Aiken from Red Fox
Go Saddle the Sea   £3.99   ISBN 0 09 953771 0
Bridle the Wind   £3.99   ISBN 0 09 953781 8
The Teeth of the Gale   £3.99   ISBN 0 09 953791 5

Book 3 in the FELIX TRILOGY

JOAN AIKEN

THE TEETH OF THE GALE

*G*rab a copy of the thrilling finale of *THE FELIX TRILOGY. It's an action-packed read – so hold on tight!*

Pulses race when brave Felix leads a rescue mission with his sweetheart, Juana. It's a deadly dangerous task – will Felix keep his head and return a hero?
Here's a tingling taster...

'Juana! Keep very still!' I called hoarsely.

My heart seemed to fall clean out of my body into the gorge below. There she was, defenceless, in deadly danger, and here I was, strung on two ropes over the gulf, with my gun strapped out of reach, useless on my back; however fast I moved, I would never be able to get back in time to save her if the bear flew at her.

The massive bear turned, at the sound of my voice, and eyed me intently. I joggled frantically on the rope, to hold its attention.

'Bear! Bear!' I yelled. 'Look at me! Look at me on the bridge. Come and get me, bear! Here I am!'

THE FELIX TRILOGY by Joan Aiken from Red Fox

Go Saddle the Sea	£3.99	ISBN 0 09 953771 0
Bridle the Wind	£3.99	ISBN 0 09 953781 8
The Teeth of the Gale	£3.99	ISBN 0 09 953791 5